She immediately reacted
to her car being hit

She jabbed at the accelerator pedal, quickly switching over to the right-hand lane. Had he thought she was in his way? Would he pass her now? This time the strong jolt threw her backward, against the headrest.

In rising terror, she attacked the accelerator. She watched her speedometer climb to sixty, then sixty-five. A quick look in the rearview mirror fueled her worst fears. The car behind her still silently stalked. Only now he seemed even closer. The next bump snapped her backward.

The beat in her ears echoed the pounding of her heart. Her eyes darted anxiously to her mirror. She could detect no other cars. None to turn to for help. In a tunnel along a freeway that was normally swarming with cars, she suddenly found herself alone with a madman.

ABOUT THE AUTHOR

M. J. Rodgers used to live in Benicia and commute to San Francisco, where she was a Financial Manager for a large corporation with headquarters in the city. She and her family now make their home in Washington State on the Peninsula across from the Olympic Mountains. *A Taste of Death* is her second Intrigue.

Books by M. J. Rodgers

A Taste
of Death
M. J. Rodgers

Harlequin Books

TORONTO • NEW YORK • LONDON
AMSTERDAM • PARIS • SYDNEY • HAMBURG
STOCKHOLM • ATHENS • TOKYO • MILAN

To my brown-eyed Alice,
who always served up
a feast for the imagination

Harlequin Intrigue edition published December 1989

ISBN 0-373-22128-2

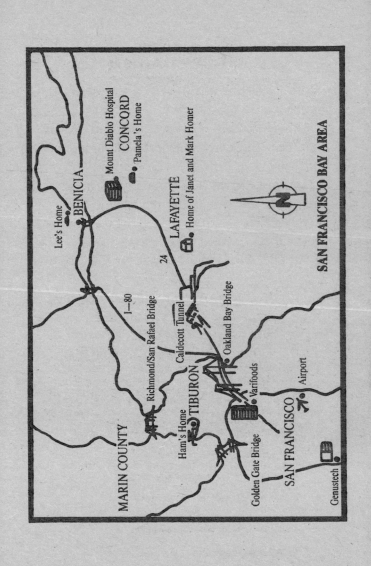

SAN FRANCISCO BAY AREA

MARIN COUNTY

BENICIA
Lee's Home

Mount Diablo Hospital
CONCORD
Pamela's Home

LAFAYETTE
Home of Janet and Mark Homer

I—80
Richmond/San Rafael Bridge

Caldecott Tunnel

24

Oakland Bay Bridge

Ham's Home
TIBURON

Varifoods

Airport

Golden Gate Bridge

SAN FRANCISCO

Genustech

CAST OF CHARACTERS

B. A. Lee—She was driven by a mysterious letter from a dead friend.

L. E. Alexander—He knew the dead chemist had been murdered and was determined to find out why.

Hamilton Jarrett—As company president, did he really only care about the bottom line?

George Peck—He controlled the lab, but had he controlled the dead chemist?

John Carstairs—Finance was his field, or was it?

Denise Williams—Would she sacrifice anything for a successful advertising campaign?

Steve Gunn—As security chief, he'd do anything the company president told him... anything.

Pam Heyer—Was she really a friend, or part of a clever cover-up?

Michael Ware—He always wanted the best. How far had he gone to get it?

Prologue

Janet hadn't meant to become a killer. She clung to that reality now as the dark, rain-swept freeway rushed at her from all sides and as the horror of her guilt threatened to drown her in its rising tide.

She battled the strong winds that beat against her small Honda once she emerged from the lower deck of the Bay Bridge. She fought to keep the car on a straight course as hard as she struggled to keep the tears from blinding her.

There was no turning back now. She had already sacrificed her job, maybe even her career. The realization that she might never find another position struck her like a clap of thunder. All the schooling—all the striving, all the years—for nothing.

Perspiration drenched her clothing, but her damp hands held tightly to the steering wheel. She had taken the right step. No matter what else had gone before, whatever else she had done, she was correcting her error, her disastrous mistake. There would be no more arguing about it, no more accusations that she was "out of touch" since her return from maternity leave. She had the evidence. If only it wasn't too late!

Her eyes darted anxiously to the folder of computer printouts lying on the passenger seat, almost as though she thought they might have disappeared. Once reassured, she looked quickly back to the road. Not many cars were keeping her company, not so close to midnight on a Friday.

She was tired, bone weary, not so much from the lateness of the hour as from the constant tension, but she knew that as the rain mixed with the oil accumulated on the pavement, the surface became slippery, dangerous. She would drive safely. She didn't gamble with her life.

But she had gambled with the lives of others. She had been stupid, blind. And at this very moment she was taking the biggest chance of her career. Defying direct orders. Forcing an open confrontation. What if she lost?

No, she mustn't think that way. Once the right people knew, she couldn't lose. Once the right people took action, the safeguards would come automatically, insuring that no more chances be taken with anyone's life. After all, that was what it was all about, wasn't it? Innocent lives?

She thought of her husband, Mark, and his unhappiness over her late-night work, of the thoughtless quarrel that her constant overtime had provoked the night before. Tonight she could tell Mark. Now that she had broken all the other rules, one more wasn't going to hurt. She'd help him to understand what she had been facing alone. She knew he would stand by her.

Yes, Mark would be there when the others turned against her. When she lost her job, her career, she would still have Mark and the children, Mark Junior and Molly. Little Molly was just learning to stand.

The thought of her daughter's first tentative attempts to stand upright on chubby legs while holding on to the coffee table brought renewed hope to Janet. Weeks of tension and unhappiness began to subside. The hands on the steering wheel relaxed.

Life could still be sweet, would still be sweet. She had made some mistakes, been guilty of bad judgment. But the worst part, the indecision, was over. True, hard times would come. But they would pass. She still had the rest of her life.

The Caldecott Tunnel loomed ahead, digging a hole through the Berkeley Hills to connect Oakland with other parts of the East Bay. Janet knew home was close now, just a few more miles. As she entered the long, dark structure, she imagined she could already see the light at the other end—the light in her kitchen where Mark was waiting for her—the light in his eyes when she told him she loved him. As she changed lanes, she was smiling happily.

The smile was still on her face when the truck collided with her car, pushing it off the slippery highway and directly into the tunnel's concrete wall. As though caught in a game of racquetball, the car bounced from wall to wall of the two-lane tunnel. Back and forth, back and forth, the pounding of the increasingly battered vehicle echoed like the beat of a deafening drum.

When it finally landed upside down in a smashed heap between the two lanes, a spark ignited gas that had spilled from the tank, and soon the wrecked car was surrounded by the orange glow of flames.

Just as the little Honda exploded, a dark green truck cleared the far end of the tunnel. It hadn't even slowed down after hitting Janet's car. The driver didn't look back.

Chapter One

It was a clear, crisp and sunny April morning—the kind of morning when little brown robins look for a puddle of water in which to bathe their wings. Such puddles were plentiful on the streets of San Francisco after the recent rains. But it was hard for a robin to find a safe bath as the stampede of cars and feet descended on the awakening city by the bay.

Lee emerged from the parking garage a couple of blocks off Market Street with a new skip in her step and energy in her movements. After a week's ski vacation in Lake Tahoe, she felt relaxed, renewed and more than ready to tackle the week ahead, in her San Francisco office at Varifoods International.

Lee knew she looked every bit the successful businesswoman in her dark blue pin-striped suit, with neatly swept-back hair. To be sure, the very light coloring of her hair, eyes and skin gave her a much more delicate look than she might have wished. But at five foot eight, the two-inch-heeled black pumps she wore added enough height to allow her to look most of her male colleagues squarely in the eye.

She said good-morning to two of those colleagues as she walked through the large glass doors facing Market Street and put her palm onto the green security panel. Somewhere within the building a computer data base checked her identification, while the guard watched the monitor's readout. He smiled his recognition as she passed through the electronic eye. She smiled back.

She saw another employee she knew and smiled, exchanging a few words with him as they shared the elevator. Reaching the eighth floor, she gave another big smile and a good-morning to her secretary, then passed through to the office that bore the sign B. A. Lee, Personnel Manager.

Actually, the smile lasted until she accessed her computer for her electronic mail messages. Then, after one quick read, it was gone.

What she saw on the screen was an interoffice memo that looked outwardly the same as all the rest. But it wasn't like the rest—it announced a death.

TO: All Employees
FROM: Hamilton Jarrett, President
SUBJECT: Employee Death
Janet Sue Homer, research chemist, was killed in an automobile accident late Friday night in the Caldecott Tunnel. Funeral services will be held at the Holy Scripture Chapel in Lafayette Tuesday morning at ten. Employees who knew Ms. Homer may be excused from their duties to pay their respects. Ms. Homer's family has asked that in lieu of flowers, donations may be sent to the Cancer Research Center.

Lee couldn't believe it. She stared at the light blue lettering on the black background of her monitor and reread the terse message. And then reread it.

Finally the momentary shock was pushed aside, and she felt the pain.

Not Janet. Not happy, sunny, full-of-fun Janet. Not the woman who had helped her kill a bottle of wine when that foolish love affair a few years back had gone wrong. Not the friend who had handed her a bottle of love potion when she was heading for Lake Tahoe just over a week ago, with instructions to sneak a few drops into any likely prospect's drink. Wonderful, funny Janet just couldn't be gone. Please, God.

Lee put her head into her hands and the tears came. "Let it not be true," she kept repeating to herself. But when she finally took her hands away, the message was still on her screen. And even when she erased it, she knew it would never really go away.

She reached for some Kleenex and blew her nose. It seemed impossible to think that she had been enjoying herself at that Friday night party up at the lodge, while Janet lay dead or dying on the highway. Absolutely impossible.

The intercom buzzed, startling Lee. In her grief she had forgotten for a moment where she was. She looked at the intercom, then pressed the lever to talk to her secretary.

"Yes, Marge."

"Lee? You sound funny. Is something wrong?"

Lee wiped away a remaining tear and took another moment to regain control over her voice.

"I'm okay, Marge. What's up?"

"I got you on Mr. Jarrett's calendar this afternoon. Will that be all right?"

For a moment Lee was at a loss. Then she remembered that the president had asked her to make an appointment with him as soon as she returned from vacation. Something about new duties. Janet's death had taken nearly all other thoughts out of her head. Thank goodness Marge never forgot such things.

"Yes. This afternoon. What time?" Lee said.

"One o'clock. And he wants you to bring his latest memo on security measures."

"I don't remember seeing a new security memo," Lee said.

"It came last week, while you were gone. Just like all the others, it was hand-delivered by Steve Gunn, our own in-house Gestapo. Ten to one he wrote it, too. You'll know what I mean when you see it. You'll find it in your In basket."

Lee didn't flinch at the crack. Ever since Hamilton Jarrett had taken over the presidential spot eight months before and brought in a new security chief, Steve Gunn, as his right hand, Varifoods International had shown strong signs of mimicking Third Reich operations.

"Thanks, Marge. One o'clock it is," Lee said as she marked her desk calendar. "And, Marge?"

"Yes?"

"Did you know Janet Homer?"

"Janet Homer? Oh, you mean the chemist killed in the car crash?" Marge said.

"Yes."

"Not personally. Why? Did you?"

Lee sighed heavily. "Yes, Marge. But I didn't know about her death until I read the electronic mail a few minutes ago. I want you to arrange for some flowers to be at the chapel services tomorrow."

"I'm sorry, Lee. I didn't realize you knew her. How terrible for you to find out this way! I'll send the flowers, but as I recall, the memo said something about donations to cancer research."

"So I'll send a donation in, too. I don't want to go against the family's wishes. It's just that I... Oh, hell, Marge, I want Janet to have the flowers. Yellow roses. Lots of them. Tell the florist to send the bill to me here. Okay?"

"Yes, Lee. I'm sorry, Lee."

Lee broke her connection with Marge and got up to get herself a cup of strong, black coffee from the pot that was sitting on the corner file cabinet. As she tipped the cup to her lips she stared out at the mockingly brilliant San Francisco morning.

But it was an internal picture she was seeing. Vivid memories reeled past like scenes from a favorite movie: Janet and herself going shopping at lunchtime, dashing to the hospital when Janet's first baby decided to come three weeks early, singing off-key at the office Christmas party two years before, hugging goodbye when Lee went on vacation only a little over a week ago.

She was feeling the loss of a woman she had called a friend. She knew of Janet's family, but hadn't really spent any time with them. No point in calling with condolences. She would see them at the funeral tomorrow. She could say what she needed to then. But what would she say?

She couldn't think about Janet anymore. The tears were threatening to come back. The pain of her death was still too new, still too unacceptable. Later she might be able to give way to her grief. Now the time was ripe to bury herself in work. She put down the coffee cup and slowly turned back to her desk.

The first thing she had to do was find that security memo somewhere in her overflowing In basket. A lot of the paper consisted of employment applications. But a lot of it was also interoffice memos, which had been printed out rather than stored in the computer. No wonder electronic mail never seemed to replace the paper flow, she thought.

Her back was starting to ache from her awkward, bent position. She finally decided she was approaching things the hard way and took the heavy pile out of the wire basket and placed it on the center of her desk blotter for easier access. As she did so, a single white envelope fell out of the heap.

It caught her attention immediately. She picked it up and looked more closely. "Lee" was written across it in bold, open script. There was something familiar about that handwriting. At the same moment that Lee recognized its author, she was tearing the envelope open. The note inside was dated the previous Friday.

Lee,
I know this must seem like an odd way to get your attention, but all my messages sent through our electronic mail system are being monitored and so are my telephone calls. I must talk to you. Something very wrong is going on—something that must be stopped. I know I can trust you. I'm beginning to think you might be the only one in this crazy place I can trust! I tried getting you at home last night, forgetting you'd still be up at Lake Tahoe. If I had your zip code handy, I would send this to your home address to be on the safe side. But I don't, so this seems to be the best choice. The minute you return, call me at home. Don't come to my workstation in the lab. It's too dangerous. And tell no one about this letter. No one.

Janet

Lee sat back in her chair, holding the letter from her dead friend and feeling at once bewildered and shocked. She re-read the phrases that puzzled her most: "Something very wrong is going on—something that must be stopped.'' What incredible things for Janet to have said! And why was going to her workstation in the lab *too dangerous*?

There was fear in the words her friend had written. Janet had composed this letter and only hours later she had died. What could it mean?

Lee shivered, but not from cold. Janet was too level-headed to be concerned without good reason. She had been trying to warn Lee about something. But what?

Lee felt the need to talk to someone, to consult someone about Janet's letter. But whom? Certainly, as company president, Hamilton Jarrett should be made aware of any possible internal problems—if that was what Janet had been referring to. And it had to be, didn't it?

No. If it was, Janet would surely have gone to her boss, to security, or even to Jarrett himself. She wouldn't have come to Lee with a company problem that could be handled by one of them. Would she? Lee glanced back at the letter still in her hands.

''I'm beginning to think you might be the only one in this crazy place I can trust.'' The words almost jumped out at Lee. And then, ''Tell no one about this letter. No one.''

A creepy feeling inched its way up her spine. Whatever problem Janet had foreseen, it was something she felt she couldn't share with anybody but Lee. But why? What was all this stuff about Janet's telephone calls and electronic mail being monitored?

Lee shook her head, confused and very uneasy. Now she had an even stronger urge to find that memo on the new security measures. She dug furiously through the large stack from her In basket. But several minutes passed before she was successful.

She grabbed it as soon as she found it. The memo was verbose, nearly two pages long. Marge had been right. Steve Gunn, the security chief, must have written it, even though it was signed by Hamilton Jarrett. Ham's messages were always much more succinct.

As she scanned the memo, Lee found that most of it was a reminder not to discuss company business with family or friends. Finally, as Lee reached the second last paragraph, she saw what might be significant.

Due to the recent check of telephone company records, it has also come to my attention that calls have been made from our business phones to numbers listed to one of our competitors, namely Tyberry Foods, International. Since there is no legitimate business reason for contact with this competitor, I must assume that such unauthorized calls are the work of industrial spies. Henceforth be advised that all company communications may be monitored without prior notification.

Lee put down the memo, noting that it was dated the previous Wednesday. Was that what Janet had been referring to?

She was feeling even more confused. Having telephone calls and electronic mail monitored was certainly a pain, but Janet had acted as if she were being singled out. Lee looked back at the letter. "*All* my messages . . . are being monitored and so are my telephone calls."

This was getting crazier by the minute. Lee didn't much care for this monitoring business, but it was supposedly being done to avoid breaches in security. Why would Janet have been singled out? Did someone think she was a security risk?

That was the craziest idea yet. Janet hadn't been an industrial spy. Lee would have sooner suspected herself. But Lee knew she wasn't addressing the real point. Janet had wanted to tell Lee something—something she wanted only Lee to hear. For heaven's sake, what?

Lee was once again interrupted by the intercom.

"Yes, Marge?"

"There's a Mr. L. E. Alexander here, who'd like to set up an appointment. He's interested in interviewing for the research chemist's position."

"Research chemist position? We don't have a requisition out for a research chemist position," Lee said.

Marge's voice had an almost apologetic tone. "We are preparing one, however, for the vacancy that occurred just this morning. Shall I set Mr. Alexander up for an appointment later this week?''

It took a moment more for the information to sink into Lee's dulled brain. The man in her outer office was applying for Janet's job! She had an immediate impression of a circling vulture. How grotesque and unfeeling could he be?

No, no, she was wrong. She had to get a hold on herself. She was acting like someone who had just lost a friend, not like the personnel manager of a major food processing company. A personnel manager was supposed to screen qualified applicants. This man didn't know Janet, didn't know how the vacancy had occurred. He was probably just some energetic job hunter looking for an opening.

And then it hit her. If this man didn't know what had happened to Janet, how did he know about the job opening? Nothing had been advertised. Suddenly, the arrival of Mr. Alexander to fill the vacancy left by Janet Homer's death took on a sinister feel.

Janet had written her a letter saying something was very wrong. Then Janet died. Almost immediately a man appeared applying for her job. The whole business was giving Lee the chills, although she had no idea why. One thing was clear, however. She wanted to know who this man was. And there was only one way to find out.

"Lee, are you still there?" Marge asked.

Lee folded up Janet's letter and put it back into its envelope. Then she folded the envelope in half and placed it in the pocket of her suit jacket.

"Yes, sorry. My attention strayed. Give Mr. Alexander an application form to fill out, and when it's completed, I'll see him."

Marge's voice was filled with barely contained surprise at the departure from normal procedure. "Mr. Alexander's application is already completed."

If there was something wrong with this eager applicant, now was the time for Lee to find out.

"Then send him in, Marge."

"Right now?"

"Right now," Lee said, opening up an empty desk drawer and sweeping in the contents of her In basket. By the time her office door was opened by her secretary to admit the applicant, Lee's desk was clean. She stood up and walked over to meet Mr. Alexander.

Her first impression was that he wasn't properly dressed for a job interview. He wore a wool cardigan over a beige sport shirt and slacks, and carried a similarly colored overcoat and umbrella. He couldn't be from San Francisco; he obviously believed the weather report's forecast of rain.

Then she looked past his attire to the man's face. She had to admit that it was a nice face.

Not one of the ruggedly handsome faces that seemed so popular on the movie screen, nor an impeccably groomed businessman's face that wore whatever expression made the boss happy. His was strong and subtle, with a steady, scholarly light in the deep-set brown eyes that watched her behind rimless glasses. His thick, straight brown hair was casually combed, and several defiant strands had formed a crisscross pattern across his forehead. He looked about thirty-five.

Lee extended her hand. "I'm B. A. Lee, personnel manager."

His hand felt large and warm as it shook hers. A firm, solid clasp. Lee was used to dealing with big men, but she sensed something extra, a quiet power within this man's casually dressed six-feet-two-inch frame.

"My application, Ms. Lee." His voice, deep and resonant, had that same solid quality.

Her predisposition to dislike, maybe even to distrust him, was quickly being overcome by his disarming manner. She wasn't sure what she had expected, but he wasn't it. The moment of truth was coming, however. She asked the question that had been burning in her mind since Marge had announced his arrival, trying to keep an accusing tone from her voice as she took the proffered application.

"Mr. Alexander, how did you come to hear about this opening with Varifoods?"

Lee saw some emotion flash behind those brown eyes. What was it?

"Actually, I didn't hear about the opening," Alexander said. "I've been in town job hunting and dropped in just to fill out an application and leave it with your office. Your secretary told me that coincidentally, a position in my field had just opened up.''

So it was as simple as that. That explained his casual clothes. He hadn't expected an interview. There was nothing sinister about him. Her suspicions had been aroused by Janet's strange letter and had nothing to do with him.

Lee exhaled some of the tension of the last few minutes. She motioned Mr. Alexander to a seat as she turned to her desk and sat down. Janet's death and her incredible letter were still foremost in her mind, but now that she had allowed this interruption in her morning, she would give it her best attention.

"If you'll just give me a moment, I'd like to review your application."

He nodded as he took the chair she'd indicated.

One part of her mind was still dwelling on the perplexities of Janet's letter, so she had to fight to put her current concerns aside in order to focus on assessing the information and the man behind it.

The first thing she noticed was that his penmanship was very neat. He didn't write out his answers, but printed everything in a block letters. Lee had noticed that many scientists did the same thing. Secondly, the information on his application showed him to be quite different from the usual applicant, scientist or not. She looked up and caught him watching her.

"You didn't fill in your complete first and middle name, Mr. Alexander. You just show the initials L. E. Is there some reason for this?"

"Yes. I don't use my first or middle name."

Lee understood that well enough. She didn't use hers, either. She glanced back over the application.

"Well, everything else looks quite complete. I want you to understand first of all that I consider a job interview a chance for Varifoods to get to know a prospective employee and a chance for the prospective employee to get to know Varifoods. So after I've asked my questions of you, I hope you will feel free to ask whatever questions you may have?"

"Yes. Thank you."

He was sitting back comfortably in his chair, entirely at ease, showing no trace of employment-interview jitters. He didn't look at all like a man who needed a job.

"Why do you want to work for Varifoods?" Lee asked.

"I believe it's a company with good potential, providing it maintains a strong research team."

Well, that sounded like a pretty stock answer from the average applicant for a research position. Lee decided she'd best probe a little deeper, to see just how average Mr. Alexander was. "What do you know about us?"

He looked as though he had been expecting the question. His answer came easily.

"The company diversified from grain milling into numerous branded consumer products three years ago, when it was bought out by Trans World Inc. Although the diversification into cereals, processed meat and cheese spreads, dairy products, fruit drinks and many more specialty items has produced steady growth, Varifoods hasn't really challenged its major rivals, particularly Tyberry Foods, International. So it can be reasonably assumed that your parent company, Trans World, is looking for more dramatic improvement."

It was an excellent answer and certainly got to the heart of her company's current thrust—and made his application all the more curious.

Lee leaned across her desk, as though by getting closer she might be able to better understand the man behind the steady, guarded eyes. "Mr. Alexander, did my secretary give you a copy of the job detail on a research chemist?"

"Yes."

"Did you have time to read it carefully? Not just the position responsibilities, but the salary, as well?"

Mr. Alexander nodded. "Is something bothering you?" he asked.

"Frankly, yes. Why would someone who has headed a division of the Food and Drug Administration in Washington want to take a one-third pay cut for a middle-level, research chemist position with Varifoods?"

His steady look did not waver.

"Simple. I would like to live in San Francisco. I'm tired of working for the government. I'd like to try my hand in the private sector, and my experience at the FDA makes such a career move possible."

A quick answer, to the point. No emotion, at least none on the surface. In her job, Lee was used to sizing up people. This man exuded a quiet confidence and consistency. Still, there was something about him she couldn't quite see, something fluid and uneven beneath the solid surface. She leaned back in her chair.

"If we were to offer you this job, it would not include full compensation for relocation from the East Coast. That is, Varifoods will financially assist new employees for major moving expenses, but such assistance rarely covers the complete costs of a move like yours. Would that deter you from seeking this position?"

"No. I'm prepared to assume the extra expenses."

He was still confident, still composed. Lee continued.

"I should also point out that chemist positions are filled rapidly because of our demanding research needs. Were we to offer you this position, we would want you to start right away. We would not be able to wait until June, when the school term ends. You may wish to consider how this midterm uprooting could negatively impact your family."

"I have no family."

He gave her another look from those steady brown eyes. But this time Lee saw a sadness around his mouth, almost as though an aftertaste of pain was still clinging to his lips.

She couldn't shake the feeling that there was a lot going on beneath Mr. Alexander's calm surface. Part of the impression came from the way those powerful hands grasped the arms of his chair.

Lee tried to clear her head of doubts. She told herself that the shock of the morning's events was causing her to lose objectivity, but the tone of suspicion and danger in Janet's letter kept resurfacing in her thoughts.

She glanced down at the application, more to regain control than because of the need to review it further. This man's education and experience more than qualified him for their research team. Perhaps her real worry should be whether Varifoods could challenge him enough to keep him.

"Is your current performance at the FDA considered satisfactory by your supervisor?"

"Yes." No hesitation in his manner, no defensive need to elaborate.

"May we contact your current supervisor at the FDA for verification of your employment and current job performance?"

"That would be awkward," he said.

"Then they don't know you're job hunting?" Lee asked.

"No. As far as they know, I'm on vacation."

"I see. Is this because you feel your employers would view you in a less desirable light, if they thought you were looking for other opportunities?"

"Wouldn't yours?" he asked.

Good point. Lee was certain that if Hamilton Jarrett found out she was looking for another job, he'd fire her on the spot. But she held back any response to Mr. Alexander's rhetorical question.

"Your situation is the same as that of many of our applicants, of course. We would not wish to jeopardize your current position. However, if we were to offer you this job, I trust you understand that employment would terminate if the information on your application was subsequently found to be inaccurate."

"Of course."

Again he had spoken confidently, easily.

"Well, I think that's all I need to ask. I'm satisfied that you are qualified in every respect. Please be assured that we will consider your application most carefully. However, as the opening has only just become available, we will be doing other interviewing before a decision is made."

"When do you expect to make a final determination?" he asked.

"Within two to three weeks. Are there any other questions I may answer for you, Mr. Alexander?" Lee asked.

"I'm called Alex, if you wouldn't mind. And yes, I'd like to know what type of research your chemists are engaged in at the moment?"

It was a reasonable request from an applicant, in a way. And yet it showed a certain naïveté about the current industry emphasis on secrecy. But then, what would an FDA biochemist know about private-sector security?

"Current research is quite confidential, Alex. Industrial espionage is a major concern to us. Even I am told only what I need to know to fulfill the requirements of my job. It would be the same for you, were this position to be offered and accepted."

Alex's question had given Lee an idea, however. She might be able to use his curiosity to satisfy her own. Janet had said it was too dangerous for Lee to go to her in the lab. But Janet was gone now. If her fear was that someone would see them talking together, that problem was gone, too.

Janet's loss was hurting Lee. The only way she felt able to overcome the pain would be to pursue the message in Janet's last letter, to find out what had been troubling her so. To do that, Lee decided, she must see Janet's workstation. She wanted to search it, to see if Janet had left any notes that might indicate what the trouble was. There was no time like the present.

Lee got to her feet. "Although I can't give you specifics on current research, I would like to take you on a brief tour of our lab, so that you will have a clear picture of what the facilities are like. I also think you should meet our chief chemist, George Peck. He would be your immediate supervisor."

"Thank you. I would appreciate that," he said. He got up to precede her to the door and opened it for her with a slight smile.

Lee rather liked the courteous gesture and slight smile. If she hadn't had Janet's mysterious message on her mind, she might have even smiled back.

"You can leave your umbrella and overcoat here, if you wish."

"They're light," Alex said, hanging them over his arm. Lee shrugged. On the way out they stopped at her secretary's desk.

Marge Klopman was sixty, barely five feet tall, with a tinge of blue in her eyes and hair. She was also the best secretary at Varifoods, or anywhere else in the world, as far as Lee was concerned. She kept up-to-date on policies and procedures and could usually tell Lee where any supervisor was—and what they were doing—at any time. Lee wasn't sure how Marge did it. One day she was going to have to ask her.

"Is George Peck in his office?" she said.

"Yes, Lee. I think he's waiting for Denise to show. But you might catch him before they get into . . . a meeting."

Lee thanked Marge, knowing she was about to say "a fight," but had caught herself because Mr. Alexander was present.

"Would you call George and tell him I'm bringing a prospective employee down?"

Marge nodded; her fingers were already tapping out the number of George's extension.

Lee led the way out of the office. With every step she took in the direction of the lab, she felt the tension mounting. She almost forgot Alex's presence as her mind kept repeating the words of Janet's letter.

Something is very wrong . . . too dangerous . . . only one I can trust . . . tell no one.

Chapter Two

Alex looked over his shoulder at the oversize, ceiling-mounted camera eye that seemed to be following him and the personnel manager down the hallway to the elevators. Briefly he wondered if someone was behind that lens, recording, watching.

He could see their images reflected in the glass, but he concentrated on hers—the light hair, the dark pin-striped suit, the high heels.

She certainly wasn't hard to look at from any angle. Her beauty was that subtle kind—the ash-blond hair, the pale skin, the eyes that seemed to reflect whatever color was around. As she'd talked to him this morning, they'd had a wave of dark blue in them, picked up from the dark blue threads in her suit jacket.

She was probably thirty, maybe a year or two older. He couldn't help thinking that she would look more natural stepping out of a Renaissance painting than a corporate boardroom. Only the deepness in her voice gave her strength away, reminding him that sometimes beauty was only skin-deep.

"What draws you to San Francisco, Alex?" she asked.

"Well, Lee... I hope you don't mind my calling you Lee?"

He watched as decision moved swiftly through her eyes. Everything he had seen so far told him she was not a woman who vacillated or who could be fooled for long. He would have to watch his step.

"Lee will be fine," she said.

"Well, Lee, a job at Varifoods and the weather brought me, mostly. I can't tell you how much I detest snow. And we had quite a bit of it this last winter."

"You don't like to ski?" Lee asked.

Alex smiled his slight smile.

"That's the difference between a Californian and an Easterner. When Californians think of snow, they think of driving to some mountain resort and skiing. But when Easterners think of snow, we think of shoveling a mountain of the stuff out of the way, just so we can get to the car."

Lee laughed lightly. The sound had a pleasant feel to Alex's ears. Then he noticed that she looked almost surprised by her own laughter, almost as though it wasn't appropriate. He wondered why.

"Oh, here come Denise Williams, our advertising manager, on a collision course," Lee said. "No doubt she's on her way to see George Peck. Come on. I'll introduce you."

Alex watched the mountain of a woman coming at him, feeling suddenly dwarfed. She lacked only about an inch to be as tall as himself, and Alex was sure she outweighed him by at least fifty pounds. Her hair, a mass of chestnut curls, bobbed around the lively and interested expression that shone out of her green eyes.

Lee introduced him as an applicant for the research chemist position, while Alex watched Denise Williams's eyes. There seemed to be the tiniest flicker of surprise, but he couldn't be sure. Then Alex shook her hand, feeling a good, firm response. This was one lady he'd never want to challenge to an arm-wrestling match.

"You're on your way to the lab?" Lee asked.

"Yes. His highness has so requested. What about you?" Denise inquired.

"I'm heading there, too. With Alex. So he'll have an opportunity to see the lab and to meet George. I thought it would only be fair for him to understand what taking this job would entail."

Denise smiled knowingly, then shook her chestnut curls.

"I don't think you're going to be able to get Alex in. Once we get to the ground floor, the security screen to the lab prohibits anyone from getting on the special bank of elevators unless their palm print has been encoded into the computer," she said.

Alex glanced at Lee to see how she'd take the news. She didn't look overly concerned. "The security guard did a manual override to let Alex through to the administrative offices. He can do a manual override to let him through to the lab," Lee said. "He's done it for me before."

Denise still shook her head. "Yes, the guards used to, but not any more. According to the latest from Gestapo headquarters, the only person who can override the palm-identification network to the lab is Steve Gunn. They rewired the guards' controls, switching everything to central security."

"That wasn't in the new security memo." Alex heard the protest in Lee's voice.

Denise shrugged. "The guards were never supposed to override the computer's electronic eye to the lab without an okay from Steve Gunn. But they got lax and went overboard, apparently. So Steve's clamped down. Now they can't override."

"What a pain," Lee said. Now Alex could see that her expression was indeed annoyed. Then she seemed to remember he was there and looked at him with a shrug of her shoulders. Her small smile was apologetic.

"Sorry, Alex. We're going through some pretty tight security measures these days. Necessary, I'm sure. But bothersome when you're not used to them. Come on, though. Even if we have to get Steve's permission, I want you to have your wish to see the lab and meet George. How else can you make an informed decision as to whether this is the place for you?"

It clearly wasn't a question she was expecting an answer to. Since Alex knew he hadn't asked to see the lab, he suddenly got the funny feeling that Lee wanted Denise to think it was his idea. But why? Was there some reason Lee wanted to go to the lab that had nothing to do with showing him around?

It was an interesting thought. Of course, Lee couldn't know he had been about to ask to see the lab, just before she volunteered to show him. Apparently they both needed to see the lab this morning.

Alex, Lee and Denise waited at the security station on the first floor for several minutes, while the guard attempted to locate the security chief within the building. Finally his image appeared on the television screen.

Alex caught a glance of the intense stare beneath the one bushy, dark eyebrow that seemed to span the man's entire forehead. A less bushy thatch of closely cropped dark hair was combed straight back. His look was stern, his words tightening his already thin lips. It was an expression devoid of humor. Even on the color monitor, the man's image seemed to project black and white.

Lee walked up to the screen and explained what she needed. Steve Gunn directed her to bring Alex in front of the screen. Alex could tell Lee was edgy and now annoyed, but she complied without comment.

Finally Steve Gunn signaled his okay, and the electronic eye was switched off from the security chief's end while Alex stepped through, then was turned back on again. Gunn told the guard to call him when Alex was ready to leave.

Alex had watched all the moves carefully. This would be a tough system to beat. He hoped he wouldn't be forced to try. As he stepped onto the elevator with the two women, he couldn't help but notice how Lee's right hand kept easing in and out of her jacket pocket. She seemed to be fingering something unconsciously. Alex got a glimpse of what appeared to be a white envelope, then Lee suddenly looked up at him as though she felt his scrutiny.

"How long have you worked here, Lee?" he asked, trying to mask his real interest.

"Nine years." A small smile. Distracted.

"And, you, Denise?"

"Just the last six months with Varifoods. But, I've worked for Trans World, the parent corporation, for several years. Where do you work now?" Denise inquired.

"The FDA," Alex said.

"You work at the FDA?" Denise repeated, a new tone in her voice and new interest in her eyes.

Alex didn't have a chance to respond. Lee interrupted as the elevator doors opened.

"Here's the lab. You're about to meet our guru of the taste buds," she said.

As soon as they stepped through the door labeled Laboratory, someone in a white coat came sweeping up to them. Before he had any time to look around, Alex found himself face-to-face with the most emaciated man he had ever seen. He was just over six feet, big-boned and bald, and maybe about forty. Skin barely covered his protruding cheekbones and chin. His thick eyebrows formed wings on either side of his forehead and his nose was large and flat. Alex had a flashing mental image of a praying mantis.

"This is George Peck, our chief chemist," Lee said. "George runs the lab, scheduling the work and evaluating all results. He has four chemists reporting to him. George, this is Alex, a candidate for the research chemist position."

A bony hand reached for his. Alex was startled both by its strength and by the alertness in the medium blue eyes that studied his face so carefully. Alex had to stop himself from stepping back in an automatic reflex action. It was as though the chief chemist had tried to come too close.

Peck's intense gaze swept back to Lee, his scientific curiosity in Alex having been apparently both aroused and satisfied by that one brief scrutiny.

"I don't have time to talk. I must meet with Denise here about the advertising schedule for our...the line we were discussing earlier. Denise."

His tone expressed a summons to the advertising manager. Alex could tell that wasn't going over well with the big woman. Her feet took root in the white tile floor.

"We already talked about the advertising schedule, George. I have everything in hand. I don't see what a further discussion would serve," Denise said.

George's expression made it clear he was displeased that Denise hadn't yet moved in the direction of his private office. "We may need to move its introduction up, depending on the results of the field test," he said.

"Move the introduction up? You must be crazy! Ham told me it wouldn't be for another two months. I've been working my tail off every night and weekend, as it is! You can't just get space in the media overnight! I've got TV and magazine spots booked! You understand, paid for!''

Alex watched Denise's color begin to deepen. If George Peck noticed, he didn't pay it any heed. He took a step toward Denise.

"Look, an earlier introduction is good news. It means the tests are going well. You've been complaining so much about how difficult it's been to keep the project under wraps, I thought you'd be delighted. Seems like you're never happy. Now, are you coming into my office to work with me on the changes, or are you going to stand there and whine?''

George Peck's eyes were as cold as his words. Alex heard Lee's intake of breath. Both watched Denise's already flushed face turn crimson. Her large hands clenched into fists, but the big woman maintained control. Although she continued to glare at George, her words to Lee and Alex were as pleasant and polite as before.

"Nice to have met you, Alex. Catch you later, Lee.''

Lee nodded in agreement as Denise followed George into his office. Alex could see she was relieved the episode was over.

Alex wasn't sure why it had happened. Obviously Denise was upset over some change in schedule. Alex had the feeling that George had goaded Denise, had deliberately said things to make her angry. Without knowing either one too well, it was difficult to tell. He wondered if Lee might open up to him about it.

"Unusual working relationship," he said and waited, but she didn't immediately take the bait. Instead she turned toward the lab, as though something else were on her mind. After a moment she sighed.

"George can be abrasive. It's best you should know that up front. Perhaps it's a good thing you saw him in action. I'm sorry he won't be available to answer your technical questions, but as long as we have the time, why don't we tour the lab? There's a kitchen in the back where the chemists, aided by the computer, mix up their concoctions. Only George and the research chemists have keys, but I can at least show you the workstations here in the big room.''

Again Alex got the feeling that Lee had some ulterior motive for being here, a motive that his presence was serving to cover. He followed her lead.

The room was large, twenty feet wide by thirty feet long. It had no windows and the walls were lined with floor to ceiling shelves. The brightness of the fluorescent ceiling fixtures also caught Alex's eye. No matter what the time of day or weather conditions, this room would always feel cheery. It would be a good place to work. He had been in enough dingy labs to appreciate controlled lighting.

There were two wide, spacious cubicles on each side of the center aisle. Alex could see the heads of the biochemists sticking out above the five-foot-high partitions surrounding the cubicles at the front of the room.

These were the men and women who belonged to one of the most creative of professions, one that sought to discover the universe's secrets. It didn't matter that they were seeking out the secrets of the stomach. The principle was the same. He always felt a high at being one of their number.

One tall dark chemist in the front lifted his head as Alex walked by. He was at least six foot two, with dark soulful eyes and a very long and full black beard. His unusual appearance, his staring eyes and the hunch to his shoulders all reminded Alex of the pictures he had seen of the monk Rasputin, intimate of the last imperial family of Russia. His nameplate said Michael Ware.

Lee was talking in a distracted sort of way about how the computer was programmed with mechanical arms located in the kitchen, enabling it to access the various chemicals and foodstuffs and mix them according to the scientific formulations of the chemists.

"The 'arms' are really vacuum tubes that suck up the various ingredients being programmed into the recipe," she said.

"So from their positions, the chemists can try out various mixtures in the computer and then go to the kitchen to taste the final product?" Alex asked.

"Taste, possibly. Or smell, or examine the texture or the color. As you know, there are only four basic tastes: sweet, sour, bitter and salty. Much of food appreciation is involved in how a product smells and looks and feels, both in and out of our mouths. And then there are the equally important features of nutrition, ease of preparation and how it fits in with our cultural biases.''

''Yes, equally important,'' Alex repeated with a smile.

Lee seemed to realize only then that she had been lecturing to someone who no doubt knew considerably more than she did on the subject. ''I'm sorry. Of course, you know,'' she said with an apologetic smile.

Alex's shrug said it wasn't important. Actually he was glad Lee had expounded on the food processing business a bit. It let him know how much she knew. That she had a good grasp of the subject did not surprise him.

But as he walked by the cubicles, Alex was somewhat surprised by the stark whiteness and meticulous neatness everywhere. Each workstation was occupied by an immaculately clad chemist bent over a microscope or computer keyboard. Their positions were so pristine, so neat. Almost too much so.

Then he saw it.

At the far back of the room one cubicle was empty. Lee had begun to say something, to turn in another direction, but Alex was no longer paying attention. Instead he moved toward the empty cubicle, almost as though it were inviting him there.

It wasn't like the other cubicles. And somehow he had known it wouldn't be. This one had happy faces and funny drawings tacked up, as if its inhabitant were rebelling against the neatness and conformity that prevailed everywhere else. Alex laughed as he read a couple of the cartoons.

Then a small gold frame set in the right rear corner caught his eye. He reached for it and found it was really two small oval pictures, connected at the center. The picture on the right was of a smiling man holding a boy who looked about four years old. The one on the left was of a tiny, sleeping baby, probably no more than a week or two old. He fingered the pictures for a moment before returning them to the back of the desk.

He was about to open the desk drawers when he became aware of Lee by his side. He turned and managed a small smile.

"I think if I were a scientist in this lab, I'd want this cubicle to be mine. It's a happy spot, isn't it?"

Lee nodded, but her look was strained and, he thought, maybe even cautious. Something was definitely bothering this personnel manager. Her hand was once again fingering the envelope in her pocket. He wondered.

Then his attention was diverted by the lifting of a dark head on his right. He saw a curious face watching him across the aisle. He decided to introduce himself and walked over, extending his hand.

"Hi. I'm L. E. Alexander. Call me Alex."

"You're an employee?" the small, round woman asked.

"I'm not hired yet, but I'm working on it."

Her short black hair bobbed up and down as she took his hand and gave it a hesitant shake. Her dark eyes studied him. "I'm Pam Heyer. You're a biochemist?"

"Yes. I'm working back East now, Pam, but I'm hoping to make a job connection here. I thought this might be the right company for me. Have you been working for Varifoods long?"

"Almost seven years."

"Then you must like the company?"

"It's okay. I haven't really worked anyplace else, so it's kind of hard to compare it." Pam shook her head, contradicting the noncommittal tone of her words.

"I understand. What are you working on?" Alex hoped his tone sounded natural, but it didn't matter. Pam hadn't heard what he said. She was clearly too interested in looking behind him.

"What is she doing?" Pam asked, almost in a whisper. Alex turned, following her gaze.

Lee was at the desk he had just left. She had just closed one of the drawers and was scanning the desktop and computer work space. She seemed annoyed by the scraps from the perforated ends of green and white computer sheets that were strewn over the desk next to the dot matrix printer. She gathered them up with a preoccupied air and bent down to deposit them in the wastebasket. As she dropped them in, she hesitated in her bent position, obviously surprised by what she saw.

Alex looked down. There, sticking out of the otherwise empty wastebasket was a small, brand-new desk lamp. Alex watched a look of confusion cross Lee's face.

Then she pulled the lamp out of the wastebasket and set it on the desk. Her movement caused the white envelope she had been fingering so much to slip out of her pocket and fall to the floor, but Lee didn't seem to notice. Alex said nothing as she plugged the lamp into a nearby outlet and flipped the switch. A small fluorescent tube in the lamp glowed obediently.

"Now why would someone bring a desk lamp into such a brightly lit room?" Pam inquired, standing next to him. Her voice was almost a conspiratorial whisper. "There's certainly no need for it. The additional light is barely discernible."

"Doesn't seem too logical, does it?" Alex said, finding that his own voice had gotten much quieter. He thought it curious that this chemist seemed suspicious of the personnel manager.

"Who sits there?" Alex asked.

Pam seemed suddenly upset, edgy. Her dark eyes avoided his, Alex observed. "Her name was Janet Homer. She died last week."

Before Alex had an opportunity to respond, the sound of footsteps drew their attention to the middle aisle. Out of the corner of his eye, Alex saw Lee reach for something at the back of the desk, then she quickly released it. In one quick, fluid movement, she stepped into the aisle to greet the new arrival. Pam immediately put her head down, as though trying not to call attention to herself.

"Hello, Steve," Lee said. "Didn't expect to see you again so soon. What brings you to the lab?"

The man was definitely the same one Alex had seen on the television screen at the guard's station. In person he was a little shorter and broader than Alex had anticipated. Lee was tall enough to look him straight in the eye. And she was doing just that.

"Just making my rounds," Steve Gunn said. "I find a security presence is a good reminder. Keeps people on the straight and narrow."

To Alex, Gunn's words sounded as though they were being shot from his mouth. His small, dark eyes darted to and fro beneath that beetle brow, as though he expected trouble to pounce at any moment and wanted to see it coming.

His posture was so rigid that he could have been wearing a board down his back. While Steve's attention was still on Lee, Alex moved into the aisle and placed his umbrella on top of the desk that had once belonged to Janet Homer. Less than a second later, Lee turned back to him.

"Well, Alex, seen enough?" she asked.

Alex nodded and followed her past the security chief toward the door. Lee had only taken a couple of steps when she swung around once more...to face Steve Gunn, who was still standing in the aisle.

"Well, Steve? Alex is leaving. You'll need to go back to your office to release the electronic eye."

The look on Steve Gunn's face made it obvious he had forgotten, but he put his head back even further as he prepared to deny it.

"I'll just have a quick look around here first," he said. "Something I came to get."

Lee shrugged and led the way back to the elevators. As they passed George Peck's office, the chief chemist and the advertising manager were just getting up. Apparently their meeting was over. Out in the hallway, Lee and Alex stood for more than a minute in silence as they waited for a free elevator. Alex had the feeling Lee had forgotten he was there. Just as an elevator came, Denise walked up.

"Glad that's over. How about you two?" she asked.

Lee nodded, but didn't say anything. Her mind seemed miles away. Alex wondered where it had gone. But as the elevator started to descend, she surprised him by asking a question.

"So what do you think?"

"If you're talking about the lab setup," he said, "I don't think it can be beat. If you're talking about your security chief, the guy looks like he eats bullets for breakfast and talks like he's spitting them out.''

Both Lee and Denise laughed.

"So you got to meet old Steve in person, I see," Denise said. "Bullets for breakfast is a good description."

"Great description," Lee amended as they stepped off the elevator.

The advertising manager shrugged her fullback's shoulders. "Well, I admit he seems to be a bit much. But if you stick around, you'll get used to him. Lee and I have. Like one of the family.''

Alex could see Lee's expression didn't mirror Denise's. He once again looked up at the wall-mounted cameras in each corridor they passed.

"One of the family?" he said. "You mean Steve's just a 'big brother' as in 1984's Big Brother?"

Lee and Denise both laughed again; this time Denise lowered her voice conspiratorially.

"Please, Alex. The hidden microphones," she said, not at all seriously. Then she turned to Lee. "You hire this man, Lee, or I'll never forgive you. We don't laugh enough around here."

Lee smiled noncommittally, then gave a sudden start as a handsome blond man with a brown mustache emerged without warning from an adjoining hallway. She sure seemed jumpy, Alex thought to himself.

"Hi, Lee, Denise," the blond man said. He extended a hand to Alex.

Lee recovered sufficiently to do the introductions.

"Alex, this is John Carstairs, our finance manager. Alex is applying for the research chemist's position, John.''

John Carstairs's light blue eyes puckered at the corners as he flashed a toothy grin at Alex from beneath his mustache. His handshake felt sweaty and tentative.

"Good to meet you, Alex. I thought I saw you folks up in the lab. Wondered what was going on?''

It was a question, but neither Lee nor Denise responded. Alex wondered what had really been asked. Since Alex's presence had been explained, was John Carstairs interested in what Denise was doing with George? And if so, why? Was there something going on here he should be taking note of?

John had obviously gotten the message that no information was forthcoming. He didn't seem disappointed, but launched instead into a discussion of a party planned for the coming Thursday night.

"Now just because my birthday and third service anniversary with old Varifoods just happen to occur on the same day as the annual party, I don't want you ladies to think you have to buy me expensive presents. Modest ones will be graciously accepted."

Lee shook her head tolerantly. "And what do you consider modest?" she asked.

"Oh, a new pair of skis. Or a ski rack for the old Chevy Blazer. You can even take advantage of the after-season sales. I won't think less of you, as long as you take off the discounted price tag."

"Big of you," Denise said. But she was smiling.

"Consider yourself lucky if you get a cake to cut on Thursday, John," Lee said good-humoredly.

"Now, Lee, I protest! When you hired me for this glorious position, you told me I could expect modest presents on a regular basis. I swear it's in my contract."

Both women looked at each other and shook their heads. Apparently they were familiar with John's act.

"You didn't read your contract right, John. What it says is that your modest *presence* is expected on a regular basis," Lee said.

Denise and John both laughed. But John wasn't finished pleading his case.

"What the hell, you know I can't spell. Still you have to admit, good finance managers are hard to find, so I suggest you both head for the stores this afternoon and..."

While John continued his protest, Alex knew it was his cue.

"Excuse me. I seemed to have left my umbrella upstairs in the lab. I remember setting it down on a desk. Must have forgotten to pick it up again. I'll have to go back."

Lee turned and looked at him thoughtfully.

"I'll come with you," she said.

"No, I think it might take both you and Denise to talk John out of his presents," he said with a slight smile. "I'll just pop up and be back in a minute. I'll meet you at the guard station."

To forestall any more discussion, he moved quickly between the closing doors of an elevator, leaving no chance for anyone to follow.

He walked quickly out the elevator doors the moment they opened onto the lab floor. The elevator right next to him was just closing. He caught sight of Steve Gunn's scowl just before the doors met in front of his face. The security chief was on his way down.

Alex didn't waste any time, but walked directly through the swinging door into the lab. George Peck was sitting in his office. Alex didn't see him look up as he turned toward the large open room where the chemists worked. Michael Ware's head came up slightly over his hunched shoulders as Alex walked quickly down the middle aisle to the empty cubicle at the end.

As Alex reached the desk, he saw that Pam Heyer, the short, dark-haired chemist opposite, had stepped away. It was just as well. He didn't want an audience. Immediately he reached for his planted umbrella and picked it up. In the next moment, he had the desk drawers open and was taking a look.

Nothing there seemed out of the ordinary—just a few interoffice memos, some writing supplies and a box of facial tissues. He closed the drawers and looked longingly up at the dark computer screen monitor. No use in turning it on. He had absolutely no idea what the internal computer system was like at Varifoods. No doubt it involved passwords and other security measures.

Then he looked over the desk, trying to remember where everything had been when he first saw it. The happy faces were still in place. The funny cartoons. The small gold frame with the pictures. The superfluous lamp was still sitting where Lee had put it, shining weakly. But what had Lee reached for, and why had she decided not to take it?

A sudden thought occurred to him. He looked down at the polished, white-tiled floor beneath the desk. He couldn't see what he was looking for. He stepped quickly around the desk, searching every corner, but it was gone. He checked the wastepaper basket, but it wasn't there, either. There was only one answer.

Someone had picked up the white square envelope that had fallen from Lee's pocket. And it hadn't been the personnel manager.

Alex made his way out of the lab to the elevator and rode down to the guard's station to join the others. But with each step the questions pounded in his ears.

Who had picked up the envelope Lee dropped? And why? Why did Lee's unconscious preoccupation with it make him think that it was something important?

GEORGE PECK had watched the tall man calling himself L. E. Alexander return to the lab and disappear into Janet's cubicle for a couple of minutes. George couldn't imagine what he hoped to find, but it was clear he was looking for something, and that was a bad sign. Whoever this Alexander guy was, he wasn't an applicant.

George absentmindedly tapped the top of his typewriter. He was sure he recognized the tall man. Could it be from that seminar in Washington, D.C. several years before? If it was, a lot of trouble could be brewing. Particularly if that personnel manager was helping this guy to infiltrate the Varifoods research team.

George's thin fingers reached into his desk drawer for a cigar. He took his time in lighting it, still preoccupied with his new problem. If he could spot this guy, so could others. That wasn't good. He needed a contingency plan.

His hand reached for the phone, then he remembered his calls were monitored. He put the receiver back and puffed on his cigar. The security chief couldn't be trusted. He'd tell Steve Gunn only what he wanted him to know, when he wanted him to know it. So for the time being, he'd best leave the building and use a pay phone on the corner. It should only take about fifteen minutes.

He rose from his chair to leave his office, but stopped as he got a glimpse of Pamela Heyer returning to her cubicle.

She'd been gone at least five minutes. Where had she been? What had she been doing? She always seemed to be sneaking around.

He frowned. She had been working directly opposite Janet. What had she seen? Perhaps it would be best to watch her for a while.

Chapter Three

Lee felt uneasy through the rest of the morning. Who had used Janet's desk? Janet's computer? Janet's printer? Who had left that lamp in her wastepaper basket? And why?

As though those concerns weren't enough, now she couldn't find Janet's letter. She had searched her pockets, her desk, her office. It was no use. She had lost it. But where?

She tried to think. She had put it in her pocket when Alex came into her office. She had gone to the lab with him, said goodbye at the guard's station and returned to her office. Could she have dropped it somewhere along the way?

The intercom buzzed. "Yes, Marge?"

"It's five to one, Lee. Shouldn't you be heading for Ham's office?"

Lee looked at her watch, not believing how quickly time had passed. Somehow she had missed lunch. She still had barely scratched the surface of her overflowing In basket. Janet's death and letter had claimed all of her attention, with the exception of her impromptu interview with Alex. And she had even used that to search Janet's desk.

But none of her efforts seemed to be to any avail. No matter how hard she thought about it, she still could not figure out what her friend had meant.

Lee thought that maybe Janet had contacted her because the problem had something to do with personnel. Had someone been treated unfairly, even had their rights violated? Had they been afraid to come forward? Had Janet decided to champion their cause?

Lee shook her head. No, somehow the idea just didn't fit the real fear in Janet's words. But what did fit?

Well, there was no time to think any more about it now. She had to see Hamilton Jarrett.

"Lee, did you hear me?" Marge asked.

"Right, Marge. I'm on my way," Lee said as she picked up a pen, pad and the new security memo.

Four flights up and she was outside the president's office. His secretary beckoned her to go in. Swallowing uneasily, she opened the door.

Hamilton Gordon Jarrett's appearance projected a personality almost larger than life. At least six foot five and two hundred and thirty pounds, his build, although partly obscured by a well-tailored, dark blue suit, promised mostly muscle. His full, red hair was only just held in check, and dark reddish-brown eyes beamed at her like brake lights beneath bushy eyebrows. The hand he extended to her, pawlike and covered with a mat of red hair right down to his knuckles, seemed gigantic.

A big, overgrown orangutan with a brain transplant from Lee Iacocca was the irreverent thought that had come to mind when she first met the new president eight months before. Her impression had not changed since, although she had only seen him on a couple of other occasions. She shook his large pawlike hand, wincing from his sharp grip.

He motioned her to sit down and then loomed over her chair as his voice growled down at her.

"We haven't talked much since I became the head of this company, Lee. I've been too busy grabbing a hold of the heart and lungs to breathe life into this old body. Personnel is just a periphery organ, as you know."

Lee didn't know any such thing. As far as she was concerned, if any factor constituted the heart of a company, it was its people. Without the selection and cultivation of good people, there was no company. However when she argued that point with Hamilton Jarrett at their first meeting, he had made it clear that he did not share her sentiments. And he hadn't done so in the nicest manner, either. Unlike Dave Erickson, the previous president of Varifoods, Hamilton

Jarrett didn't appreciate opinions that differed from his own.

"My time's been well spent," he went on. "I know the strengths and weaknesses of every vein and artery in this old company. I'm its brain. Its heart. Its new blood. Its guts."

Lee was glad she hadn't had any lunch. This image that Ham was so fond of was not only beyond her capacity to appreciate on a literary level, but also threatened to make her sick.

"I'm telling you this so you'll understand that nothing operates without my knowledge, my drive, my approval. I know everything that goes on. Nothing can be kept from me."

Lee wondered if Hamilton Jarrett was trying to give her a not-so-subtle message. The missing letter suddenly came to mind. Had she dropped it in Steve Gunn's presence? Had he picked it up, read it and taken it to Ham? Was Ham expecting her to confess to having received it?

Lee tried to calm her jumpy nerves. Ham had never struck her as someone who would pull any punches. If he really thought there was something wrong with her receiving such a letter from Janet, he surely would have come right out and said it, wouldn't he? Besides, how could it be wrong?

"I know everyone is fond of calling me the 'Big Ham' behind my back. But what they don't know is that I like it. I've even told Steve to encourage it. After all, I believe what Shakespeare said. Life is a stage. And it's the big Hams of this world who dominate life's stage and make it shake and pulsate."

As Hamilton Jarrett paused to look down at her, Lee realized that she had let her imagination get the better of her. Ham knew nothing about the letter. He was just trying to imbue her with his philosophy.

Maybe she should tell him. If something was wrong within the company, and everything about Janet's letter said there was, surely Hamilton Jarrett should be told? He was an uncompromising man, true, but he was still the president of Varifoods.

Her former boss's words echoed in her ears: *"He's a mover, a real shooting star and Trans World is grooming him*

*for the top echelons where they like 'em tough. He has a
different management style. You'll learn a lot from him."*

Despite her thoughts or maybe because of them, she returned Hamilton Jarrett's look directly and with serious
consideration. If she told him, should it be now or at the end
of whatever it was he wanted to say?

"You'd best also understand that I tolerate no disloyalty.
People are the easiest things to replace," he went on.

Lee looked down at the memo in her hands, trying to bite
back her retort to his totally insensitive comment. Thoughts
of telling Hamilton Jarrett anything were fading rapidly.
Dave Erickson had said she'd learn a lot from this man.
What he hadn't said was that she wouldn't necessarily like
what she learned.

"I see you brought the new security memo. I want you to
take your pen right now and underline what it says about
not discussing company business with anyone, including
other employees without a need to know," Ham told her.

Lee complied, although she felt adult enough to get the
message without this underlining business.

"Good. Now commit it to memory. Too many lacka-
daisical attitudes exist among the employees of this company. They'll be no more fraternizing with the enemy. This
company is at war, and we take no prisoners."

She nodded at the look of expectation in his purposeful
stare. He glanced away, seemingly satisfied.

"I take everything that happens here personally. My
people don't work for Varifoods—they work for me. My
people don't concentrate on pleasing some unknown stock-
holders or the public—they concentrate on pleasing me.
Remember that when you interview candidates for positions here. Instill it in them. And keep it in mind as you assume your new duties."

Finally they were getting to the real reason for this meeting. Lee listened as Jarrett went on.

"My predecessor performed all the public relations
functions of this company, and he did a passable job. But
it's not a job for the president. And it doesn't entail enough
work for another full-time manager. So I've decided to give
the responsibilities to you."

Oh, goody, Lee thought. *Just what I needed. More work and in an area I know nothing about.*

As though hearing her silent protest, Ham continued. "I know you have no experience as a public relations manager, but you're familiar with the food processing industry. Erickson and your previous bosses considered you an outstanding performer, capable of looking past interfering details, seeing the big picture. Which is good. Big pictures must always be kept in mind. Remember that."

Hamilton Jarrett looked away from Lee once again to stare out the floor-to-ceiling windows of his massive corner office. His gaze took in the view of San Francisco Bay and the Golden Gate Bridge, much as though he too was seeking the big picture he had just mentioned.

"You also have an M.B.A., which tells me you have at least been exposed to public relations concepts. But you'll still have to prove yourself to me."

Ham's reddish-brown eyes returned to her face.

"Despite what any of your previous bosses have said about you, your continued employment here will rest solely with me and how I assess your performance. After all, you haven't had much to do, just being a personnel manager. Adding public relations should test your mettle."

Lee was tasting blood as she bit her tongue. *Oh, Dave,* she thought. *How could you accept a position on the board of directors of Trans World and abandon me to this orangutan? Somebody who neither values nor understands good employees?*

"As the new public relations manager for Varifoods," Ham went on, "you'll be expected to respond immediately and intelligently to any queries about our products and processes from the board of directors, regulatory bodies or the general public. I accept no excuses. There are no second chances and there is no time to erase mistakes."

Hamilton Jarrett was again pausing to study her, Lee saw. She was beginning to feel the strain at the back of her neck from having to look up at him from her seated position.

"I'm leaving town tonight on confidential business. I'll be back Thursday night for the party. I'll keep in touch in case you get something you can't handle. But if you can't handle something, you'd better have a good reason why not. Is that clear?''

''Yes,'' Lee said.

''Good. I'll call you at ten tomorrow morning.''

''I won't be here at ten,'' Lee said.

Hamilton Jarrett looked at Lee as though she had just spit on his foot. ''Why not?'' he asked.

''Janet Homer was a friend of mine. Her funeral is tomorrow morning,'' Lee said.

She didn't miss the quick frown and twitch at the corner of those reddish-brown eyes. What had generated his discomfort? Was he embarrassed? Or was he really so unconcerned about his employees that all he felt when one died was annoyance?

''How did you know Janet Homer?''

Something about the way Ham asked that question caused a chill to run down her spine. Although she couldn't say specifically why, she was suddenly very glad that she had not volunteered the information about Janet's letter.

''I got to know Janet just as I've gotten to know many of Varifoods' employees—around the office, at company events.''

Ham didn't seem satisfied with her answer.

''The woman worked as a research chemist in the lab. I hardly think you two would run into each other 'around the office.' ''

Lee was on the defensive now and she knew it. Ham's voice was even enough, but there was an underlying quality to it that she didn't like. For some reason her friendship with Janet disturbed him—and that disturbed Lee.

She got the sudden impression that she had waded into a lake that was too deep. A disturbing feeling of danger surrounded her, but she fought to control her voice, her expression.

''When Dave Erickson was president, he used to sponsor a yearly picnic at his home for all employees. I met Janet there several years ago.''

Those reddish-brown eyes stared at her for a full minute. Lee looked back, her gaze steady and unblinking. Finally, the big man turned his eyes away.

"Leave a message with my secretary if anything comes up tomorrow that I should know about. While I'm away I'll call you directly each morning at ten."

His tone and manner were so nonchalant that Lee wondered if she had imagined the unpleasant exchange they had just had.

Ham picked up what Lee recognized as a computer copy of a personnel record. She didn't have to guess whose. He read it for several minutes before saying anything. Curious behavior, she reflected. It was almost as though he thought it necessary to take an even closer look at her.

"Your records show that your full name is Bernard Allen Lee. That's obviously a man's name. What possessed your parents? Were they so disappointed you were a girl they pretended not to notice?"

This was one subject that Lee did not want to discuss. Why was Ham bringing it up now? Was he trying to show a personal interest in her in his own gruff way? Something about the man made Lee doubt it.

"Hard to tell," she replied.

"You never asked them?" Ham's tone was disbelieving.

"I never asked them."

She knew that the way she answered would tell him that she didn't like to be questioned about her personal life. For the first time in their conversation, he moved from his standing position before her and went to sit behind his desk. Lee thankfully lowered her head. Her neck muscles registered their relief.

She couldn't read his position change or the look he was now giving her. For a moment he seemed to want to prolong the interview, to regain something that he had misplaced during their brief exchange of words. But whatever it was, he apparently thought better of it. Maybe he just didn't want to waste any more time on her.

"See my secretary outside. He will give you my written instructions. Follow them."

Lee stood and turned, aware that she was being dismissed. She had reached the door before he sent his final message.

"Good luck." His tone was almost encouraging.

Lee turned back at his words, thinking how much more at ease she would be feeling if he had projected that attitude through their entire conversation. But that obviously was not the style of this man. He'd deliberately set out to keep her off balance—first a stern recitation of standards with the dire consequences of the slightest mistake—and finally a tardy token of support.

Maybe this was how he treated everyone. Maybe he had just dumped her into the coop with the other chickens to join in pecking frantically for the occasional seed. But however well he succeeded in plucking her feathers, Lee knew she wouldn't show it. If she proved to have no other talents in this new capacity as public relations manager, her poker face would serve her well.

Lee curled her lips in a brilliant, confident smile. "Thank you, Ham."

As she turned once more to leave, she didn't miss Ham's look of surprise, mingled with something like mistrust.

HAMILTON JARRETT SAT for a full minute after Lee had left his office, just staring at the closed door.

The woman was an enigma. He couldn't seem either to intimidate her or to get her to release the air of reserve she held like a shield. Those things had bothered him from the first.

But she did her job well, kept her end running so smoothly that he hadn't had to concern himself with it at all. Not that it was good to let her know it. Patting people on the back just made them soft, gave them too high an opinion of themselves. Better to get them on the edge, grateful for every occasional crumb of praise.

Besides, if they weren't too sure of themselves, they were a lot less likely to cook up trouble. He had told George that. He had warned him to be a strong manager. But George hadn't been strong enough. At least not strong enough for Janet Homer.

Fortunately, she was one problem that no longer existed. But how many more did he have? Finding out that Janet and Lee had been friends opened up a whole new arena of trouble. What if the damn chemist had talked? The thought brought a new frown to his already wrinkled brow.

He buzzed his secretary.

"Yes, sir?"

"Get me Steve Gunn. Now."

"BUT IT WASN'T an accident, Willy."

"I don't care what it was or wasn't, Alex. You had no right to just take off. Have you forgotten we're already overburdened? Do you know what your absence is going to mean to the rest of the staff?"

William Hansen's voice pounded clearly over the line, belying the three thousand miles that separated them.

"I can't help it. I can't just let it go and pretend it didn't happen. Dammit, she's dead!" Alex said.

Willy must have heard the desperation in his voice, because his own grew more even, less agitated.

"Cars crash every day. The police have labeled this an accident. Woman just lost control of her vehicle. Probably fell asleep at the wheel. There's nothing you or I or anybody can do now. You do see that, don't you?"

Alex stopped pacing and clasped the drapes on the window of his hotel room as if he were clasping the shoulders of his supervisor, trying to get a message through.

"I tell you I spoke to the police. I know why they said it was an accident, and they were wrong!"

"For God's sake, Alex, how can you be so sure?"

Alex exhaled, trying to regain some calm, to control the emotion that was coloring his voice.

"Willy, I already told you she called. You have to understand, she asked for me. Something was wrong, desperately wrong. She told me she needed to see me right away, couldn't discuss it over the phone."

The line was quiet for a moment. Alex hardly noticed. The churning of his insides was giving him no respite, no time for reflection. He had been able to retain an outward calm for only so long. Now the pain was coming out.

"You knew this Janet Homer personally?" Willy asked.

Alex straightened, released the curtains from his grasp and resumed his pacing.

"We were in school together. We shared some times, even after she moved to the West Coast. She was... Sally's sister."

"Sally's sister? Damn. I'm sorry, Alex."

"She was a good person, Willy, a straight shooter. If she told me something was wrong, it was because she needed my help, my professional help."

"But, what *exactly* did she say was wrong?"

Alex tried to read the tone of Willy's voice. It seemed to have lost its original argumentative quality, even showed some interest.

"She didn't say. She said she couldn't say. She wanted me to fly out to talk with her. You understand? She felt it was that important."

"What did you tell her when she called?"

Alex's shoulders slumped beneath the weight of his answer.

"I told her I couldn't come immediately. We were fighting a deadline on approval for a new drug. You remember, Dawson Pharmaceuticals, the one we finished late Friday night. I said I'd be there, I mean here, by Saturday afternoon."

Alex's fingers raked through his hair and came to rest on the back of his upturned head. His eyes watched the ceiling.

"If only I..."

"If only you what? If only you'd dropped everything and grabbed a plane? What time did she call you? Didn't you say just after three o'clock on Friday? That made it after noon in San Francisco. She was dead twelve hours later. Are you trying to convince me you could have stopped it? You could have prevented her from losing control of her car?"

Alex pressed his hand against the wall of his room, almost as though he were trying to hold it up, he reflected wryly.

"She didn't lose control. It couldn't have been an accident. Something was wrong at her company. She called me to report it. Then twelve hours later she's dead. Doesn't that sound a little too coincidental to you? Don't you have any curiosity about what it was she was going to tell me?"

Now Willy's tone was full of protracted patience.

"Alex, we're the Food and Drug Administration, not the FBI. Your friend worked for Varifoods, and their parent corporation is Trans World. That's a large, reputable firm. It's not as though we're dealing with some fly-by-night drug company smuggling in some bad narcotics from south of the border."

Alex shook his head.

"Being big doesn't insure honesty, Willy. Far from it. Have you forgotten those falsified test results we got from that large pharmaceutical firm on its new barbiturate? Any reference to hair loss had been deliberately omitted from the data. Took a lot of very angry—and, if I need to remind you—bald men and women to alert us to that side effect. This wouldn't be the first time a big company tried to cut some of our corners," Alex said.

"Cut corners? What corners? This isn't a drug company we're talking about. Food manufacturers are not required to provide us with their recipes or formulations, and we don't approve finished food products."

Alex was losing his fight for control over his voice. "You act as though we have no responsibility for food. You know it's our job to insure health standards, to approve new additives. You know as well as I that food acts within the body just as a drug does. And, just like bad drugs, bad food can kill."

"Alex, Varifoods' processing plants have gone through all the regular inspections and consistently passed. They have not applied for approval of a new additive. So, even if there is an internal problem within the company, we simply have no say in the matter."

"No say in the matter? Do we have a right to take a chance here? Hope that everything is okay? Damn it, Willy, Janet was a top chemist. She wouldn't have been so upset without good reason. If there is something wrong at Varifoods, and I truly believe there is, how could you live with yourself if you did nothing?"

Alex could almost hear the tension at the other end of the line. He imagined Willy rubbing the top of his balding head with the splayed fingers of his right hand, a habit his boss always had when they disagreed.

"When are you planning on coming back?"

Alex exhaled. Although Willy hadn't admitted it yet, he was going to give him a chance. "I don't know. Not until I find out the truth."

"And what do you believe is the truth, Alex? That someone killed Janet Homer? Someone who was afraid of what she was going to tell you? Do you really believe she held a secret so sensational that she was murdered for it?"

Doubt threatened to dull Alex's response; it was natural when one was faced with something as unthinkable as murder. But Alex had faced the unthinkable before. He had a burning, intense need to fight back, to do something constructive. And this time he had a chance. Thoughts of the opportunity were driving him now. Whatever he might find at the end of this road no longer mattered. He must still make the journey.

He leaned over and rested white knuckles on the nightstand next to the bed. "Whatever the truth is, I'll find it. I've got to Willy. Please understand, I've got to."

Another uneasy silence momentarily strangled the line connecting the two men.

"Alex, is this because of Sally? Because there was nothing you could do then? Are you trying—?"

"Please, Willy, no psychoanalysis," Alex interrupted before his boss got too far.

"Okay, okay. I'll put the couch away. But promise me you'll call every day, and that you'll fill me in on everything you learn and on everything you're about to do. Before you do it. I don't want to be left holding the bag on this one. Promise."

"Come on, Willy. I can handle this."

"I didn't say you couldn't handle it. I just asked you to promise to call and keep me informed."

"All right."

Willy must have heard the slight reluctance in Alex's voice.

"'All right' isn't good enough, Alex. Not this time. Promise me, or I won't grant you the leave. I mean it."

Alex thought over Willy's request. The older man was trying to keep him out of trouble, because when Alex got into trouble, it generally meant Willy and the department got into trouble, too. And Willy was first, last and always watching out for his tail. Thirty years in government service had ingrained his attitude.

Not that Alex blamed him. Taking a chance and losing was hard. He had lived through the consequences before. But that was what being a scientist was all about—thinking of what was possible and going for it—and sometimes being wrong.

"Alex, did you hear me? I want your assurance you'll keep me informed. You've got to understand, it's the only way. Emotionally, you're already in over your head. Don't you see it?"

His boss was probably right about that. Alex knew his emotions were running pretty high. Better just to agree and get on with it.

"All right. I promise, Willy."

Alex dropped the telephone receiver as though it had become too heavy. He moved to the window and leaned against the sill. The morning sun had gone to shine elsewhere. Gray drizzle oozed out of the late-afternoon sky. It didn't matter. He wasn't seeing it.

He was seeing Janet's happy face—and the graphic photographs of the car crash and fire that the police had shown him. He hoped the accident investigators were right when they said everything had happened so fast that Janet probably never knew what had hit her.

He had told Willy he would stay until he found the truth. His afternoon at the police station had only convinced him that despite their final report, Janet's death was no accident.

But if he was to find the truth, where should he look? In his mind, there was only one place that could hold the answer to Janet's death: Varifoods. And one person: maybe a certain executive by the name of B. A. Lee.

Her behavior had seemed suspicious from the first. Supposedly a busy personnel manager, she had dropped everything and seen him immediately when she found out he was applying for Janet's so recently vacated job. Even her secretary had found that unusual.

And why had she used him to gain access to Janet's desk? That had obviously been her real reason for inviting him to tour the lab. Why was she hiding that fact from the other employees? What was she hoping to find in Janet's desk, or maybe cover up?

Alex's eyes refocused on the images of Market Street spreading before him. His room on the second floor of the Sheraton Palace Hotel gave him a view of flickering streetlights, tall buildings and anonymous heads that scurried beneath him in a fast-moving blur.

He dug his hands into his pockets as the contrasting memory of Lee's direct look came to mind. He had liked that direct look. He had liked her.

But Lee's behavior seemed to point to her involvement in Janet's death. She knew something. He was sure of it. And he was also sure he would find out what she knew.

Chapter Four

The old brick chapel of the Lafayette cemetery perched precariously on the pinnacle of a green hill. Cars in search of a parking space circled its perimeter. And the large numbers of people who entered carried umbrellas, sure of the prophecy being preached by the heavy rain clouds lingering above.

Lee had driven her black Fiero to the funeral directly from her home in Benicia. As she parked it and walked into the chapel, she felt a tension headache coming on. She dug into her purse for an aspirin and found a water fountain at the entrance. She hadn't slept much the night before. Thoughts of Janet and the mysterious letter kept waking, kept pressing in on her.

She had decided to approach Mark, Janet's husband. She was going to get him in some quiet corner and ask him what had been bothering Janet at work. Perhaps Mark would know.

Of course, it might not be that easy. She didn't really know Janet's husband. They had met in person only briefly in the maternity ward five years before, when his son was born. Mark Junior had decided to surprise his mom by coming nearly three weeks early. Janet had been at work. It was such a surprise that Lee had only just gotten the expectant mother to the hospital when the youngster made his entrance.

Janet had kidded later that it was because of all the aerobics she had done through her first pregnancy that Mark Junior decided to rush the doctor's estimate of the date of his birth. She'd insisted her son just couldn't wait to see what all the jumping around was about.

Lee found herself smiling at those memories, until she saw the little dark gold head of the five-year-old boy bobbing up and down in the front pew and heard him ask his daddy if that was Mommy in the closed casket. And then Lee began to cry.

They were tears of pain, not of release. The words of Janet's letter held her by their gravity and urgency. She was caught in the mystery surrounding her friend's last day on this earth. And until that mystery was solved, Lee knew she would not be able to release her grief, would not be able to say goodbye to her dead friend.

At some point later both the eulogy and Lee's tears had stopped. She was one of the first to step out of the chapel, although she did not immediately follow the crowd out to the grave site. She was waiting to see if she could catch Mark's eye.

She saw one of the chemists from the lab, Michael Ware, descending the stairs, his long hair and beard accentuated even more by his dark clothing. He had been around Varifoods a long time. She knew him enough to say hello, but that was about it. He always carried such a sinister reserve about him that he looked right at home at a funeral, she reflected.

Finally Lee saw Mark come down the steps, his dark head bent, his slim shoulders curved downward, holding on to Mark Junior's small hand. A stout older woman was next to him, carrying a little pink-clad girl about eight months old.

Molly, Lee thought. The reality of the motherless little girl brought a new sadness to Lee, a sadness with deep roots in her own past.

And suddenly she knew she couldn't. She simply couldn't approach a man who had just lost his wife and bring up Janet's worries at work. It would be callous, unfeeling. No matter how much she needed answers to her questions, she must not ask. Not now. Not today. Not of the man next to the white casket.

So instead she followed the procession of mourners to the grave site.

As the casket was being lowered into the grave, she diverted her attention to the faces among the large crowd, curious to see which other Varifoods employees had come.

She recognized Pam, the short, round chemist who occupied the cubicle opposite Janet. She also saw the carrot top of Tom Borden, the new chemist she had hired just four months ago. It was natural for them and Michael Ware to be here. They had all worked with Janet.

Then she caught sight of John Carstairs darting through the crowd. Almost directly behind him was Denise Williams. How odd! She hadn't realized that either of them had known Janet. They had said nothing yesterday morning about her death. Of course, as she thought back, she hadn't said anything to them, either.

It was then that thoughts of the missing face made Lee wonder. Hamilton Jarrett was still out of town on business, so she hadn't expected him to be present. But surely George Peck, Janet's immediate supervisor, should be here?

As though he had read her mind, Steve Gunn spoke from behind her. "Not everyone could come. It's a busy time around the lab."

She turned to face the security chief. His sharp features, black hair and eyes might have been softened, even humanized, if he smiled. But he was, as always, standing at attention, staring straight ahead, avoiding direct eye contact.

He reminded Lee of a wild animal when he did that. Wild animals—and a lot of humans—equated a direct look with intimacy or aggression.

"I'm glad you found the time, Steve."

The security chief's expression was noncommittal. "I make it my business to be a part of everything that goes on at Varifoods, and everything that happens to its employees."

Lee decided to try another approach, to determine the feelings of the man. "Did you know Janet Homer?"

His answer was a bit slow in coming. There was the smallest twitch in his right cheek, like a tensing of the jaw. Lee had noticed it before. It was as though something was jabbing the security chief, trying to get out, and he was only just holding it back.

"I knew her, just as I know all the employees who work for Varifoods. It's my business."

Concern for Janet certainly wasn't evident in his response. Lee turned back to watch the casket come to rest, no longer able to bear the unfeeling words from the stoic security chief.

Why was he here, if he hadn't really known or liked Janet? And if he had, what was preventing him from saying so? She personally didn't care for the strong, silent types. She liked a man who not only felt the right emotions, but could also let them be seen and heard when the occasion warranted it.

She looked around and spotted Mark standing at the foot of the grave. His head hung in grief. Would he be willing to try to solve Janet's mystery, too? Maybe in a few days she could send him a note. Ask him to call her. And then...

All thoughts of contacting Mark were suddenly dispelled when she saw the face of the tall man standing behind him. The disheveled dark brown hair, the bespectacled scholarly eyes. It was the applicant for Janet's job! L. E. Alexander. Alex.

She was so shocked that she just stared at his slightly bent head for a full minute as close members of the family leaned over to drop little bunches of flowers onto the casket.

Slowly her thoughts started to take form. The man had lied to her! He had shown up at her office the first business day after Janet's death, pretending not to have known her—yet here he was at her funeral!

She had been dismayed when he headed so quickly for Janet's desk in the lab. But that was only because she had hoped to distract him elsewhere, so that she could search the desk herself. Now his actions were taking on a more sinister air. Why had he rushed to Janet's desk? Could it possibly have had anything to do with the warnings in Janet's letter? What kind of awful game was he playing? Oh God, what was happening?

Suddenly he started to move forward. Lee stepped back behind Steve Gunn, almost as though she was afraid Alex would look up and see her. She watched in a new mixture of confusion and wonder as he bent on one knee and gently laid a single, long-stemmed yellow rose on Janet's casket. The deepening shadows of the overcast day could not hide the tear that shone on his cheek.

Then Lee knew. He was friend, not foe. Whatever the reason for his strange behavior, he had cared about Janet, her Janet. She watched as he rose and stepped back into the circle of people now turning away from the grave.

New questions flooded Lee's mind. How did this man know Janet? Why had he come to her office and applied for Janet's job? Why had he said nothing about knowing her dead friend?

As the mourners dispersed over the next few moments, Lee lost sight of Alex. She was heading in the general direction of her car, preoccupied with sorting out this new information, when she suddenly heard her name called. She turned with a start to see Mark approaching her.

"It is Lee, isn't it?" he asked. He was two inches taller than Lee, but today looked closer to her height because of the noticeable slump to his normally erect shoulders. He gazed at her with deep, brown eyes.

She smiled and offered her hand. He gave it a restrained shake.

"Yes, Mark. I didn't know if you'd remember. The last time we met, you had something much more important on your mind."

Mark patted the little golden head at his side in acknowledgment.

"Jan spoke of you often, Lee, with affection and respect. Did you see how the yellow roses you sent filled the chapel? After seeing them, I was almost sorry we didn't encourage more flowers. Jan always loved them so, particularly the yellow roses. She always thought they were so sunny and..."

Mark stopped talking, a sick, hollow look entering his eyes. Lee turned her head, not able to bear the raw pain. Instead, she looked down at the little boy clinging to his daddy's pant leg. Mark Junior looked up, staring at her with Janet's bright blue, curious eyes. It was the look of those eyes that decided Lee's next words and overturned all her previous decisions.

"Mark, sometime soon I'd like to talk with you about Janet and her work at Varifoods. You see, she had indicated to me recently that something was wrong. Something serious. I'd like to talk to you about it. I know now is not the time. Will you call me when you're ready?"

Lee reached into her purse and brought out her business card. She found a pen and circled her home telephone number and handed the card to Mark, looking again at his face. He took the card, but before he could respond, a voice bellowed from behind Lee. She felt herself jerked around by a determined hand on her shoulder.

"You got your pound of flesh! You and your rotten company! Wouldn't let her keep decent hours, so she could come home to her family! Insisted she work herself into exhaustion. Killed her, you did! My little girl is dead! My grandchildren have no mother now! Are you satisfied? Are you?"

Lee recognized the stout older woman who'd held Janet's little girl, Molly, throughout the ceremony. Indeed, the little pink-cheeked girl was still propped up in the woman's arms. She was rubbing one of her big brown eyes, beginning to cry, undoubtedly frightened by her grandmother's angry voice.

"Now, Mother Windermere..." Lee heard Mark begin to say.

"Don't interfere, Mark!" Mrs. Windermere told him firmly.

Lee was taken back by the woman's verbal attack. She couldn't understand what was happening.

"I'm so sorry about Janet, Mrs. Windermere," Lee said. "I'm the personnel manager at Varifoods. I don't—"

"Pam Heyer told me who you are! I know what your company has done! Look at these children you've orphaned. Come on, big, brave Personnel Manager, take a good look!"

Lee kept telling herself that this couldn't be happening. Janet's mother couldn't possibly be blaming her for Janet's death. Had the world gone mad?

Mark Junior had also begun to cry at the sound of his grandmother's screaming and his father bent to pick him up. For a moment Lee just stood there staring dumbly at the older woman's angry face. What could she possibly say?

"This won't help, Mrs. Windermere. And you know Jan wouldn't want it," Alex's voice said as if out of nowhere.

He had come up silently, so silently that Lee hadn't even heard him approach. Now he was standing right next to the distraught woman and putting one arm around her shoulders. Instead of protesting as Lee thought she would, the woman just laid her head on the tall man's large shoulder and began to cry softly, bouncing the sobbing Molly between them.

Lee looked at Alex and found him staring at her over the bent head of his mother-in-law. His expression seemed to ask a question, but Lee had no idea what it was.

Not sure whether Mrs. Windermere might begin her accusations again, Lee decided she'd better leave. She mumbled something in the way of a goodbye to Mark and nodded her head in Alex's direction. Then she took off for the car. On the way there, new questions swarmed in on her.

Why did Mrs. Windermere think the company had overworked Janet? What did all these references to late nights and exhaustion mean? Was Janet on her way home when the accident occurred? Had she been kept late at work? Was the lab on mandatory overtime? If it was, why hadn't she been informed? Could this be what Janet had been trying to tell her in the letter?

So many questions. And if anything about Mrs. Windermere's accusations was true, Lee wanted to know. But it looked as if she would have to start investigating to find her answers. Where to start? Before she opened the car door, she looked around for Steve Gunn. It occurred to her that if employees from the lab had been working late, he certainly would know. But the security chief seemed to have evaporated into the heavy air.

She didn't know what kind of car he drove. Perhaps he had already left. If he hadn't, she knew she would have to conduct a foot search that would take her back to the grieving husband, back to the angry mother.

Lee didn't feel quite up to that. She decided to see the security chief later at the office and find out what she could then. Now she felt an uncharacteristic need for the safety and solitude of her car and slipped into the comfortable, fleece-covered seat of her small black Fiero.

Lee started in surprise at Alex's voice as she finished closing the car door. "Lee, please. Wait a minute."

Once again he seemed to come out of nowhere. He must have followed her; yet when she had looked around a moment before, Lee could have sworn he wasn't there. Lee turned her car key into the Accessory mode in order to let down the power window.

"Yes?"

Alex crouched against the side of her car, one of his large, strong hands resting on the driver's door, over the rim of the open window. He seemed to be studying her for a moment, as though he were still trying to decide something.

Lee felt the need to speak, to relieve her own uneasiness at being watched so closely. "Thank you for what you did back there. For helping Mrs. Windermere, and me," she said.

His broad shoulders gave a small shrug. "She didn't mean what she said. It was the grief talking. Janet was her last child. I hope you can understand that? Maybe forgive her?"

Lee nodded as she looked at Alex's suddenly bruised-looking mouth and wondered what made it look that way. It reminded her of the sadness that had haunted his lips during his interview the previous day. But just as she became aware of its presence, it seemed to disappear.

"Could we go somewhere to talk?" he asked.

Lee looked up into those steady brown eyes so close to her own and felt a small disturbance in her equilibrium. She tried to right herself from the momentary imbalance, sure that the combination of this man's quiet power and sad mouth had caused it, but unsure why that should be so.

"Can I expect an explanation about yesterday morning?" she inquired.

He exhaled. "Yes."

It was the right answer. Lee looked around at the large number of people heading for their cars. The patter of raindrops had begun to hit her windshield.

"I'll open the passenger's side. We can talk here," she said.

Alex shook his head. "I think maybe somewhere away from here would be best. I'd rather no one from Varifoods saw us together. There's a little coffee shop off Mount Diablo Boulevard, near the 24 freeway. Will you follow me there?"

Lee felt rather than heard the urgency in his voice. It sent a chill up her spine as she received the message in his expressed desire not to have employees from Varifoods see them together. She nodded without hesitation. This was one conversation she would have gone almost anywhere to have.

Alex stood up and walked down to the end of the parking lot. Lee watched him get into a dark brown Chrysler compact, then followed him the few blocks to the coffee shop. They met inside and got a booth in the back. After the waitress had poured their coffee, Lee leaned back expectantly, watching her companion's face.

"How did you know Janet?" she asked.

"We were in college together, must be at least thirteen, fourteen years ago."

He paused and glanced out the window. Lee realized it wasn't the rain he was seeing, but a past that had included Janet. After a moment his eyes moved back to her face, back to the present.

"Hard to realize so many years have passed since then," he said. "Memories make it seem like yesterday."

Lee liked the gentleness in his voice. "You were very close, weren't you?" Lee asked.

Alex nodded. "How did you know?"

"I saw you place the yellow rose on her casket. I saw you cry. I knew then I could trust you. That's why I'm here now."

Alex's look was slightly uneasy. Obviously he had not realized that she had been on hand to view his unguarded moment.

"I wasn't aware a man's tears could impress a woman so much," he said, too evenly, too quietly. Lee knew then that her comment had been too offhand; it needed further explanation.

"It's not the crying that counts. I've seen men cry before without having it affect me. I'll never forget my cousin's face when the electricity went off during a Superbowl game one January. There he was at six feet, one hundred eighty pounds, twenty-two years old, standing in front of the darkened television screen and bawling like a baby. And frankly, that's what he reminded me of."

Lee took a sip of her coffee before continuing, watching the very nice face of the man in front of her.

"You see, Alex, it's not the fact that you were crying. It's why you were crying that was important to me."

Alex looked at her and smiled his small smile. Lee found herself staring into his brown eyes and feeling her toes grow warm. She tried to collect her thoughts.

"So you met Janet in school?" she repeated.

"Yes. As sophomores we got partnered in chemistry and found we worked well as a team. She was very good. Helped me keep my average up. But it wasn't just the academics that attracted me to her. She loved life and that showed in everything she did. After the chemistry class was over, we still saw each other, doing the things friends do like studying together and taking in a movie on weekends."

"And after college?" Lee asked.

"We went to different graduate schools. Still saw each other, although not as frequently. But it wasn't the quantity that counted. When I needed a friend, she was there. Even after she met Mark, and Sally and I—"

There was a flash of pain across that nice face as he interrupted himself. Lee waited, but he didn't finish his sentence. Instead he asked a question. "Tell me about your friendship with Janet."

Lee realized that Alex had gotten into a sensitive area and was seeking to refocus the discussion. She was curious about Sally, but somehow knew she shouldn't pry.

"It was an office friendship mostly," she said. "The kind where you get together and go shopping on your lunch hours, occasionally stop for a drink after work and share news.''

''Did you ever work closely together?'' he asked.

''No. We met at a company picnic nearly six years ago. Since Janet was only five foot four and I'm five foot eight, the judge thought it would be funny to team us up for an old-fashioned sack race. Janet and I were game, though, because we both knew it was all in fun. We really tried to win, too, but another team came in first. I liked Janet right away. She went all out to win, but when we didn't make it, her first thought was to go and congratulate the two who had.''

''Yes, that sounds like her. I remember the time . . .''

Alex and Lee went on to share reminiscences of Janet, of their happy times with their lost friend. Being able to talk about Janet so openly with someone who had also cared for her made Lee feel better. She thought her companion looked as if he felt better, too.

''Who are you? Really?'' she suddenly asked.

He seemed a little surprised at her question.

''I'm really L. E. Alexander. Alex. All the information on my application was correct. I didn't lie to you.''

''But the application itself was a ruse, wasn't it? You have no intention of seeking a job with Varifoods, do you?''

''Only if necessary,'' Alex said.

Lee shook her head. ''I don't understand. What does that mean?''

Alex's eyes seemed to grow brighter for a moment. ''That means that I'll do whatever I have to to find out why Janet Homer was murdered.''

The room seemed to tilt in front of Lee's eyes. She closed them, placing her hands on the table, trying to steady herself, trying to think through the shock of his words. When she opened them, she knew that the blood had drained from her face.

''Murdered?'' Her voice was weak, barely a whisper, even to her own ears.

''Drink some coffee. You look pale,'' he said.

He took her hands and placed them around her coffee cup. His touch was warm and strong. Lee felt it penetrate the numbness. She lifted the cup to her lips and swallowed a large gulp.

When next she spoke, she was back in control. But she felt that the protest in her words lacked substance.

"How can you say such a thing? Janet's death was an accident."

Alex seemed to understand her need to deny. His tone was patient.

"It was close to midnight last Friday when Janet's Honda hit the side of the Caldecott Tunnel, turned over several times and caught fire. The police went over the car thoroughly. They found some dark green paint on her left rear fender. Inside a dent."

Lee swallowed nervously as the import of the paint and the dent registered. "A dent?" she repeated.

"Another vehicle collided with hers, pushing her off the road and into the tunnel's wall."

As soon as Lee heard the words, she got a clear image of what Alex was saying. In her mind's eyes she saw all too vividly Janet's white Honda being hit by a nondescript, dark green blur.

"Another vehicle hit her?"

"Yes," Alex said. "It must have happened that way. Her husband told me he drove the car only the day before. It didn't have any dents or green paint then. And there wasn't any green paint in the tunnel that she could have hit when her car was crashing. It came from another vehicle. And it came that night."

"But why did the police label it an accident?" Lee asked. She didn't want to believe what she was hearing but at some level she had begun to wonder if Alex was right.

Alex adjusted his almost invisible glasses, looking somewhat frustrated.

"The car was smashed up pretty bad and scorched by the fire. The police kept insisting it was only a speck of paint. They thought that a speck of paint could have been missed by her husband, could have even been from a minor accident that Janet had sometime Monday."

"Had they gotten a report of such an accident?" Lee inquired.

Alex shook his head. "No. But by itself it wasn't enough, because minor accidents are often not reported. The police told me they looked at what they considered the facts of the case: no other tire marks were present in the tunnel. The pavement was wet, slippery. There were no witnesses to the crash. Janet's body wasn't badly burned. The autopsy showed she had no drugs in her, no alcohol."

"And that's why they filed it under Accident?" Lee asked.

Alex nodded. "The authorities wanted to believe it was an accident. That explanation was just so much easier than anything else."

Lee nodded in understanding. "Yes, the easy way out."

Alex leaned forward in his chair. "But it wasn't an accident, Lee. I'm certain."

Lee looked at the steady brown eyes. Yes, she could see he believed it. But could she?

"Why, Alex? Why would someone kill Janet?"

Then he leaned back and studied her face, as if he were expecting something. His next words mirrored that expectation. "I was hoping you could tell me."

She shook her head. "Why do you think I would know?"

"Because of what you said to Mark back there at the funeral. You told him Janet had found something wrong at Varifoods. You told him you wanted to talk to him about it."

"Mark told you?"

"No. I overheard. I had only spotted you a moment before in the crowd. Your presence at the funeral surprised me. I started to follow you. You see, up until then, I thought you might have had a part in it."

"You thought I would hurt Janet?" Lee's tone was incredulous.

Alex looked uncomfortable. "You have to understand. I didn't realize you were a friend of Janet's. Not until I saw Mark go up to greet you. Not until I overheard your conversation. If you had had a part in any wrongdoing, you certainly wouldn't have been so open about approaching Mark to discuss it."

"But even if you didn't know I was a friend, how could you possibly believe I could hurt her?"

Those steady brown eyes watched Lee. "You acted rather oddly yesterday, insisting on interviewing me right away. Then I realized you were trying to convince Denise Williams that I had requested the trip to the lab. I knew you had your own reason for wanting to go there. And then when you searched Janet's desk the way you did. I . . ."

"You saw me search Janet's desk?"

Alex nodded. "I thought you might be out to destroy evidence that might be lying around. Evidence of what Janet had found wrong at Varifoods."

"So you knew about Janet's discovery? But how?" Lee asked.

"Because Janet called me about it Friday," he said.

Lee leaned forward in her chair. "She did? Oh, Alex, what did she say?"

"She said she wanted to see me. That she had to see me. She said that she couldn't be specific over the phone, like she expected someone might be listening. She did tell me that something was very wrong. Something serious."

Lee shook her head, disappointed. "That was all? Those were her exact words?"

"No. Not exactly. It was more like: 'I've found out something. Something terrible. I must talk to you right away. I must stop this before it's too late. I can't talk now. Not on this phone. Can you fly out? Come to my home?' At least that's what I remember. I may have some of the words wrong."

Lee was trying to digest what she heard.

"And you're sure she meant there was something wrong at Varifoods?"

"Yes. There's no other explanation. Although geography separated us, we were still good friends. Family, really. You see, I married Janet's sister."

"You're married?"

The words were out before Lee could take the disappointment from her tone or wonder why such information should cause her disappointment. Fortunately Alex didn't seem to notice. Instead the sadness captured his expressive mouth again.

"Not anymore. But I'm digressing. The important thing is that Janet's call wasn't generated from a personal problem. I heard the fear in her voice. She knew about the work I do at the FDA. I'm sure she called me because she thought I could help her solve the problem."

Alex's words echoed her own reaction to Janet's letter. There had been fear in it, too. But Lee found herself sidetracked for a moment, as she thought about Alex's marriage to Janet's sister. Janet had never mentioned her. Lee had seen no woman other than Mrs. Windermere with Mark, either in the chapel or later at the grave site. Where was Janet's sister?

Lee wanted to ask the question, but something held her back. He'd said he wasn't married anymore. Were they divorced? Looking at the strong, sensitive face before her, Lee couldn't imagine the wife of such a man wanting a divorce.

She suddenly realized she was thinking these thoughts because she was very attracted to Alex. It came as a bit of a surprise, perhaps because her mind had been so totally preoccupied with Janet's death. Conscious of the attraction now, she reminded herself that she should get her mind back to the topic of Janet's call.

"Your application showed you are a division manager at the FDA. Do you have a speciality?"

"Yes. My field is neurobehavioral toxicology."

"Neurobehavioral toxicology? I'm not sure what that means."

"Basically, brain and nervous system poisoning," he said. "But I doubt my speciality means anything. Janet would have called me no matter what area the problem was in."

"So you think Janet found something wrong at Varifoods, perhaps some violation of FDA standards, and because she was unable to get the violation corrected internally, she contacted you for assistance?" Lee said.

"That's exactly what I think. I also think that someone stopped her getting my assistance," Alex said.

Lee felt her eyes widen involuntarily. "Are you saying that Janet died because of something wrong she had discovered with Varifoods?"

The steady brown eyes stared unwaveringly into hers. "Yes. That's exactly what I'm saying."

"But that would mean that somebody at Varifoods..."

"Murdered Janet," Alex finished for her.

Chapter Five

John Carstairs had watched Lee follow the man who called himself Alex to a coffee shop. His curiosity was getting the better of him, but he knew there was no way he could hear their conversation. He had a sophisticated listening device that, if pointed in the right direction, might have allowed him to sit across the street and still pick up their words, but he had left it in his truck. That was a rotten piece of luck.

At least he could do other things. He took the license number of Alex's car. He could have it checked and find out who the man really was. It was a cinch he wasn't an ordinary job applicant, as Lee had pretended.

It was also a cinch that whatever the big secret was, the personnel manager seemed to know about it. She could even be orchestrating it. Otherwise, why was she searching Janet's desk? Strange. Maybe very clever. He never would have figured her.

He checked his watch. If Alex and Lee stayed in the coffee shop a while, he'd have time to get back to San Francisco and search her office. Her secretary would be going to lunch soon. Maybe if the personnel manager thought she had covered up well enough, she might have gotten sloppy and left something around. It was worth a try.

He started up his dark blue Corvette and felt a surge of power as the engine growled back at him. He had a dirty job, but then somebody had to do it. He smiled.

"YOU UNDERSTAND, Alex, that I recognize the logic of your conclusion. It's just that it's so hard to accept that someone at Varifoods, someone I know, is a killer!"

After three cups of coffee, Lee and Alex had decided that they should order lunch or face being thrown out of the coffee shop. A bowl of hot soup and a sandwich sounded pretty good to both of them. But as Lee tried to tackle her soup, Alex could see that their topic had taken care of her appetite. It had taken care of his, too.

He watched her face, very pale against the black of her suit jacket, the silver colors of her blouse darting in and out of her unusual eyes. It was a lovely, intelligent face. He was glad he could trust its owner.

"But you suspected something, Lee. You must have. Otherwise, why were you searching Janet's desk?" he asked.

She sighed. "Janet managed to drop a letter into my In basket. It was dated Friday, the day she died. It contained a lot of the same type of message that she gave you over the phone. Phrases like 'something very wrong is going on,' and that I 'might be the only one in this crazy place' she could trust. It also said it was 'too dangerous' for me to go to the lab to see her. She wanted me to call her at home."

"Why didn't she call you at home?" Alex asked.

"I was on vacation up at Lake Tahoe. I only got back Sunday night. When I walked into the office Monday, I read about Janet's death in an office memo and found her letter."

Alex exhaled. "So that's why you acted the way you did. But don't you see? That letter confirms just what I was saying! May I see it?"

Lee shook her head sadly. "I lost it."

Alex suddenly recalled something white falling from Lee's pocket.

"Was it in a folded envelope in the right pocket of your suit jacket?" he asked.

Lee looked at him as though he had psychic powers. "Yes."

"It dropped out of your pocket when you leaned down to take the lamp out of Janet's wastebasket," he said.

"At her desk? You saw it? Oh, no. That means the leaning crew got it last night."

"No, it doesn't," Alex said. "It was gone when I went back to retrieve my umbrella."

"Someone picked it up? Who?" Lee asked.

"I don't know. All I know is that when I went back, it was gone."

Lee licked her suddenly dry lips. "But, Alex, that means someone must have picked it up deliberately. And if they read it, they know that Janet was trying to get in touch with me, trying to tell me what was going on. Who could have done it?"

"Did anyone at Varifoods dislike Janet? Or seem to be jealous of her? Or display anything that seemed negative about her?"

Lee shook her head. "As far as I knew she was well liked. The only time I ever heard her saying anything negative about another chemist was when she made some offhand comments about Michael Ware."

"The Rasputin look-alike?" Alex asked.

Lee smiled. "I never thought of that image before, but it fits him perfectly. Yes, Michael, our Rasputin look-alike. Janet thought he was a bit too haughty."

"Did she mention anything specific?" Alex asked.

Lee waved her hand dismissively. "It was just little things. He sulked if he didn't get the best projects. He always demanded the best vacation dates on the calendar, even though he was third in seniority," she recalled.

"The chemists have to stagger their vacations?" Alex asked.

"Yes. Only one can be gone at a time, so that's why his grabbing the best times annoyed Janet. She also told me he was always going behind their backs to report infractions to the chief chemist, George Peck. He constantly complained about Janet's cubicle not being as stark and stripped as the others. Apparently George had issued an edict in that direction, but Janet just ignored it."

Alex leaned back in his chair.

"Okay, Michael Ware might have taken your letter from Janet. Who else was in the lab from the time you dropped it until I went back and saw it was gone?"

Lee recited the names. "Steve Gunn. George and Denise. The other chemists, Pam Heyer and Tom Borden. I suppose any of them had an opportunity."

"You're forgetting someone," Alex said.

"Who?"

"John Carstairs, the finance manager you introduced me to when we got off the elevator."

Alex watched the recognition register on her face. "That's right! He said he'd seen us in the lab. He was up there, too!"

"Who do you suspect?" Alex said.

Lee shook her head. "I've absolutely no idea. If I could only find out what Janet was trying to warn us about. Perhaps the 'what' would point to the 'who.' It had to threaten somebody so much that he, or for that matter she, was willing to kill to keep it quiet. What could be so serious?"

"What are the research chemists working on now?" he inquired.

Lee shook her head again. "It's on a need-to-know basis, Alex. And it's been determined that I don't need to know."

"But can you find out?"

Lee thought for a few minutes. "I can find out if what Mrs. Windermere said was true—if Janet and the other chemists were working overtime. The computer has all those records."

Alex shrugged. "Actually, Mark already told me that Janet had been getting home late almost every night since she returned from her maternity leave two weeks ago. Frankly, that's all he knew about the business."

"She was working late?" Lee exclaimed. Alex could tell the information surprised her.

"Yes. You didn't know?"

"No. I had lunch with Janet twice the first week she came back. I do remember asking her how it felt to be back, and she said it was more tiring than she remembered. But she said nothing about overtime. I would have remembered.

You see, technically, George Peck can't have his chemists work overtime without my approval. Technically.''

"You say that as though you expect he might have done it, anyway."

"Yes. He might have. He was shorthanded when Janet went on her extended leave. He might have been making up for lost time. I won't know for sure until I check the computer."

"But if he knows you can check the computer, why would he take a chance and do it?"

"Actually, George doesn't know I can check the computer. He requested and got a programming change three months ago, placing everything in the lab's purview under a separate file matrix, accessible only through his and the chemists' separate security passwords. Even his employees' time records went into it. It's a closed system. Not even the payroll programs can access it. He inputs separately into the accounting system's files to generate his employees' paychecks."

"Then how can you access the time records?"

Lee leaned over her untouched soup and lowered her voice.

"I've been playing around with the Varifoods computer system since it was first put in, more than five years ago. We've had two enhancements, both of which I ordered. There's not much I don't know about the system now, including George's programming change. Every password is encoded in the file's configuration. I have no trouble in finding them."

"You're a computer hacker!" Alex said.

Lee smiled at the term. "No, not really. I just got curious and started to experiment. Then I took some classes here and there and experimented some more. Computers are like toys—fun to play with. Still, I'm only familiar with the one at Varifoods."

"Yes, but fortunately that's all we need. What happens if you find George's employees have been working overtime without your approval? Are there any penalties?"

Lee shrugged. "Under our past president, definitely. Particularly if George required the overtime without paying them. But Hamilton Jarrett, our new president, pretty well lets George Peck run his own show. He was the one who approved George's programming changes."

"Why is that, Lee?" Alex asked. "Just different personalities between this Jarrett guy and your previous president?"

"Yes, they're as different as Abraham Lincoln and Genghis Khan. I guess I don't have to tell you which is which. But it's not just that. Jarrett has only so much time to prove himself to the Trans World board. They're looking for us to pull ahead of the Tyberry food line, just as you intimated in your interview yesterday. I think Hamilton Jarrett has given George free rein, so to speak, to come up with something competitive."

"And do you think George can?" Alex inquired.

Lee shook her head. "I don't know. I don't like to sell people short, but he's been at Varifoods longer than I, and he's never impressed me as innovative. From the little I've overheard around the chemists, they consider George a very unimaginative plodder. The exit interview I had with a good chemist about five months ago was filled with disappointment."

"Well, this George Peck certainly had a good research chemist in Janet," Alex observed.

Lee nodded. "Absolutely. The others have very good backgrounds and talent, too. But I don't know if George knows how to use his people. My feeling is he puts them down more than he encourages them."

"That reminds me. I talked to Pam Heyer at the funeral."

"Oh yes, she's the chemist that had a position across from Janet. I don't really know her," Lee said.

"She seems okay," Alex said. "I explained to her that I was Janet's friend, and that Janet had warned me something was wrong before she died. Pam told me she thought that there was some trouble in the lab after Janet returned from her maternity leave. But just then Denise Willams came walking by, and Pam clammed up on me."

"Was the trouble between Janet and George?" Lee wondered.

"I didn't have a chance to find out. As I said, Pam shied away when Denise came by. I don't think she wanted to be seen talking to anyone. I did get the feeling Pam was a friend of Janet's, and she wasn't too fond of George. By the way, was George's goading of Denise typical of how he treats people in general?"

Lee sighed. "George has never been a particularly likable person, but Ham's preferential treatment has rapidly pushed his peevishness into antagonism."

Alex felt himself frown; this was all very confusing.

"What's bothering you?" Lee asked.

"I'm not sure. But it's strange that this Ham, whom you liken to Genghis Khan, would put so much faith in George Peck if Peck has no track record, isn't it? I mean considering it spells success or failure for your new president?"

Lee seemed to be considering his words.

"Now that you mention it, I do believe you're right. Ham replaced our old security chief within a month after taking over, and brought in Steve Gunn. Said the old chief hadn't impressed him. But he positively dotes on George. He could just as easily have brought in a real go-getter to lead the research team. Why didn't he?"

"Maybe George Peck charmed Ham," Alex said.

"Charm and George Peck are a contradiction in terms. Even before Ham came along to inflate his ego, he was hard to get along with. I've always tried to avoid him."

"Except when you braved his company to introduce me, so you could get a look at Janet's workstation. By the way, I never asked you, did you find anything in Janet's desk?"

Lee shook her head. "No. Someone got there before me."

"What makes you say that?" Alex asked.

"The computer had been used. Perforated edges of a printout still lay across the desk. And there was a small desk lamp in the wastepaper basket."

"So that's why you looked so confused. You were wondering who had used Janet's desk. Any thoughts about it now?"

Lee seemed to think for a moment. "It might not be anything sinister at all. It might have just been one of the other chemists. Although I still can't think why they would have had to use Janet's desk, when they had their own.''

"What were you reaching for, when Steve Gunn interrupted?"

Lee shook her head. "You sure saw a lot. I'd like to think I'm better at concealment than I obviously was on that lab tour."

Alex heard the feigned resentment in her tone. He smiled.

"Sorry. I guess because you didn't suspect me, you let your guard down. When you want to, I'm sure you can be the epitome of discretion."

Alex liked the little smile on her face that his comment generated.

"So what were you reaching for?" he repeated.

"Actually, I was going to take Janet's pictures of Mark and the children, so I could return them to Mark today at the funeral."

"You thought better of it?" Alex asked.

Lee nodded. "Steve startled me. I thought I'd best not take anything with him around."

"You don't like Steve, do you?" Alex surmised.

Lee took a moment to consider Alex's question. "'Don't like' is probably too strong. Let's just say I'm not comfortable around him. He's Ham's man. I'm sure he'd do anything the president told him to. People who follow orders that blindly bother me."

Alex nodded his understanding. "I got the same feeling. Is he good at maintaining security?"

"Maybe. But I'm not sure it's all necessary. I recognize the need for confidentiality in the food processing business, but I think someone like Steve Gunn goes at it the wrong way. You see, if employees really want to smuggle a company's secret formulas out, they're going to find a way. You have to remember, we employ some of the best minds in the industry. Frankly, I'd be disappointed if they couldn't outsmart a security system!"

Alex laughed. "So how do you maintain confidentiality?"

"Maybe I don't have the answer. But I think the right approach is to make their job so interesting and rewarding that they have no desire to betray the company that treats them so well.''

''I like your way.'' Alex smiled.

Lee smiled back, obviously pleased with his compliment. Alex liked the way her smile felt, sort of warm and gentle. It had been a long time since a smile had felt that nice. He shook himself slightly, trying to bring his attention back to their topic.

''Now what were we discussing before? Oh, yes, why did you say someone got to Janet's desk first?'' he asked. ''Couldn't Janet have used the printer? Thrown the lamp away?''

Lee was about to disagree, then seemed to think better of it. ''I never got a chance to read a newspaper report of Janet's death. Didn't you say she was killed around midnight?''

Alex nodded and waited expectantly.

''Well, then, maybe it was Janet who used the lamp. I kept thinking she would have left sometime between five and six. But if she was working overtime...''

''I see no reason for Mark to lie about such a thing,'' Alex commented.

Lee was obviously concentrating. Alex watched the tiniest of frowns mar her smooth, white forehead.

''Okay. The cleaning crew comes around eight and leaves before nine o'clock, because that's when the lights go out. Now, if Janet was in the lab after them, she might have been the one who printed something out and left the scraps on top of the desk. I'll know if she was there when I check the computer. As I mentioned before, the computer keeps a timed record of all employees' comings and goings.''

''But if it was Janet, why did she need a lamp?'' Alex asked.

''Why indeed?'' Lee said, clearly confused. Then Alex saw the sudden flash of her eyes and heard the excitement in her voice. ''The lighting, of course! That's it!''

''That's what?'' Alex demanded.

''Here, let me explain,'' Lee said. ''Let's say Janet was there in the lab Friday night after the cleaning people. She has work to do. The computer automatically turns off all room lighting after the cleaning crew leaves at nine o'clock. The only exception is when security is informed of late-night workers and reprograms the lighting by dialing in a code for a particular section of the building.''

Alex nodded as he saw what Lee was getting at. "So to keep the lights on, security dials in a code. But Janet has a lamp to do her work by, so we know that the lights weren't on! And by inference, that security was never notified. Janet was there without their knowledge!''

"Right! Janet was in the lab without authorization. And if what we're thinking is true, then Janet went there to get something out of the computer. Something she printed. That would explain the scraps of perforated edges from her printer. There's only one reason why she would have been in the lab without authorization and waited until late at night to print something out.''

Alex nodded. "It had to be the evidence of whatever it was she found wrong at Varifoods!''

Lee nodded her head excitedly. "We've got to find out if Janet was really there. I've got to get to the computer right away!''

"When will you know?'' he inquired.

Lee looked at her watch. "It's half-past noon already. It will take me about thirty-five minutes to drive into San Francisco at this time of day and find a parking space. Probably another five to ten minutes to get from the parking lot to the office. Playing with the computer a maximum of, say, thirty minutes. Where can I reach you?'' she asked him, starting to get to her feet.

"I have a room at the Sheraton Palace. I'll stay by the phone this afternoon,'' Alex told her, rising from his chair.

"Okay, I'll call you from the office just as soon as I know. No, wait. The call could be monitored. I'd best meet you after work, say around six. I'll come to the hotel lobby and have the desk clerk ring your room.''

"Okay. And since you haven't eaten much lunch, I'll take you to an early dinner.''

She smiled and nodded. He helped her on with her raincoat, noticing the soft curve of her neck as she lifted her hair to let it rest outside her collar.

They paid their bill and then hurried to their respective cars, trying to keep from getting too wet. An earnest downpour had begun. Lee waved to Alex as she got into her car and buckled up. He watched her drive away.

He wasn't in any hurry to get back to his hotel room. He had until six after all. Fatter and fatter raindrops landed loudly on his windshield, their percussive beat curiously soothing. He laid his head against the headrest.

Sleep had been almost nonexistent the last few nights; he'd kept reliving Janet's call, the urgency he had heard in her voice. And Janet's words had kept getting mixed up with Sally's call—one that had been placed to him nearly five years ago—a call that he had also answered too late.

Alex closed his eyes, willing away the punishing images of the past. The weight of Janet's murder still oppressed him, but it wasn't as crushing a burden since he had been able to share it with Lee.

Thoughts of Varifoods' personnel manager brought a small, unbidden smile to Alex's lips. There were lots of things about Lee that a man could admire. She was very attractive in many ways.

But the most important way, as far as Alex was concerned, was how Lee treated people. Alex had really appreciated her desire to give Varifoods' employees interesting and rewarding work in order to gain their cooperation, rather than waving a security stick over their heads to gain compliance.

And when he had felt exposed and uneasy about being seen crying at Janet's funeral, she had made him feel comfortable, even special because of it. What had she said? It was what you cried about that was important, not the fact that you cried.

Yes. And it was what you cared about that was important, too, not just the fact that you cared. Lee obviously cared about the right things, he concluded.

He closed his eyes and felt himself drifting off, her smiling face a clear memory.

As she drove away from the coffee shop and headed in the direction of the 24 freeway westbound, Lee realized that she felt a lot better than when she had gotten up that morning.

She knew why, too. She had been able to share her thoughts about Janet's mysterious death with someone she could trust. With Alex.

He was still a bit of a mystery, though. Imagine being married to Janet's sister! Wondering again about what had ended the marriage, something Alex had said earlier finally registered. It was after Mrs. Windermere's harsh words, when he'd approached Lee's car. He had mentioned something about Janet being Mrs. Windermere's last child. Did that mean that Janet's sister had died, too? Was that how the marriage had ended?

How tragic. Perhaps that was why such a sadness clung to his lips sometimes. How it had happened? Illness? Accident?

Her mind was still occupied with her musings when the Caldecott Tunnel suddenly loomed in front of her, giving her a queasy feeling in the stomach.

Lee had always disliked long tunnels. She felt as though the carbon monoxide from a thousand car exhausts lingered within, ready to choke any driver who dallied too long.

It was in one of the eastbound lanes of this very tunnel that Janet had had her accident last Friday night. Only if Alex was right, it hadn't been an accident, after all. It had been murder.

Lee shivered. Murder wasn't an idea she could get used to. She just couldn't accept it yet. How could anyone do such a thing?

The motive. That would be the key, if it really was murder. That was what she had to figure out. She and Alex. What were the reasons people murdered? She thought of the seven deadly sins she had read about somewhere.

Pride, anger, lust, gluttony, envy, covetousness and—oh, yes, sloth. She remembered them all. But which one had been the motive for killing Janet? Perhaps if she took them one by one?

Pride. Had Janet discovered that someone had falsified credentials? Or was she threatening to expose the improper or unscientific work of a fellow chemist? Seemed unlikely.

Anger. Maybe Janet had been given another chemist's project and improved on it, thereby making the first chemist mad? No, that seemed pretty flimsy, too.

Lust didn't seem to fit at all. Maybe it was too simplistic to think that the old vices still lay behind current motivations. The computer age seemed to demand more sophisticated passions. But what would make someone deliberately set out to hit Janet's car and force her into a concrete wall?

Lee was so immersed in her reflections that when the car hit her from behind, she had to struggle for a moment to determine what was real and what imagined. Then the car hit her again, and reality loomed only too vividly.

Chapter Six

She could immediately hear the pounding of her heart as her body reacted to the impact. An inner voice was trying to tell her to be calm. She still had control over her car. The driver behind her must realize his mistake by now. He would understand that he was following too closely and would pull back.

But the fact that the bumping of her car had begun at the same time as she was visualizing Janet Homer's accident unnerved her. Somehow the two events seemed intertwined, as though sinister forces were at hand. Tension strapped her shoulders.

She scanned her rearview mirror. The headlights of the car behind her beamed like two hungry eyes. The face of the driver was indiscernible. The darkness of the tunnel obscured anything that might identify him or his vehicle.

For one more hopeful moment, she kept the thought that it had all been a mistake. After all, it had been a quick, sharp bump. Maybe he was just an inattentive driver. Maybe he had had too much to drink too early in the day. Maybe his judgment was impaired. Then all hope vanished as he bumped her again. And again.

She jabbed at the accelerator pedal, quickly switching to the right-hand lane, then slowing down again. Had he thought she was in his way? Would he pass her now? This time a strong jolt threw her backward against the headrest.

In rising terror she attacked the accelerator. She watched her speedometer climb to sixty, then sixty-five. But a quick look into the rearview mirror only fueled her worst fears.

The car was still behind her, stalking her—only now he seemed even closer.

The next bump snapped her backward again. The beat in her ears echoed the pounding of her heart. Should she lean on the horn and make a lot of noise? Her eyes darted anxiously to her mirrors. She could detect no other cars—none in front of her vehicle—none behind her pursuer—none to turn to for help. In a tunnel along a freeway that was normally swarming with cars, she suddenly found herself alone with a madman.

Should she step on the brake? At this speed he wouldn't be able to respond quickly enough to avoid a collision. She would be prepared, while he would be caught unawares.

No, that was foolish. They could both end up badly injured, if not dead. All she could really do was maintain her current speed and hope she could make it to the other side.

She felt another bump. It seemed even harder this time, aimed at her left rear fender, almost as though the vehicle behind her was trying to shove her into the side of the tunnel.

The side of the tunnel! Just as Janet had been pushed! She floored the accelerator, now trying blindly to get away. Perspiration poured down her back. Her hands ached from their tense grasp on the steering wheel as her tires began to screech through the tunnel's gradual turn.

Another bump. She had to hold on. The windshield wipers screeched across the dry glass. She wanted to reach down to turn them off, but couldn't. She just couldn't chance removing her hand from the steering wheel. Not even for a second.

Another bump jolted her body. She tried to concentrate on keeping the car steady, the wheel as straight as possible. *That's right,* she thought. *Just move it steadily along. Don't think of anything but controlling the car.*

Another bump taxed her concentration. She fought to regain her balance. Then she was bumped again. And again. She was beginning to despair, to panic at the thought that this might never end. Somehow she was going to be in this tunnel forever, pursued and pushed until the madman behind her succeeded in running her into the tunnel's side and to her death!

Finally she saw the small circle of light ahead. She was coming to the end of the tunnel! Slowly, ever so slowly, it grew. At last she emerged into the rain-drenched sky of early afternoon. Lee felt spent but incredibly relieved. She had survived!

She immediately tried to pull over to the right, looking for a place to stop the car. Some instinct told her she had only been in danger as long as she was in the tunnel. She didn't know why, but she was sure.

A vehicle streaked by, but she didn't notice. All she felt was the overwhelming need to pull over. She had to find a vacant spot on the shoulder of the freeway. She had to find a place where she could regain her composure, her control. But traffic was merging from the twin tunnel on her right. She couldn't get over.

There was no choice but to continue to the first off ramp leading to the outskirts of Berkeley. An eternity passed before the sign finally loomed up in front of her. She pulled onto a half-moon shoulder at the end of the ramp, turned off the ignition and set the brake.

Then she closed her eyes and let out a long, deep breath. She rested her head on the steering wheel and thought of nothing. Gradually her hands began to release their grip, until finally they fell like heavy weights into her lap. The tension between her shoulder blades began to ease.

Maybe a minute passed. Maybe a half hour. In her enforced state of relaxation, Lee couldn't judge which. But the next thing she knew was that someone was tapping on her window. Reluctantly she turned her head and opened her eyes.

His knuckles were large, and the face behind them was just a blur through the rain-swept glass, but Lee could see his uniform. He was a policeman, and he was saying something. She lifted her head and tried to concentrate on the words.

"Are you all right?"

Lee opened her mouth, and was surprised when nothing came out.

"What is it? What are you saying?" His voice was loud, its tone probing. It seemed to shake Lee enough to activate some brain cells. She pressed the button to let down the window. It didn't work. For a moment Lee looked at it stupidly. Then she turned the key to the Accessory position and tried again. The window responded obediently.

"I'm all right." Now that she had said the words, Lee realized she did indeed have herself back in a tenuous balance. The recent terror had gone, leaving in its wake a vague feeling of unreality. She looked around, feeling as though she were floating in a bubble.

"You're illegally parked here, miss. I'm afraid you'll have to be moving on."

"I'm sorry, officer. But I just had a dreadful experience. Someone was following me in the Caldecott Tunnel and bumping my car. Some madman was trying to push me against the tunnel's wall."

The officer looked at her in surprise. He wasn't wearing a raincoat, and he was getting quite wet as the rain grew heavier with each passing second. He had probably gotten out of his car, thinking his message to her would just take a minute. More than a minute had already passed.

As he stood there, apparently digesting Lee's words, he seemed to be torn as to what he should do first. He looked up as though seeking an answer from the heavens. That seemed to work. His rain-soaked face returned to hers.

"Can you drive?" he asked.

"Yes," she said, though her head was shaking.

Now the officer shook his head at the conflicting message.

"Why don't you get out of the car and ride with us?" he suggested.

Lee gave the idea momentary consideration. "No. Really, I'm all right. I can drive." This time her body language did not contradict her words.

"Then follow our car to the station house. We'll take your statement there," the now thoroughly drenched policeman said.

Lee looked back, and saw another officer getting equally wet at the right rear corner of her car. At his partner's signal, both men returned to their vehicle and drove away.

Lee followed, her automatic reflexes taking over for her dulled brain. Only one conscious thought got through. She now knew Alex was right. Janet Homer had been murdered.

STEVE GUNN walked into his office and took off his soaking-wet raincoat. He hung it up and reached his hands to his equally soaking hair to squeeze out some of the excess moisture. He jumped at the unexpected knock on his door.

"Come in."

The door opened to admit his young, thin and timid-looking secretary, carrying some paper towels she had apparently been keeping in her desk. She extended her hand as though she were making too modest an offering to a god.

"Will these help?"

Steve took the towels and waved her away. She scurried out of the office like a little mouse. Steve's expression reflected his disgust.

He couldn't stand cringing women. They made a man look foolish, weak. He liked a woman who stood straight and confident; that was the kind of woman who challenged a man. That was the kind other men admired—the kind he wanted. After all, the woman a man was seen with told other people a lot about him. Other men measured his importance by her. These signs were crucial.

The towels soaked up the excess moisture from his hair and face. He threw them into the wastebasket and circled his desk, but before he sat down, he turned on his video screen. Lee's empty office was immediately reflected on his monitor.

Varifoods' personnel manager was the kind of woman who would suit him. He had felt it when they first met. Tall, attractive. They would look good together. Her obvious avoidance of him had only made her more desirable. Nothing easily obtained was ever satisfying. He had begun to make his plans.

Steve leaned over and switched off the screen, shaking his head. Now all those plans had to be scratched. She was proving to be a risk. The boss's instructions were clear enough, and he would carry them out faithfully. Too bad. But there were always more women out there. Plenty more.

Steve sat back in his chair and took out his notepad. He had to check out this guy who had been with Lee. Of course, he already had an idea of what he was going to find. His spy at Tyberry was already in place. He'd just give him a call.

IT WAS NEARLY THREE O'CLOCK when Lee finally got to her office. Marge said hello with a look of inquiry as she handed Lee her telephone messages, but Lee only nodded as she walked straight into her office and closed the door. She didn't want to talk in general, and she specifically didn't want to discuss where she had been.

She walked around her desk and sat down in the chair, resting her head in her hands. Physically she felt okay, but emotionally she felt like tenderized meat, thoroughly beaten and flattened. The police had been polite but skeptical, even suspicious of her story after a while. Perhaps she couldn't really blame them.

She had been too forthcoming, telling them right off that she had been attacked by the same person who had attacked and killed her friend, Janet Homer. Naturally, when they checked and found the report on Janet labeled Accidental Death, they had begun to doubt Lee's entire story.

Perhaps if she had been in control she could have convinced them. Now she could see herself chattering at twice her normal speed, two octaves higher than her normal tone to the ever-patient sergeant who was taking her statement.

He had tried to slow her down, he had even tried to believe her. But in the end she could see he didn't. And that was all her fault. In her agitation, she hadn't even been able to give him a description of the vehicle, much less the driver. No make, no model, no color, no nothing.

Where had her wits been when she drove out of the dark tunnel? Well, that was a silly question. At that point she had had no wits. All she had been able to think about was stopping the car and collapsing. Yet all she'd have had to do was look into her rearview mirror at the vehicle that emerged behind her. She could have seen what it looked like and maybe even who was driving.

But her recent panic and her overwhelming relief at surviving the attack had pushed all other thoughts from her mind. She hadn't looked back. And that was the reason she'd had nothing to give the police.

It was an explanation, but not an excuse. Not in her mind. She had made a big mistake by allowing herself to fall apart and let a killer get away. Maybe she'd even allowed him to come back another day.

Damn.

She tried to put aside her error. Beating herself down this way was nonproductive. She had to refocus on the important task of finding this maniac, this murderer, and uncovering the reason for Janet's death. She had to begin with the computer time-ins. She sat up straight and turned toward her screen.

Lee easily found the access codes she needed and slipped into the separate storage matrix for the laboratory. She brought up the computer time records and began scanning them for entries made during the last two weeks. A frown creased her forehead.

It couldn't be, but there it was. According to these records, Janet hadn't worked late one night since her return!

"Well, I'm glad to see you finally made it in!" Denise Williams said from the doorway. Lee jumped at hearing the unexpected voice, not even aware that the door had been opened.

"For God's sake, Denise, knock next time. You gave me a start!"

"I did knock. Twice. Didn't you hear me? What's wrong with you? What are you so jumpy about?"

Denise had started to come around the desk, so Lee hit the Clear key and turned to the advertising manager.

"I'm sorry, Denise. I guess it's Janet's death that's unnerved me. By the way, I didn't realize you knew her."

"I didn't," Denise responded.

Lee was disturbed by Denise's answer. She beckoned the big woman to take a seat beside her desk.

"If you didn't know Janet, what were you doing at her funeral?"

Lee watched the other woman's face. She was yawning, seemingly undisturbed by the contradiction between her words and actions as she sank heavily into the offered chair.

"What I meant is that I didn't know her well, just enough to say hello when I went down to the lab. She was in George's office one morning a couple of weeks ago, when I went over to give him some advertising materials. We were introduced then. Of course, I heard the gossip when I came aboard six months ago."

"Gossip? What gossip?" Lee asked.

"Well, the gossip about Janet and George, of course."

"Janet and George? What are you talking about?" Lee demanded.

Denise looked at Lee as though she were trying to make up her mind about something.

"No, I guess you wouldn't have heard. People only pass gossip on to those who'll listen. Even now I'm getting the feeling that I've said too much. Maybe I'd best be leaving."

"You stay right there, Denise, and tell me what this is all about."

Denise hadn't made any effort to get up. She leaned back in her chair and studied Lee's face for a moment.

"Well, the story goes that George and Janet had a fling."

"I don't believe it," Lee said.

"I found it difficult to believe, too, particularly after I met Janet. And I'm sure you agree George isn't exactly Mr. Hunk, certainly no Ham Jarrett. But sexual attraction is a funny thing. Who knows what turns some people on? George is smart, ruthless, and he's got power. There must be something to his reputation."

"His reputation?"

"Uh-huh. Mind you, it all happened before I came to Varifoods. I understand Ham sent Steve around to quietly advise all the pursuers of office hanky-panky to knock it off. There were quite a few."

"I can't say I disagree with the errand, but how did he know who they were? I didn't have a clue," Lee said.

"You wouldn't. Remember, Lee. People only see what they look for. Anyway, the story as I got it is that Steve made sure the fooling around stopped."

"How did he do that?"

"He told those involved that the next time an employee was found playing around with another employee, they'd both be fired and would never work in the industry again. Everyone knew he meant it. Ham has enough power to do it, you know."

"Then what you're telling me about George isn't current news?" Lee asked.

"No. Ancient history. So you can imagine that the stories have been distorted with time. George apparently had a few other office flings before Janet, but most of the talk was about her."

"Because she was married?"

"Yes, and because George is, too, and because she worked for him. And because everyone thinks the child she had about eight months ago was George's."

"Dear heaven." Lee shook her head in disbelief.

"No, Lee. 'Dear heaven' had nothing to do with it. It was plain old office lust."

Lee deliberately ignored Denise's graphic clarification. Office gossip would never convince her that Janet had had an affair with George Peck.

"It just doesn't make sense, Denise. None of it. George didn't even attend the funeral," she said.

Denise shrugged her broad shoulders. "You've known our chief chemist a lot longer than I have, so you should also know that old George can be a real creep when he sets his mind to it. And he sets his mind to it often."

"All the more reason Janet wouldn't have anything to do with him," Lee remarked.

"I didn't realize you knew her so well. What's this all about, anyway? What's bothering you?" Denise asked.

Lee thought about what she could tell the advertising manager and decided that part of the truth wouldn't hurt.

"At the funeral today, Janet's mother started yelling at me. She blames Varifoods for Janet's death."

Denise scratched her eyebrows, as though she had developed a powerful itch. "Really? And how was the company supposed to have killed her daughter? By making her eat our stale products?"

Lee ignored the sarcasm in the other woman's voice. "She implied the company overworked Janet, forced her into exhaustion."

"Is that all? Well, she's probably right," Denise said. "We're all overworked. We'll probably all fall asleep at the wheel going home one of these nights, and smash ourselves into oblivion. That includes you. When I left at nine o'clock last night, I saw the light burning under your door. You're as foolish as the rest of us, overworked and underappreciated."

Lee shook her head.

"Ham has added to my responsibilities. That's why I was here late. But it doesn't make sense in Janet's case. I reviewed the computer-recorded checkouts for the night she died. They show she left at six o'clock with the other chemists, signed out with her palm print just like the rest. And she hasn't worked a single hour of overtime since she came back from her leave. Why does her family think we overworked her?"

Denise looked at Lee with an understanding smile.

"Don't be naive. The woman was obviously using work as an excuse for getting home late. You just proved she wasn't here. She probably had something going on the side. Happens all the time."

"A man?"

"That's where I'd put my money."

Lee shook her head emphatically. "Look, even if I thought Janet capable of an affair, and I don't, I think it highly unlikely she would be pursuing an affair with an eight-month-old baby at home, not to mention a handsome son and an adoring husband. I'm having difficulty believing that surrounded with that kind of love, she'd be out looking for something else. What was she missing?"

"Look, I don't know. There are people out there who are never satisfied. Maybe Janet Homer was one of them. I realize you were her friend, and I'm sorry. But you can never be sure about anyone. And I mean anyone.''

"Her mother was so angry. So . . .''

"Oh, come on, Lee. She was unhappy. She was looking for somebody or something to blame. She probably—''

Denise was interrupted by the buzzer from Lee's secretary.

"Yes, Marge?'' Lee said.

"George Peck is on the phone for Denise. He seems very anxious. Can she pick it up?''

Lee looked at Denise who nodded.

"She will, Marge. Thanks.''

"Put him on the speakerphone, Lee,'' Denise requested.

Lee did and Denise said hello. No answering hello came from the chief chemist, however. He went immediately to what was on his mind.

"Do you have those new advertising placements ready? I've been waiting for twenty minutes. I'm not waiting much longer.''

The threat in his voice was unmistakable. Denise shook her head, drawing her lips into a tight line. "Yes, George. I'm on my way.''

Lee switched off the voice connection, and Denise started to get to her feet.

"Excuse me, Lee, but as you've heard, I've been summoned by our chief chemist and creep. Would you believe that he told me we wouldn't be getting together on this until tomorrow morning? Now he calls around, tracking me down, and puts on a big act about my keeping him waiting!''

"What would happen if you didn't show? What was he implying when he said that he wouldn't wait much longer?'' Lee inquired.

"That he'd go to Ham, of course. That he'd accuse me of not cooperating. That's the latest major sin in our little congregation, if you haven't heard. Not cooperating.''

"And Ham would believe him?''

"Believe him over me? Oh, yes. Ever since our chief chemist presented samples of our new product line, the boss thinks he walks on water. Can't do enough for him.''

Lee's eyebrows rose. "I don't understand. We have a new product line? Which one is that?"

Denise looked suddenly ill at ease, clearly wishing that she could take back what she had just said.

"Lee, forget what I just said. Please. I have to be going now. I'll talk with you later."

Denise moved quickly to exit Lee's office, only to collide with the blond man who had just opened the door.

"Hi and goodbye, John," she said.

Denise's departure was not well received by John Carstairs. His hands went up, as though he were tempted to forcibly restrain the advertising manager.

"But you can't go!" he exclaimed. "I've been searching for you everywhere. Ham told me to get together with you about some special financing not reflected in the annual budget. He's expecting some tentative figures today. He'll be calling for them in less than an hour."

"Got no choice, John. I have a prior commitment. If you want to wait in my office, I'll try to get back as soon as I can."

Denise smiled apologetically and walked out of Lee's office, leaving behind a plainly unhappy man.

"Denise is on her way to the lab. I guess we both caught her at a busy time. And speaking of busy, I have to be getting back to work," Lee said.

"Give me a minute first, Lee. I've been meaning to talk to you. Why is Ham making you the public relations manager in addition to personnel manager? Doesn't he understand the amount of work involved in both positions?"

"If you're trying to get on my good side, John, you've just succeeded. But to answer your question, no. I don't think Ham understands the work involved."

John sat down, uninvited. "Don't worry. After he gets my figures from the first-quarter fiasco, he'll rethink his decision."

"Why's that? What's all this first-quarter fiasco business about?"

"Well, maybe I shouldn't be telling you this, but our fearless leader has already gotten himself into a bit of financial trouble. Seems he wasn't paying close enough attention to the status reports I've been sending him. He came in way under budget for the first quarter.''

Lee was sure she hadn't heard right.

"Wait a minute. I thought underspending one's budget was the whole idea of properly managing company funds,'' she said.

John shook his handsome, blond head and flashed the bold, white teeth beneath the light brown mustache.

"Popular misconception among the uninformed. Men on the move must go over budget to prove how hard they are working to increase the company revenue, particularly in the first quarter. Otherwise the guys at corporate headquarters might just cut their budget for the rest of the year.''

Lee listened to John with some amusement. Of course, it wasn't really funny, and John's bright smile didn't have its origin in mirth. It was all part of business life to be constantly playing games with numbers and with people.

"So, after the Big Ham realizes he has to increase expenses, I imagine he'll reconsider doubling up on your responsibilities. You see, it would be to his benefit to add a new public relations manager.''

"Thanks for the tip, John. I hope you're right,'' Lee said.

"You can count on it. And now that I've told you my secret, why don't you let me in on yours?'' John suggested.

Lee looked at his face. His expression was perfectly serious.

"What am I supposed to know?'' she asked.

"About the new product line, of course. Everybody's talking about it. What's all the secrecy for, anyway?'' he asked without a moment's hesitation.

He really had a charming face. Lee wondered fleetingly if Ham would have someone like John go around and test out his employees' discretion. She willed away her suspicions and tried to think up an appropriate response. Technically she didn't know anything. What Denise let slip a few minutes before had been unintentional.

"John, I don't know about a new line. What have you heard?''

Lee managed an expression of polite interest and waited to see its effect. He studied her openly as he leaned back in his chair. It was a determined scrutiny. Something sharp and quick dwelt behind that relaxed charm. Why hadn't she ever noticed it before?

"Another time, then," he said, getting to his feet and walking toward the door. A somewhat abrupt departure, Lee thought.

She puzzled over his question and the reason for Denise's secrecy. Ever since Janet's letter the morning before, everyone seemed to be acting strangely. Most of it was probably her imagination. But she hadn't imagined the bumping incident in the tunnel.

Now it looked as though she and Alex had been wrong about Janet working late. Could Denise have been right? Could there have been another man?

No. Every time Lee thought about Janet's husband and children, she just couldn't imagine her out looking for something else. None of it made any sense.

She turned back to her screen. Janet had written the letter to her and called Alex at work on Friday. If whatever had been bothering Janet had something to do with the lab, then maybe some computer files might have been deleted in an effort to cover up. It was worth a look.

She studied the history of file activity since the previous Friday. It had been brisk that day, slow on the weekend, and had picked up again Monday. Altogether very discouraging.

She had hoped to find a huge purge of incriminating data, a cover-up. But none of the major programs had been altered. Nothing substantial had been deleted, only one old access code had been phased out, and there had been a two-line alteration in the entry and exit security system for the lab.

An alteration in the security system? Her hopes renewed, Lee's fingers flew across the keys.

Chapter Seven

Lee's pulse began to quicken as she searched through the program change in the security system. It had something to do with the logic associated with the in-and-out verification of a palm print. Lee studied one of the added lines. It seemed to eliminate a previously built-in five-second delay.

Her eyes scanned the rest of the programming language. What had the five-second delay done? Then she realized that before a palm print was registered in the time record, it could be canceled within five seconds by a conflicting entry.

She looked back at the second added line of logic. It prevented a second signing out before a corresponding signing in. So each Out had to have an In.

That seemed strange. She reread the program. Prior to the addition, each palm-print identification In had had to be matched with the corresponding Out. But there were no instructions for what would happen if two palm-print identifications were made for Out and only one for In. That was probably because no one anticipated someone coming back into the lab without signing in.

So prior to the addition, someone could sign out, somehow reenter the lab without signing in, and then re-sign out—and the computer would ignore the second one. But how was it done? How could someone leave the lab and then reenter without the guard noticing and the computer registering the entry?

Lee decided she needed to investigate. She left her office, took an elevator to the lobby and walked over to the guard's desk. He looked vaguely familiar.

"Hi. I'm Lee, the personnel manager."

"Yes, Ms. Lee. I remember seeing you on several occasions. Can I help with something?"

"I'm curious about how the security system works for the lab. What information do you get when I place my palm print on the green identification screen?"

"Same as that for the screen at the entrance to the administrative offices. Go ahead and walk through the lab's electronic eye and I'll show you. Be sure to put your palm print on the screen first, of course."

Lee placed her hand on the screen, walked through the electronic eye and back to the guard's desk to read the information on his monitor.

B. A. Lee
Personnel Manager
Female
Five foot eight
One Hundred Twenty two Pounds
Blond Hair; Light eyes
No Distinguishing Marks

As she read the last entry, the screen went blank.

"It's visible for only a few seconds," the guard said. "We have to keep our eyes focused on the monitor in order to catch it. If the palm print wasn't cleared, the word Unauthorized would flash across the monitor, and anyone attempting to pass through the electronic eye for the next three seconds would activate an alarm."

"Is this information from the palm print on the Out or In identification?" Lee asked.

"Doesn't matter. It's the same for either."

"But how does the computer know whether I'm signing in or out?" Lee wanted to know.

"The computer reads the direction of your hand," the guard said. "If your palm is pointing toward the building, as it would be when you enter, then the computer records an

In entry. Conversely, if your palm is pointing away from the building, then the computer records Out."

"I see. What would happen if I came in and then left immediately? Let's say within just a few seconds?"

"Why would you want to do that?" the guard asked.

"Oh, I don't know. For the sake of discussion, let's just say I forgot to mail a letter in the mailbox at the corner. I lay my palm down on the In green security screen, walk through the suspended electronic eye, and then remember I have to mail my letter. So I turn around and lay my hand on the Out green security screen and pass through the suspended electronic eye again. What would the computer record as my In and Out entries?"

The guard shook his head. "I don't know."

"Well, let's see," Lee said. She passed out of the lab's security screen, through the administrative office's security screen and back out and in again. Then for good measure, she passed out of the administrative offices and in and out of the lab's security screen.

The guard was shaking his head. "I don't know what you're trying to prove, Ms. Lee, but there's no way I can access the computer to find out what effect all this in-and-out business has."

"That's all right. I can. By the way, do all the security guards have regular shifts?"

"Three in every twenty-four hour period. Eight to four. Four to midnight. And midnight to eight. The central column here is always covered."

"But what about lunches? Breaks?" Lee asked.

"We might be gone a few minutes, here and there."

"It's after four now. Do you usually work the four to midnight shift?"

"I guess. But I've worked them all at one time or another."

"When do you normally take your break on this shift?"

"Oh, between six and six-thirty. There's often an outflow of employees between five-thirty and six. I wait until they sign out and then I generally take a ten-minute break. Walk around a bit to stretch my legs."

Lee was getting the glimmer of an idea. She looked around the lobby. On either side of the electronic eyes were rest rooms.

"So people could come in or out without your noticing them?"

"Yes. But everything that's happened will be recorded. And if anyone tries an unauthorized entry, the alarms go wild."

"You can't cut the alarms off from here?" Lee asked.

"No. It's on automatic. We can monitor, be on hand in case of trouble, but if the security of the system is violated, the police are called automatically, and you can hear the racket for blocks around.

"Has it ever happened?" Lee inquired.

"One night a couple of months back. While I was on break, one of the employees brought his kid with him. I guess he was going to show the little guy where his daddy worked. Well, anyway he signed in with his palm and then walked through the suspended electronic eye with the little guy over his shoulders. Immediately the sirens blared in their ears. He told me later it sounded like the start of World War III. Cops were at the door in minutes, and the Big Ham followed very soon thereafter."

"Poor little kid," Lee said. "Must have scared him to death."

"Actually, I think the old man was shaking worse, figuring he'd lose his job and all. But the Big Ham just sort of laughed. Patted the little kid on the head. He even thanked the employee for verifying the alarm system worked so well."

"But if his dad had carried the boy, what kind of sensor picked the youngster up and set off the alarms?" Lee asked.

"As the president told me that night, it was a heartbeat sound sensor. It picked up two heartbeats, where there should have been only one."

Lee was still shaking her head as she made her way back to her office. With all this elaborate security, one would think they worked in an ultrasecret weapons factory instead of a food processing company. She headed directly for her computer.

A few minutes later, she had checked her numerous In and Out entries and established how they had affected her time record within the building. It was most illuminating.

Marge buzzed her on the intercom and said good-night. Startled, Lee looked at her watch and saw it was a quarter to six. It was time for her to gather her things and start for the Sheraton Palace. Fortunately it was only a few blocks away. She had a lot to tell Alex.

"WELL, as the old saying goes, I've got some good news and some bad news," Lee said.

They had just finished an early dinner at the corner restaurant on Market and New Montgomery streets in the Sheraton Palace complex. The atmosphere was restful and the service unobtrusive, but Lee had been so starved that she couldn't really judge the quality of the food. It was only after she cleaned her plate and sat back that she was ready to talk. Alex seemed to understand. He had waited patiently until coffee was served.

"Let's hear the good news first," he said.

"Well, I'm pretty sure we were right about Janet being in the lab late Friday night."

"Pretty sure? Didn't the computer records confirm it?"

Lee stirred some cream into her coffee.

"Actually, the computer records show Janet left at six with the other chemists. And not just last Friday. The computer shows she worked regular hours ever since she returned from her maternity leave two weeks ago. But I think the records are wrong."

"They've been altered?" Alex asked.

"Not exactly. Remember that I told you I'd be surprised if our chemists couldn't figure a way to beat the security system?"

"Yes?" Alex said in a questioning note.

"Well, I think that's what happened. I checked the security system programming this morning. Two changes were made over the weekend.

"First, the five-second delay in the storage of In and Out timings has been removed. Until now, if someone had walked into the building and out again within five seconds, the In and Out palm prints would cancel themselves out, and there'd be no record in computer memory."

"And?" Alex asked.

"And up until the second change, as long as an authorized In palm print was matched to an Out, the identification was satisfied. So someone could register several Out prints in succession without a corresponding In, and the computer would just ignore them. All it was interested in was matching at least one Out to every In."

She could see that Alex was frowning. "I understand what you're saying, but I don't see that it explains how Janet could stay late without reflecting her correct time in the computer records."

"Well, this is purely conjecture, but you remember the layout of the lobby at Varifoods? The single guard in the center, with the separate green security screens on the right for entry to the bank of elevators leading to the lab, and the other green security screens on the left for entry to the bank of elevators leading to the administrative offices?"

"Yes, I remember it clearly," Alex said.

"Let's say then that Janet signs out with her palm print, along with the other chemists somewhere between five-thirty and six. She either leaves the building with them or goes into the ladies' room there in the lobby and waits."

"Waits for what?" Alex asked.

"The guard to take his break. Then she goes back through the green security screen, only she immediately places her hand on the opposite screen, the one pointing to the outside of the building. With the five-second delay factor, the computer would have matched the entries, understood they canceled each other out, and never put them into memory."

"So for purposes of the time record, Janet would never have been shown going back into the building," Alex concluded.

"Exactly," Lee said.

"But what about when she left? Wouldn't the computer have picked up her time then?" he asked.

"No. Remember, until the second logic change in the programming, excessive Out entries had no effect. When

Janet signed out as she left the building, her entry would have been ignored, because the computer already showed her as Out.''

"And these changes were made over the weekend, right after Janet died, which means they had found out how she was getting in and wanted to correct the problem before others figured it out, too," Alex said.

Lee nodded. "Yes. But the logic changes weren't only made on the lab security system. The administrative offices' security system was also altered. I checked it this afternoon. I guess they, whoever 'they' are, decided to play it safe all around," Lee said.

"Who could make such programming changes?" Alex asked.

"Several people could authorize them. Ham certainly, Steve, George, Denise, even John, I suppose. Although since they relate to security, my bet would be on Steve."

Alex was moving uneasily in his chair and looked uncomfortable.

"Lee, I don't want to sound like an alarmist, but if someone at Varifoods is trying to plug any loopholes in their security system, and if this someone killed Janet, it could be the same person who picked up Janet's letter where you dropped it in the lab. This someone could be nervous about your friendship with Janet. They might think you know something. They might even..."

Alex stopped, so Lee finished for him.

"Make an attempt on my life? You're not being an alarmist, Alex. That was the bad news I mentioned earlier. You see, I know you were right when you said Janet was murdered, because whoever killed her tried to kill me. This afternoon."

"What?"

Lee could see she had shocked him. As clearly and unemotionally as she could, she told Alex about the bumping incident in the Caldecott Tunnel after she had left him at the coffee shop in Lafayette. And she didn't leave out her failure to notice anything important that would have convinced the police that it was an attempt on her life.

When she finished, she raised her eyes and saw him watching her worriedly. He put one hand on her arm.

"Don't think less of yourself just because you were too frightened to think straight. You had just survived a savage attack. And you survived by using your wits and not panicking. You controlled your car through a curving tunnel, even while the car was being hit repeatedly. I think you did very well."

At that, and upon seeing the warm, worried look in his eyes, Lee felt somewhat better. It was so good to have him to talk to about these things. She wondered briefly how it would feel to be folded into those strong, solid arms, drawn closely to that broad chest. But his next words drove such thoughts from her mind.

"I'm at a loss, Lee. You're in obvious danger, and yet the police aren't convinced. So it's pointless to appeal to them for protection. You have to try to get out of this mess and go on an extended vacation, maybe even take a leave of absence. You've got to get far away from San Francisco—before it's too late. You see that, don't you?"

Lee didn't like the sound of what she was hearing. "No, I don't see anything of the sort. I can't back off until I find out what's wrong at Varifoods. It's too important. Someone has already killed to keep it quiet. Killed Janet, my friend."

"That's precisely my point! They've killed and they're willing to kill again. It looks very much like you're next on the list! Get out now, while you can!" His tone was no longer even. There was a definite edge to it, and Lee saw something flash behind those steady brown eyes.

Maybe at some other time she might have tried to be more sensitive about the frustration in his voice. Right now, however, all she could think about was that he was insisting she stop investigating Janet's death. And she wasn't about to do that.

She tried nonetheless to fight the emotion that was tightening her vocal cords. "How could you think I'd give up? Do you really expect me to run and hide? What do you take me for?"

"A fool, if you don't listen to me!"

His hand now gripped her arm tightly, almost as though he were attempting to control her. That was a mistake.

Her voice suddenly fell as a new emotion took over. It seemed more quiet and controlled, but she spoke through clenched teeth.

"Is that so, Mr. Alexander? And I suppose you're going to run quickly to the nearest exit, now that the going has gotten a little rough?"

Alex was obviously still upset. He didn't seem to fully appreciate the change in Lee's voice. "Of course I'm not running. I came to find out who killed Janet, and I'm not going back until I do," he declared.

"That's exactly why I have to stay, too. Janet was my friend."

"Someone is trying to kill you. That makes a big difference," he continued.

Lee's next words were an open challenge. "So if someone bumps your car tomorrow in the Caldecott Tunnel and tries to kill you, you'll take the next plane out of town and forget the whole thing?" she demanded.

Alex's look told Lee that he knew where her logic was going; it also told her that he wasn't going along for the ride. He leaned closer as though she were hard of hearing, grasping her arm even more tightly.

"Of course I won't take the next plane out. I'll have the presence of mind to turn around and see who it was!" he exclaimed.

Lee yanked her arm from his grasp; bruised pride brought her to her feet. He had struck where he knew it would hurt. Her tone was icy. "I'll say good evening now, Mr. Alexander."

She reached into her purse and brought out enough money to cover the expense of her meal. She threw it onto the table, adjusted the strap of her purse over her shoulder and stalked out of the restaurant.

She was so angry that the cool night air felt like a salve on her burning skin. She hadn't believed Alex could be so hurtful. He'd told her she had handled the tunnel episode well, but at the first moment of challenge had thrown her failings into her face in an effort to coerce her into believing she was no challenge to Janet's murderer.

She knew she couldn't match this murderer's ruthlessness. She couldn't be conniving and deceitful. But she wasn't powerless, either. And she wasn't going to let anyone make her feel that way! She could challenge this murderer, whoever it was, by using both her intelligence and her position at Varifoods. And she was going to do just that!

She was a block down the street, making her way toward the parking garage, when she heard her name called. Because she knew who it was, she ignored the voice. She had nothing to say to Mr. L. E. Alexander. He called again. Still she ignored him. Then she found him walking by her side.

"What do you want?" she demanded, in a tone more of challenge than inquiry.

"You forgot your coat," he said mildly.

Lee stopped abruptly as she realized he was right. Her anger had warmed her up so much that she had failed to notice. Without saying anything, she stretched out her hands. But Alex held the coat away from her. "No. Not until you listen to me. Please."

Lee hated being coerced into anything. This man had already tried that tactic once. Didn't he ever learn? She started walking again. "Keep the coat," she told him, her anger and determination not to give in suppressing all other emotion.

She had gone another half block before she realized he was keeping pace with her. "I'm sorry, Lee. That's all I really wanted to say. Please stop and let me give you your coat back. Please."

She was still angry, but he did have her coat. And it was a nice "Please." She stopped again. "All right. Give me my coat," she said.

He stepped in front of her. "I apologize for what I said. It was very insensitive, stupid. I let my temper get the best of me. I didn't mean it. You were very courageous in the tunnel. I just...don't want you involved, Lee, because I don't want you to get hurt."

His face was mostly in shadows, but Lee heard the sincerity in his voice. She would never respond to intimidation, but tenderness got her every time—her anger was melting away. She reached again for her coat, but he was still holding it.

"Let me help you put it on. It's cold out tonight."

He helped her locate the sleeves and lifted the garment over her shoulders, letting his hands linger there as he looked into her face. His fingers felt warm and strong through the fabric.

"Lee, are you determined to go on with this?"

Lee sighed; her anger could find no place at the gentleness of his tone and touch. "Alex, I must. I'm not the stuff of which heroines are made. I know that. But I've never run away from anything in my life. And I can't see myself doing it now."

"It's not safe," he reminded her.

"No, it's not. I realize that. But the police aren't likely to offer me protection when they don't believe the danger exists. So as I see it, the only way I can ever be safe is to find out who killed Janet and try to see that person brought to justice. Otherwise I'll always be looking over my shoulder. Can you understand that?"

He gave her shoulders a slight squeeze and stepped closer. This time his voice was even gentler, deeper. "Yes. I understand. Will you let me work with you? For Janet's sake? I think we'd make a good team."

Standing so close to him, Lee found herself very aware of his body, its heat warming the air between them. She felt a similar heat from the hands still resting on her shoulders and had to resist a strong urge to reach out and touch his chest.

"Yes," she answered. They would make a good team for more than just this investigation, she reflected.

"Good. Come on. I'll walk you to your car," he said, dropping his hands and turning to walk beside her.

"Can you hire me right away for Janet's job?" he inquired.

Lee tried to focus on his question. She could still feel the imprint of his hands where they had lain on her shoulders. Obviously he had been doing some thinking while she indulged her attraction for him. She tried to be objective.

"No. That would cause suspicion to fall on you immediately. I need to interview a few more candidates, go through the outward signs of a routine search. Probably the earliest I could offer you the position would be two weeks. Then there would be another week's delay, as your references were checked and your identification processed through the system.''

Alex was obviously disturbed by the prospect of a delay. ''I don't know, Lee. We can't wait two to three weeks. Janet's voice sounded urgent when she called me, as if whatever she was worried about was going to happen soon.''

''Well, I could have you back on a follow-up interview,'' Lee suggested. ''But I wouldn't be able to get you into the lab. It would look too suspicious if you went back a second time.''

''Yes. I'm afraid I'll have to stay in the wings for a while. Meanwhile the burden for finding things out is going to rest with you. You mentioned before that you knew the computer system pretty well. Do you think you could access the work the chemists are doing?''

''Sure, I could access it, but there's no way I could understand it, so what's the point?''

''Well, you could print it out and bring it to me,'' Alex proposed.

Lee shook her head. ''Do you realize how much chemical research is stored in that computer? Briefcases or parcels of any kind are not allowed in or out of the offices. Even if I could print out a file and smuggle it underneath my coat, I'd have no idea what files to select, which ones could be important.''

Alex was quiet for a minute.

''Then there's no way of getting around it. The only way out of this little dilemma, Ms. Lee, is for us to become lovers.''

Lee was sure she hadn't heard right. ''What was that?''

They had reached the front of the parking garage, and Alex was standing in the light. She could see the smile on his face, but the tone of his voice was serious.

''You heard right. It would give me a reason to call for you at work, a perfect cover to come up to your office. You could access the files. I could read them. We could sit side by side, so that if anyone happened to walk in, I'd just lean over and give you a kiss. They'd probably get embarrassed and leave."

Lee shook her head, although the idea wasn't particularly displeasing. "But lovers so fast? Do you think anyone would believe it?" she queried.

"Of course they would. Happens on TV all the time. Besides, all they'd have to do is see me kiss you, and they'd be convinced."

"I'm not so sure a kiss would be that convincing," Lee said doubtfully.

"You haven't seen one of mine yet," Alex said lightly, with a dash of humor that Lee noticed. They were approaching Lee's black Fiero. She wasn't sure how she should respond. The thought of a convincing kiss from Alex was somehow very exciting. A cold wash of reality interfered with the idea, however.

"I'm afraid it's impractical," she replied. "I have three interviews scheduled for tomorrow morning. You can't be sitting in my office while I conduct them. Even if people thought I'd fallen madly in love, no one would believe that I would be so unprofessional."

She opened her car door and slipped behind the wheel. "If you want to get in, I'll drive you back to the hotel."

He nodded and moved to the passenger's side. By the time he had fastened his seat belt, he had apparently come up with a new idea.

"All right, how about my coming by and bringing you lunch tomorrow? I'll be your considerate lover, who understands you have a lot of work to do and can't leave the office. We can eat while we go through the files. How's that?"

She considered it. "Yes. That might work. My last interview should conclude approximately eleven-thirty. What about eleven forty-five?"

"It's a date. Have any culinary preferences?"

"Just something that's not likely to spill on the keyboard. Shall I drop you in front of the hotel?" she asked. They were starting to pull into New Montgomery Street.

"If you wouldn't mind, let me out at my car. It's in a garage off an alley, halfway down the block. See, right there on the left."

"Are you going somewhere?" she inquired.

"I thought I might like to drive around for a while," he said.

Lee pulled in at the garage. Alex turned to look at her.

"You will be careful? Someone has already tried to kill you, remember. He may try again," Alex said.

Lee nodded. "I'll be careful. Remember, I'm not the stuff of which heroines are made."

Alex got out of the car and leaned back in. "You could have fooled me," he said and took hold of her hand, bringing it to his lips for a quick kiss.

Lee felt the warmth travel up her arm and looked at him in surprise.

"Just practicing to be your lover," he said, smiled and released her hand.

Lee watched him walk up to his car, which was parked just to the right of the entrance. From the tingling throughout her body she knew he didn't need any practice. She drove off.

Alex started his car and immediately turned in the direction of Lee's fast disappearing Fiero. He would have liked to have told her he was going to follow her home, but wasn't sure how she would have taken the news. She was one independent lady.

Tonight he had found that out the hard way. She wasn't the kind of person who could be bullied into anything—not that he had meant to bully—at least not consciously.

But when she'd described how someone had tried to run her car into the side of the Caldecott Tunnel, while he snoozed in the coffee shop parking lot, he had lost his objectivity. All he'd been able to see was Sally's dead, chalk-white face and the pictures of Janet's charred and twisted automobile. All he could still feel was the horror that it had almost happened again. To Lee.

As he followed her onto the Bay Bridge, his stomach still churned. He knew that without her help, he had a slim chance of finding out who had killed Janet and what the secret was that she had wanted to expose. Yet as much as he ached to know those things, he couldn't jeopardize Lee's life to find the answers.

She was just too willing to place herself in danger, and there didn't seem to be much he could do about that. Once again, the old, helpless feeling crept over him, and he pounded the steering wheel with his right palm in pure frustration.

He wondered at the strength of his feelings for the attractive personnel manager. Wherever they were coming from, he would have to put them aside. He and Lee were up against a dangerous adversary. He would need to keep his wits about him at all times.

Chapter Eight

Lee finished her third interview by eleven-thirty. She was just showing the applicant out of her office when a call came in at Marge's desk. From the look on Marge's face, Lee could tell something was up. She waited at her secretary's station until Marge put the caller on hold.

"Lee, this is an urgent call from a Lieutenant Roger Morris of the Seattle Police Department. Ham's secretary had it transferred down here. It seems Ham left no number where he can be reached, and the lieutenant says the information can't wait."

"Give me a minute to get back to my desk and then put him through," Lee said.

As she made her way to the telephone, Lee's mind was full of questions. Why would a police captain from Seattle need to talk with her so urgently?

"We've had a case of food tampering here, with a foreign substance. One of your products," Lieutenant Morris said.

Lee's heartbeat started to race along with her thoughts. Could this have something to do with Janet's warning? Was someone at Varifoods tampering with the ingredients in their products? She willed her voice to remain even.

"What product? How was it tampered with? Was anyone injured?"

"It's your Cool and Light iced tea mix, twelve-ounce glass jar. Our lab isolated the chemical haloperidol. Man who ingested it suffered a seizure. His condition is critical. Only case so far. We're testing the other bottles off the shelf at the grocery store where it was purchased. I'll be talking with the press this afternoon. Thought you might want a company representative to be here."

"Yes. Do you have the coding from the bottom of the jar? Good. Got it. Thank you for calling. I'll be on the next plane."

By the time she hung up, Lee had accessed the computer and identified the manufacturing plant that had bottled the adulterated iced tea mix. She made several quick calls in succession, the last of which got her a reserved seat on a flight out of San Francisco to the Seattle-Tacoma airport.

She placed a call to Ham's secretary and gave him in the basics of the call, to pass on when next Ham called in. She also sent back-up electronic mail messages to Ham and to the legal department, just in case.

Then she picked up her purse and stopped at Marge's desk, quickly briefing her.

"Shall I cancel your appointments for this afternoon?" Marge inquired.

"Yes. And for tomorrow, just to be on the safe side." Then Lee remembered about Alex. "Dammit!" She checked her watch. It was eleven thirty-five.

Marge looked at her. "What's wrong?"

"It's Alex. My... friend. He's bringing me lunch here in ten minutes. We were going to sit in my office and eat it. But I can't wait. I won't be able to explain what's happened. The plane leaves from S.F. International in fifty minutes. I've got to go now to catch it."

"Alex? Do you mean L. E. Alexander, your applicant on Monday?"

Lee heard the surprise in her secretary's voice. She looked away, feeling uncomfortable. "Yes. We've sort of gotten to know each other in the last day or so."

Marge's eyebrows went up but she didn't say anything, just waited expectantly, a very interested look on her face.

"Tell him why I had to leave, Marge. Explain it to him?"

Marge's voice held the smallest trace of amusement. "Of course, Lee. Any personal message you want me to pass along with the explanation?"

"Personal message? Like what?" Lee asked.

"'I'll miss you, darling,' or 'love and kisses'?''

Lee tried not to grin. "You're close to being fired, Marge," she said as she made her way to the door.

"Nonsense. You couldn't operate without me, and you know it. See you tomorrow. Call if you're not going to make it in."

Lee nodded and ran for the closing elevator.

DENISE WILLIAMS stepped off the elevator and stopped in surprise as she saw L. E. Alexander standing there, talking with Lee's secretary. Curious, she stepped to a partition, where she could hear what was being said without being seen.

"We were going to have lunch together. Are you sure she left?"

"Yes, Mr. Alexander, I'm sure. She told me about your luncheon engagement, but some urgent business came up. She's on her way to the airport. Left no more than ten minutes ago."

"I don't understand. She told me we'd have to have lunch in her office, because she couldn't be away from her desk for an extended period. Are you sure this trip is business and not something personal?"

"Mr. Alexander, I know you're disappointed. But there's no reason to be concerned. Lee has just been called away on business. She may be home tonight—maybe not until tomorrow. I'm sure she'll be in touch."

"Marge, are you telling me everything?" Alex asked.

"Everything I can, Mr. Alexander."

"Where can I reach her?"

"I can't give out that information," Marge replied.

"Well, what was this urgent business all about? At least tell me that," Alex requested.

"Look, I can't. Please understand. You don't work for Varifoods. Company policy prohibits me from discussing company business with you."

"Can I at least get into her office and leave these roses there?" Alex said.

"I'll take the roses and put them in a vase for her, Mr. Alexander. Just leave them with me."

Alex frowned and dumped his packages onto Marge's desk. "You might as well take these two lunches, too. I hope you enjoy lobster," he said, sounding upset.

Denise moved farther back along the partition as Alex emerged from the secretary's office and quickly stepped into an elevator. Marge called after him.

"Mr. Alexander, I'm very sorry. Please try to understand. Lee didn't want . . ."

Marge didn't say any more; the elevator doors had closed behind Alex. Denise stood in her hidden position, considering what she had seen and heard.

Could Lee possibly be involved with the tall, handsome chemist?

Yes, from what Denise knew of the proper personnel manager, she could imagine her falling for his kind of scholarly charm. But not so soon. What was wrong with Lee? Denise had wanted to talk with her about the letter she had received, but now she was wondering if it wouldn't be more prudent to go elsewhere.

Well, Lee wasn't in, anyway. Maybe she could catch her the next day. But with everything at stake, she had to talk to someone. Ham was out of town. So there was just one thing she could do. She made her way to the lab.

"You understand, George. He's getting thick with Lee. This Alexander guy was at Janet Homer's funeral, too. Why would he be applying for Janet's job, unless . . . ?"

"Yes, Denise. I get the point. Actually, I suspected this guy from the minute he walked in here. I told you I remember seeing him at that seminar. Why don't you go talk with Steve? If you suspect Alexander, then Steve's little network should prove valuable."

"So you're not going to do anything?" Denise asked.

"I've done what I could. Now go talk to Steve and leave me alone. I have work to do," George said imperiously.

Denise left, though she was anything but satisfied. Having Alexander roaming around was too dangerous. Steve had better be in the mood to take some action, or she'd have to do something herself.

ALEX SAT BACK on the bed in his hotel room, munching on some take-out chicken chow mein. He was hungry. He hadn't had a chance to eat all day, but his disappointment was giving the food a bitter flavor—his disappointment and his growing worry over Lee.

He had checked with all the airlines at S.F. International, but none of them would verify that she was a passenger on a flight going out.

Where was she going in such a hurry, anyway? According to Marge, she had left her office no more than ten minutes before Alex arrived. Why couldn't she have waited to tell him what had come up? He closed the containers and pushed them aside.

She hadn't returned to the office. He had waited until after six and still she hadn't showed. He had managed to find out her address and had driven all the way to her home in Benicia to see if she was there. She wasn't home, and her car wasn't in the garage.

Finally he had given up around ten and returned to his San Francisco hotel room with his Chinese take-out—and the taste of defeat.

He flipped the remote control to activate the television set. The eleven o'clock news was going strong. He listened for a minute to international problems. Then he pushed the Mute button, deciding it was time to fulfill his promise and check in with Willy. He dialed his boss's home number from memory. A sleepy voice answered after the fourth ring.

"Hi, Willy. It's Alex. How are you?"

"For God's sake, Alex, it's after two in the morning. You woke me up. I wish you'd remember the three-hour time difference."

"I'm fine, too." He heard Willy exhale his exasperation.

"Okay. You're fine, too. As a matter of fact, I'm glad to hear it. Particularly after the long-distance call that came in this afternoon."

"What call?" Alex inquired.

"Somebody wanting to verify that L. E. Alexander worked for the FDA and what he did. Who's checking up on you?"

Alex immediately thought of Lee, then shook his head. She would have told him. No, it had to be someone else, and that made him uneasy.

"Who was it, Willy?"

"Didn't say. The voice was muffled. Couldn't even tell if it was a man or woman."

"What did you answer?" Alex asked.

"As long as whoever it was didn't volunteer a name, I just said I never heard of you," his boss replied.

Alex frowned. "Well, I guess it doesn't matter what you said. I wish I knew who it was, though."

"What are you doing to make someone check up on you?" Willy wanted to know.

"I think I may be making a murderer uncomfortable."

"So you're still riding that horse, huh? Okay, what have you found out so far?"

"Not a whole lot. Except that Janet had been working late at the lab and not letting her company security team know. Whatever she was looking into must be pretty heavy stuff to have her mistrust them."

"Are we talking illegal additive here?" Willy suggested.

"Possibly."

"What does her family think?"

"She wasn't allowed to discuss her work with her co-workers or family. Company policy," Alex told him. "But she did write an interesting letter to a friend in the company, the personnel manager. It was dated the day of her death and said pretty much the same thing she said on the phone to me."

"You've talked to this personnel manager? You trust him?"

"Not him, her. And yes, I do. She was a friend of Janet's. It looks like she's a target, too. We're working together to find out what happened. At the moment, though, I'm worried, because I can't seem to find—"

Alex stopped in midsentence; suddenly he was looking at the the topic of their conversation. There was Lee on the eleven o'clock news, with a microphone shoved into her face.

"Can't find what?" Willy asked in his ear.

"Can't talk now, Willy. Call you tomorrow," Alex said quickly, dropped the receiver onto its cradle and repressed the TV's Mute button to obtain sound.

She stood straight and erect in front of the cameras. Her long hair was gathered in a soft blond roll around her head. Her large eyes reflected the gold of her blouse. He was both relieved and happy to see her. She was all right. His hours of worrying had been for nothing.

It was the reporter's question that Alex first heard.

"What is this drug, haloperidol, the one that was found in your company's iced tea, Ms. Lee?"

A drug found in a Varifoods product? Alex sat up, his interest in the subject almost equal to his relief at seeing Lee.

"It's classified by the FDA as a strong tranquilizer. It's used primarily to control psychotic thinking and abnormal behavior disorders."

Her voice projected well; its depth and clarity sounded familiar. He could tell that she wasn't reading from any notes, and knew that what she was saying was accurate. She had obviously done her homework well.

"How did haloperidol get into your company's iced tea mix?"

"The police believe the bottle in question was removed from the shelf, the seal broken and the drug added. The residue of several pulverized haloperidol tablets was found in the remaining iced tea mixture. All the other bottles on the shelf were undisturbed, their seals intact, their contents unadulterated."

"We understand the police have a suspect in custody, a man recently released from a mental institution. Our sources say he had a grudge against the grocery store owner. Was he on this drug?"

"Yes, the police released that information a little while ago. The suspect's doctor has said he was using such a prescription. That is one of the reasons the police are questioning him."

"If that's true, why has Varifoods recalled all of its iced tea mix?"

Her eyes widened in surprise at the question as she continued to stare into the camera.

"We're not taking any chances. What the police think has happened and what may later be proved to have actually happened could be different," Lee responded.

"But isn't your company going to lose a lot of money recalling this product from the shelves, when it might not even be necessary?"

Lee was still looking directly into the camera. "Better we lose some money than place our customers in danger, wouldn't you say?" she suggested.

There was a slight pause before the next question. The camera lens remained on the unwavering look in Lee's eyes.

"How is the victim?"

"Mr. Joseph Claremont suffered a seizure. I saw him at the hospital just a few moments ago. The doctors told me he's out of danger, and they don't believe he has sustained any permanent damage. He will be kept there under observation for several days."

"Is a seizure a normal side effect of this drug?"

"No. But Mr. Claremont unknowingly ingested a large quantity within a few minutes. His body had no opportunity to build up a tolerance, and the shock to his system brought on a temporary seizure."

Alex watched her in renewed admiration. She was forthright and genuine, and it came across. She represented her company well. But were they as guiltless as she portrayed them?

Alex was feeling uneasy again. The iced tea had been doctored. Had some psychotic really done it? Was it just coincidence that after Janet found something wrong at Varifoods, something deadly shows up in one of their products?

Now the camera was focused on the station's reporter. Alex could just catch her words, identifying her as belonging to NBC Broadcasting, Channel Five, Seattle.

So that was where Lee had gone in such a hurry. But why? Wasn't this something the president should be taking care of? Why would a personnel manager take on such an assignment? And why couldn't she have called him?

The telephone rang, as if on cue. He picked it up and answered distractedly.

"Alex, is that you?" Lee's voice asked.

His tone sounded harsh even to his own ears. "Lee! For God's sake, why didn't you call sooner?"

"Alex, I'm sorry. Things happened so fast, I didn't have a moment to call before the press conference. Let me tell you what happened. For starters, I'm in Seattle."

"I know. I just finished watching you on the eleven o'clock news."

"Alex, you sound funny. Is everything all right?" she inquired.

"No, everything isn't all right. How did you let yourself get roped into this Seattle thing, when you knew we were supposed to go over the files today at lunch?"

"Alex, it isn't a question of letting myself get roped into it. It's my job. Didn't Marge explain?"

"All Marge explained was that you were called out of town on business. She wouldn't tell me what business or where you had gone. I don't call that an explanation. And since when does a personnel manager handle a press conference?"

Lee's voice was beginning to sound irritated, too. "Alex, I'm the public relations manager for Varifoods as well as its personnel manager."

Alex couldn't keep the challenge out of his next question. "Oh? Since when?" He was angry because he had been worried, and he knew that he was taking it out on her.

"Since Monday afternoon," Lee replied, now a bit more than irritated. "Ham gave me the added responsibilities. I can't say I'm exactly happy about it. But when I heard a drug had been found in a Varifoods product, I was eager to fly up and check it out personally. I thought it might have something to do with Janet."

"Well, did it?" Alex asked, aware that there was still an edge in his voice, although everything Lee was saying made sense.

Lee sounded as though she had heard the edge. "Alex, back off! I'm not a child. I've been conducting my business affairs quite successfully for many years without your approval!"

The line between them remained silent as Alex tried to regain his inner balance. Would he appreciate being questioned this way? No. So why was he treating Lee to the third degree? He exhaled and tried again.

"I'm sorry, Lee," he said in a more natural voice. "Does there seem to be a tie-in?"

Lee's voice also softened, he noticed. "No. The police are pretty convinced it was an isolated incident. I've been with the lab chemists since I got here. They've opened other jars from the grocery store and others in the area. They're certain that the doctoring was not done at the Varifoods plant. I've called for inspections throughout the bottling department. Everything has checked out okay."

"Is that all?" Alex demanded, once more disturbed.

Lee sighed. "Yes, Alex, now what is it. What is really bothering you?"

Alex exhaled, trying to control his emotions. "Look, Lee, I'm sorry. I know you don't deserve this. But I've been so worried. I've been looking for you everywhere today. I kept thinking about that attempt on your life yesterday, and then when I couldn't find you, I thought maybe..."

The line fell quiet again as Lee thought over his words.

"Yes, I see that now. I was wrong not to call, Alex. I could have left a message at your hotel. I wasn't thinking straight. I'm the one who should be apologizing. How can I make amends?"

Alex audibly warmed to her words. "By keeping me informed of everything from now on, Lee. By letting me stay close until this thing is over. Very close. Please."

There was a slight pause on the other end of the line. Alex wondered what she was thinking. He had said "very close." How was she taking that suggestion?

"Okay. I'll be home tomorrow, around two in the afternoon. I hadn't planned on going into the office, but heading straight home to Benicia. It's 105 Tustin Court. Could you meet me there around four-thirty?"

"You have something in mind?" he asked.

"Yes. There's a party at Ham's home in Tiburon at six. Maybe you heard Denise, John and me talking about it on Monday?"

"The one to celebrate Varifoods' anniversary?" Alex asked.

"Right. Friday is a company holiday," Lee said. "It marks Varifoods' twenty-fifth year. Thursday night's party might give us a chance to mingle and ask questions. All the chemists will certainly be there."

"Good. I'd like to have a shot at getting some of them alone, particularly Pam Heyer. If you'll recall, she said she thought something was wrong ever since Janet returned from her maternity leave. Maybe she knows something that could be helpful," Alex suggested.

"Or maybe she's in on whatever happened to Janet," Lee replied. "I keep wondering why Janet didn't want to confide in her about what she thought was wrong at Varifoods."

"Yes, that thought has crossed my mind, too. And she was suspicious of you, which automatically makes me trust her less," Alex observed.

The line fell quiet before Lee spoke again.

"That was nice, Alex. Sort of like 'Your enemies are mine.' Thanks," she said with an audible yawn.

Alex smiled. He suddenly felt a great deal better. "So tomorrow at four-thirty?" he asked.

"Yes," Lee confirmed. "Good night. Good dreams."

"You, too," he said and hung up, but didn't feel tired. He felt relieved and almost . . . happy. It wasn't a word he had thought about in a long time. Happiness had proved elusive in the last five years. But knowing Lee was all right and that they had a plan for the next day seemed to have brought it back within reach.

Suddenly he had an appetite for cold chow mein.

LEE WAITED for Alex until five o'clock, growing more worried by the minute. She had called his hotel three times in the last fifteen minutes, but there was no response from his room. Where could he be?

She took off her high heels and started to pace in her stockings. The thick living-room carpet felt good beneath her feet, but she didn't pay it any attention. All her concentration was on Alex.

Had she gotten the times mixed up and told him five-thirty when she meant four-thirty? She had been pretty tired. It had been a full day.

Fortunately, the psycho had confessed to doctoring the iced tea mix that morning. The poisoning victim was doing fine, and would recover completely. Varifoods had been exonerated of all blame.

She wanted to tell Alex these things. She wanted to go over the Seattle poisoning and fully discuss their plans for the evening before it was time to start for Ham's party. That was one reason why she had suggested they meet at four-thirty.

It was getting very late. She looked at her watch again and wondered whether she should try his hotel one more time. She reached for the phone, then jumped as it began ringing in her hand.

It was Alex.

"I got a flat tire on the 780 freeway, a couple of off ramps before yours. I'm sorry I didn't call sooner, but not knowing the area too well, I ended up taking the long way around to find a phone."

"Where are you?" Lee asked, very relieved.

"In front of a twenty-four-hour 7-Eleven store, staring at an off ramp that says Sixth Street."

"I know where it is. I'll be there in five minutes," Lee said.

"I should have a garage come out to fix the tire. Any recommendations?"

"Don't waste your time calling," she said. "I'll drive you to one. See you soon."

Lee arrived within her five-minute prediction and saw Alex standing beside the pay phone, looking absolutely wonderful in a well-fitting dinner jacket, while he unknotted a kite string for two eight-year-old girls. She pulled the car up alongside and he got in, waving goodbye to the two girls. They were obviously sorry to see him go. Lee drove away.

"So you lead them on by fixing their kite string and then break their hearts, is that the story?" she suggested, feeling in a playful mood now that she knew he was all right.

Alex smiled. "I see I can't hide anything from a sophisticated woman like you. Not that I want to, the way you look in that dress. You don't happen to have a knotted kite string I can fix for you, by any chance?"

Lee felt her pulse quicken at his words. Playful or not, his message was unmistakable.

"I'm afraid I'm all out of knotted kite string," she said, not really sure what she meant.

"Well, a knotted heartstring will do as well. You've never been married, have you?"

It was a direct personal question. She had been asked it many times before and had a well-rehearsed answer. It started with the importance of her career and ended with her reluctance to disrupt her perfectly ordered life. But for some reason that answer didn't feel appropriate on this particular occasion. She found herself just saying, "No."

"You're not interested in marriage?" Alex asked.

"I've never found anyone I really wanted to marry," Lee said. It was the simple truth. She wasn't sure why she was telling it to Alex, however.

"No one's broken your heart?" he inquired.

Lee shrugged. "A bruise or two, maybe. A couple of years ago I dated the same man for about a year. I felt quite . . . disoriented when it ended."

"What happened?" Alex asked.

"Nothing. That was the trouble. He was very introspective. When I finally managed to get him to talk about the future, he told me he didn't believe in long-term commitments. He explained he wanted to take every relationship in his life a day at a time. That included his relationship with his boss, his doctor, his stockbroker, his dog and me." Lee felt herself smile at the admission. "As I recall, he listed us in that order, too."

Alex laughed. "You're shaking your head, as though you still can't believe it."

"What I can't believe is how I could have dated him for so long without understanding how he felt. I took his small displays of affection as just the tips of a deep and dynamic mass of desire waiting to erupt and sweep me off my feet. I never realized that the little emotion he showed was all that was there. Perhaps that says more about my shallowness than his.''

''You know that's not true,'' Alex told her. ''You saw in him what's inside you—strong emotion. That's what makes being loved by the right person so important. If you want commitment, he has to want commitment. You have to get back what you give, or you'll always feel cheated.''

Lee nodded, pleased with his understanding.

''It's better to keep life at arm's length,'' he added. ''Get fewer bloody noses that way.''

At that, surprise flashed through her, and she noticed that the sadness was back on those expressive lips. How hard had life hit him? she wondered.

Her attention was distracted as she drove into the garage. Alex explained to the mechanic that the rental car had neither spare tire nor tools to replace a flat. The mechanic nodded and went to get a hydraulic jack and lug wrench.

''We'll have to lead him to the car. Once the tire's fixed, we can drive back to your place, leave your car—or the rental, if you'd prefer,'' Alex proposed.

''I'd like to go to the party in my car,'' Lee told him. ''Dependability is a big issue with me.''

Alex nodded. ''Me, too. They don't make these Fieros anymore, do they?'' he commented as he leaned against its high-gloss hood.

''No. And I'm taking good care of mine. Who knows? One day it might even be a classic, just like the old T-Birds.''

Alex nodded. ''Could be. I like the car. And it certainly runs better than my leased car. It's been running rough since I got it. No spare is the last straw. I'll turn it in tomorrow and get another,'' Alex said.

The mechanic climbed into his truck and waved to them. Lee and Alex got back into her Fiero, and Alex began to give her directions.

Lee entered the 780 freeway, backtracked, took another exit and reentered, so as to come up behind Alex's disabled car. She started to slow down as Alex pointed to the side of the freeway ahead.

''There it is. The dark brown Chrysler.''

No sooner had he said the words then Lee saw a flash and heard a roaring in her ears. She hit the brakes, throwing them both toward the windshield as the car Alex had just pointed out exploded before their very eyes.

Chapter Nine

"The explosion was deliberately set?" Lee asked.

After an hour of questioning by the Benicia police, Alex wasn't smiling. He sat down next to her on one of the beat-up wooden chairs of the police station's waiting room almost as though he was too tired to stand.

"Police won't say what set it off. Maybe they don't know yet. They just told me to stay around, while they check out who I am. No reason for you to wait. You should be getting to the party."

"Alex, I can't just leave you here."

Alex smiled. "I called the rental agency. They're going to send someone over with another car. I think they're worried it might be the company's fault."

Lee licked her dry lips. "It isn't, though, is it?"

He reached over to take her hand. "Let's not jump to conclusions. The car didn't seem to be running properly from the moment I picked it up. And for the last day or so I've had to stop for gas every few miles. Gas line probably sprang a leak. I'm just glad no one was hurt when the thing blew."

Lee wanted to believe that was the explanation. She wanted to believe it so much that she agreed to go to the party as though nothing had happened, as though Alex hadn't just missed being blown up in his car.

"When you're cleared by the police and the rental car comes, will you join me at the party?"

"Yes. Here's some paper and a pen. Write down the address and how to get there. I shouldn't be too far behind you."

Lee took the paper and pen and complied. She looked up to catch Alex watching her with those steady but worried brown eyes.

His voice sounded concerned and rather nice. "Maybe I'm wrong. Maybe you should wait here until we can go together. I don't like the idea of your being there alone."

She thought about his words as she looked at her watch. It was already seven-fifteen, and the drive would take well over an hour. She shook her head.

"If there's something to be learned at this party, then I'd best be there to learn it. Come when you can."

She got up to leave the waiting room; Alex rose with her and held the door for her. They walked to her car, then he turned to take her hand.

"Watch yourself, Lee. And please, don't leave the party until I get there."

Lee nodded as she looked up into his concerned eyes. Alex leaned over and kissed her lightly, his lips barely brushing hers. She felt that light kiss vibrate all the way through her.

He smiled as he stepped back to open the car door. "Just practicing," he said.

BY THE TIME Lee arrived at Ham's Tiburon home, it was packed with the employees of Varifoods' San Francisco office. The closest parking space she could find was at the bottom of a hill a block away.

A maid took Lee's coat at the impressive all-glass entrance. Laughter and music blared from her left. As she walked in that direction, she stepped down into a huge, bold red room. Anywhere else, it would have been considered bad taste, but in Hamilton Jarrett's home the gaudy decor seemed somehow appropriate.

A band played on a raised platform at the end of the room, their deep red shirts perfectly matching the plush carpeting and velvet drapes.

The atmosphere was murky with the cigarette smoke that always seemed to accompany alcohol and loud music.

Everyone was chatting away and trying not to spill hors d'oeuvres or drinks on dinner jackets and evening dresses.

Lee was looking around to see whom she recognized in the large crowd, when she heard a familiar voice to her right.

"Well, if it isn't Ms. Public Relations!" John Carstairs exclaimed as he walked up to her. "Caught your act on TV last night. Not bad, not bad at all. Maybe you should be getting a replacement for the personnel manager position and stay in PR."

"You always seem to know the right thing to say, John. Thanks."

He smiled. "Let me get you a drink. What will it be?"

"White wine, please."

John went to get her drink from the bar that had been set up in the middle of the room. While he waited his turn in line, George Peck approached her. His dinner jacket hung on his large, bony frame like a suit on a hanger, Lee thought. And although spouses and "significant others" were always invited to the annual company party, Lee could see George's wife nowhere in the crowd.

Actually Lee didn't blame her. George always seemed to drink too much and get too friendly with other women at these events. His wife had probably decided that this year she just wouldn't stand around and watch him play the fool.

"Come on, Lee. Dance with me. We'll discuss chemistry," George proposed, his arms outstretched in her direction.

Lee noticed that his sharp blue eyes did not appear to reflect alcohol consumption, although his body seemed to be swaying a little. Either he was only pretending to drink or he hadn't been at it long enough.

"You'd find me a poor conversationalist in chemistry, George. Definitely not in your league. Besides, in case you hadn't noticed, nobody is dancing."

"They're just waiting for us to start. And don't worry about the chemistry. It's just a matter of mixing the right ingredients. I'm sure I could stir you up."

Lee didn't like the innuendo, nor his purposeful stare up and down her body. She didn't like them at all.

"Get lost, George. Real lost."

George smiled smugly at her words, but his arms no longer reached toward her.

"Or what? You'll call on that big lover of yours? Alex, isn't it? Where is he, by the way? Where is this chemist from the FDA?"

Lee tried to swallow her surprise. Where had George heard that? Did he know Alex was here to investigate Janet's death? Why did he sound so smug? And why was she reading a challenge into his words?

She mustn't panic, mustn't let him see how his words had upset her. The best defense was a good offense.

"You'd best keep your lecherous voice down, George. I understand Ham doesn't tolerate employee fraternization of any kind."

The smug smile didn't leave his face.

"The only people who have to follow rules are the ones who lack the power to make them. Ham won't do a thing to me. In case you haven't noticed, I've got the big man in the little palm of my hand."

His voice was too confident, his manner too easy. Lee had the uncomfortable feeling that this last boast might have a lot of truth in it. Somehow she didn't want to pursue the thought.

John returned with her glass of white wine, encouraging her to join him in the room next door, where the band's music wasn't so loud, and where a buffet had been set up. She accepted gladly, thinking that even King Kong would be preferable to the continued company of George Peck.

"Old George say something to offend you?" John asked, as they both got plates and began to help themselves to the food.

"Is it that obvious?"

Her companion laughed. "He can be a bit too much at times, but I suppose everyone has his place in the scheme of things. You know what they say about these genius types—eccentric and all that."

"Describing George as eccentric is about as accurate as describing Attila the Hun as impolite."

John laughed again, showing a lot of teeth—and very little substance, reflected Lee. She was beginning to sense he was much more of a political animal than his job title implied.

"Do you really think George is a genius?" she probed.

"Ham sure sings his praises. And he's not the most effusive of men when it comes to compliments. Apparently George's newest brainchild is a winner."

"Newest brainchild?" Lee asked.

John's eyes gleamed behind his suddenly transparent mask. "Come on, Lee. You know. The new line."

They moved away from the table and sat down in some nearby chairs. Lee was no longer interested in food, however.

"That's the second time you mentioned a new line, John. What's it all about?"

"Well, if that's the way you've got to play it—but frankly, I find all this secrecy stuff a real bore, don't you?" he opined as he popped a small sandwich into his mouth.

"Yes, very boring, John. So tell me what the story is behind this new line," Lee suggested.

But John was looking at Lee a little absently now, as though his thoughts had packed and gone on a trip.

"I wish I knew," he said with a wishful air.

"Did you ever get to see Denise about that budget matter?"

His eyes focused more clearly on her. "That budget matter was the funding for the new line."

"I thought it might be," Lee said.

John gave her an accusing glance. He obviously thought she was pumping him. Then he just shrugged, as though it didn't matter if she was.

"We got together on Wednesday. Not that it did any good, of course. The specifics are so buttoned up, I don't even know what I'm supposed to be allocating the dollars for. All I ended up with is a lot of projected expenses and no offsetting revenue."

"When are you supposed to get the missing information?" Lee inquired.

"Hopefully Monday. Denise said she'd call. Something about the results of some tests being verified. I really wish I could know sooner. I wanted to take next week off and get in some skiing before the season ends. Doesn't look like I'm going to get a chance now. What does that look on your face mean?''

"It means if you're fishing for information, I don't have it," Lee told him.

"But you knew Janet Homer, the chemist who was killed last Friday?" he asked.

Lee couldn't hide her surprise at his question.

"Yes. Janet and I were friends. What has that got to do with what we were talking about? This new line?"

John smiled very cleverly.

"Oh, nothing. Probably. I was just curious when I saw you at the funeral. You and your new...applicant for Janet's job. Wasn't sure if it was an official appearance."

Lee was taken aback to find that John was so observant. Maybe it was time for her to stop letting him surprise her.

"Yes, Alex realized he knew Janet from school. He thought it would be appropriate to attend, too. How did you know Janet?" Lee asked.

"We met when I first came to work at Varifoods three years ago. I saw her up at Lake Tahoe a few times skiing. She got pretty good. Her husband was a little klutzy, though."

"So this was before she got pregnant and went on her maternity leave?" Lee asked.

John nodded. "Yes. A group of us from Varifoods got together and shared cabins two seasons ago, just like one big happy family. I'm sure you ski. Didn't you see the notice on the bulletin boards?"

"Yes. But I was involved with someone then who didn't ski. I didn't want to drag him along, because I knew he wouldn't enjoy it."

"Are you a good skier?" John inquired.

"Not really. I spend most of my time freezing my tail off waiting for the ski lift, and the rest of it falling down the mountain. I don't seem to learn my lesson, though. I keep going."

His laugh was cool and polished. "You'll have to come with me next time. I'll teach you how to get down the next mountain standing up. I taught Janet, and she was real good by the time I was finished.''

"You taught Janet? I didn't realize you were that close," Lee commented.

Something glittered in John's light blue eyes. "I teach all the pretty women at Varifoods. It's the least I can do for my company."

His comment was good-natured enough, but by now something about John was bothering Lee.

"When did you see Janet last?" she wondered aloud.

"Oh, I guess when I came by to talk with George about a week ago. I said hello, but she seemed preoccupied and didn't even want to go for a cup of coffee. I don't get over to the Market Street office very often. As you've no doubt noticed, we finance wizards are on Bush Street now," John replied.

"That's right. Your group was moved out. I remember now. You used to have offices right down from the lab. How long have you been at the new quarters?" she asked.

"At Bush Street, six months. Ham, in his infinite wisdom, moved us out just two months after he took over. He thought we were too close to his precious lab. Must have thought our breathing would contaminate the samples."

John's voice had a noticeable edge now. Lee sensed that there was no love lost between the finance manager and the president of Varifoods.

"I didn't see Ham when I looked around a few minutes ago. Do you know where he is?" Lee asked.

"No," John said in a very stilted manner. "But I think you're about to find out."

Lee realized that he was looking intently over her shoulder. She turned—to see the stern countenance of Steve Gunn.

"The boss would like to see you."

"Ham?"

"In the library. I'll show you the way."

She put down her unfinished drink and plate of food and followed the stiff-shouldered security chief through the crowded room and down a relatively clear hallway. When they were nearly at the end, Steve paused and pushed a recessed button adjacent to an almost hidden door.

Lee heard a buzzing sound, and the door opened to reveal a small elevator. Steve moved into it and she followed.

The quiet security chief continued to look straight ahead as the elevator slowly took them to the next floor. His expression was grim, as though he were going to an execution. Lee wondered briefly if he ever smiled.

When the pulley mechanism had grown silent, Steve opened the door and preceded Lee out of the elevator. Halfway down a deserted hallway, he paused and knocked on a double door. Without waiting for a response, he opened one door and beckoned Lee to enter. She did so, and heard the door close behind her.

Hamilton Jarrett stood before her in evening dress. His white jacket and ruffled shirt accentuated his thick red hair and deep-set eyes. It was the first time she had seen him since Monday afternoon's sermon of the gospel according to Ham. Looking at him now, she had to admit that he presented an appearance some women might find attractive.

"Good evening, Lee. Thank you for coming. Here, sit in this chair. I want to talk to you."

Lee moved forward into the large, masculine room. Its walls were wood-paneled, with a massive, redbrick fireplace trimmed in black wrought iron. The oversize black leather chairs and couch looked tough, very much like their owner. Thick, red Persian rugs lay upon the highly polished, dark wooden flooring.

She sat down, feeling almost lost in the oversize chair, but Ham continued to stand. He had a glass of red wine in his hand.

"I've been watching my television here in some surprise. Oh, I got your cryptic note about what was happening and what you planned to do. Legal tells me you kept them fully informed. I must admit, I hadn't really expected such a smooth handling of the matter. You were...good. Very good."

He paused only briefly.

"So this tampering incident may have been a blessing in disguise. In any case, it's given me more confidence in you.

Your response was polished, professional, effective. You looked and sounded good on television. Your last boss said you had good instincts. Now I believe him.''

Lee didn't feel that his last comment deserved a response. She knew she should relish the praise, but somehow she didn't. She had done the right thing, and everything had gone smoothly. But what if she had done the right thing and, for some reason beyond her control, things had *not* turned out well? Looking at the hard man before her now, she was sure she would have been fired. Something was wrong when you had to be lucky, as well as talented, to keep your job.

"There's something else I've learned about you, however. Something that your last boss did not warn me about.''

Ham's pause raised the hairs on the back of Lee's neck. A little voice told her he was playing his manipulation game again, and she refused to play into his hands. She deliberately stood and smiled confidently at her boss. In her high heels, she didn't feel his height nearly as intimidating.

"And what have you discovered, Ham?''

His reddish-brown eyes burned brightly, and he pursed his full lips—in surprise? Speculation?

"That you're setting yourself up for failure, Lee. Just when you could have opened the door to immense opportunities.''

A knot began to tie itself uncomfortably in her stomach. She thought about sitting down again, so that she wouldn't be so close to the glow in the reddish-brown eyes. But she couldn't manage the movement without some awkwardness, and awkwardness at this moment would be disastrous. She had to stand her ground.

"You say that as though you think I'm deliberately trying to fail,'' she said. "Why should I do such a thing?''

His small smile told Lee that he had been expecting her question. He had manipulated her, despite all her efforts not to be.

"Don't ask me, Lee. You're the one consorting with the enemy.'' He took a sip of wine, then placed the glass on the table beside him, never taking his eyes off her face.

"What do you mean?" she asked, trying desperately to control her voice and expression.

His small smile vanished into the straight, hard line of his mouth.

"You know exactly what I mean. I told you that I am aware of everything that happens at Varifoods. Did you think you could hide this relationship from me?"

He had to be talking about Alex. Lee didn't know how much the big man standing before her really knew, but she must be careful not to make assumptions, not to disclose information unnecessarily. She fought hard to gradually paint a light smile upon her lips, to keep her voice low and even.

"Humor me, Ham. Who is the enemy? And what is the relationship?"

She could see that her bluff was disconcerting him and felt a sudden surge of hope. He was so used to people deferring to him that he was unprepared for a challenge.

"Are you going to try to tell me you aren't passing information to this Alexander guy?" Ham demanded.

Lee's tone crackled as if discharging static. "Alex is the enemy? Pass information to Alex?" She continued with as much surprise in her voice as she could manage. "What information would that be, Ham? How many people we employ? How much we pay them?"

She watched him rummage through a number of facial expressions as he sought the right one. Lee waited in silence, hearing the ticking of the watch on her wrist.

"All right. The information you possess isn't exactly classified. What *are* you doing with the guy then?" he probed.

Lee really liked the look that finally emerged on Ham's face. If she could just keep up the offensive, she might get through this. She held her head high.

"Look, Ham, I'm as susceptible to a good-looking man as any other woman, and Alex is a good-looking man. Once I decided he wasn't suitable for a job at Varifoods, he became fair game. He's neither an employee nor a prospective one. In other words, he's none of your business."

After that bold speech, Lee turned and walked toward the door. She almost made it.

"Wait a minute," Ham said.

Her hand was just turning the knob. She held on to it for support for a moment before turning back to face the big, red-haired man and looking at him with what she hoped was cool detachment. It became harder and harder to do so as he walked toward her. He stopped less than a foot away.

"You're wrong when you say something isn't my business, Lee. Everything about anybody who works for me is my business. Why did this Alexander guy go to the Homer woman's funeral?"

Lee had to fight to keep her voice even. "Because he knew her. He told me they went to college together."

There was a challenge in Ham's voice now and a new gleam in his eyes. "Do you know where he's from?"

"Of course. It was on his application. He's from the East," Lee said.

"No, Lee. Wrong answer. He's from the FDA," Ham said. One of his huge paws slid over her arm, as though he were getting a hold on his prey. Lee tried not to flinch, not to yank her arm away.

"And what does he do for the FDA, Lee?" The reddish-brown eyes bored into her and she fought a rising panic.

"He's a division manager."

Ham almost smiled, and his tone grew sarcastic. "And you found an FDA division manager unacceptable for the position of research chemist at Varifoods?"

Lee's heart was racing. She kept trying to remember that "offense" was the operative word. If she could just get back onto the offensive, she might survive this terrible encounter. She threw all her remaining strength into her voice.

"Of course! He was way overqualified. Varifoods could never have challenged him. We would have paid him relocation fees, taught him all our research methods—and lost him in six months to a competitor offering more money and a higher position. And he would have taken our secrets with him! Do you think I'd jeopardize my company by doing anything so foolish?"

Ham stared down at her. Just for a moment his grip tightened on her arm. Then he let her go, and his angry, hard look dissolved into disturbed reflection.

"Yes, of course. You're right. To hire him would have been a mistake." He spoke as though a great truth had dawned. Then he moved away from the door where Lee still stood and returned to his drink.

Lee turned to leave once more. This time her shaking hand got the door open before Ham spoke again.

"Don't go, Lee. Come have a drink with me first. I'm glad to hear you have the company's interests at heart. We have some celebrating to do tonight."

At this point, Lee felt she could sure use a drink. But this man was the last person she wanted to see on the other end of a celebration toast. And she didn't know how much longer she could control the shaking that threatened to overtake her. She had to get out.

"Some other time, maybe," she said, as she walked quickly through the open door and shut it behind her. She almost ran to the elevator, stepping in and closing the doors as though she expected Ham to follow. Her whole body was shaking as she rode down to the first floor. She got out and looked down the hallway toward the crowded and very noisy room.

No. She couldn't go back there. Not yet, anyway. She needed to find a place where she could stop shaking, where she could quietly regain control. There was a door to her right that led out to a large deck overlooking the Golden Gate Bridge and the lights of San Francisco. The coolness in the night air had driven Ham's guests inside. Lee was thankful. It was a perfect place to be alone.

She stepped quietly onto the deck, closing the door behind her, then walked over to the rail, pressing her palms against the rough, weathered wood. Her heartbeat gradually began to slow.

Several minutes went by as Lee concentrated on the city lights and breathing in the fresh, salt-laden air. She deliberately blocked out all other thoughts. A light, friendly breeze lifted some strands of hair across her face. She swept them back as they tickled her nose, noticing at the same time that her hand wasn't shaking anymore.

Her newfound sense of peace was gradually replaced by an awareness that the breeze was now quite chilly. She was just turning to go inside when a shape suddenly emerged from the shadows. She started, then relaxed when she recognized the figure.

"For God's sake, Steve! You scared me. How long have you been there? Why didn't you say something?"

The cigarette between his lips glowed as he inhaled. Smoke was blown out of his mouth as he spoke.

"You looked like you were enjoying the view. I know I was."

Lee wasn't sure if the security chief's words had some more subtle meaning. She decided to ignore them.

"I didn't know you smoked, Steve."

He took one last drag, then crushed the smoldering cigarette between his bare hands. Lee thought that if his action was meant to impress her, it had failed miserably.

"I didn't know you picked up strange men," he said.

Lee knew immediately that she didn't want to have this conversation. She started to move past Steve toward the door, but he stepped in her way.

"He's using you," he said.

"Who are you talking about?" she asked, although she was pretty sure what was coming.

"Alexander. The guy who applied for Janet Homer's job. The guy who put flowers on her grave."

His words weren't a surprise. It seemed that Alex was making a lot of people at Varifoods uncomfortable. But Lee wasn't ready for another round of interrogation. She tried to step around Steve, but once again he moved to block her way. She was growing irritated, but was willing to play his little game if it would help her to get rid of him.

"Okay, I'll bite. How could Alex possibly use me?"

Steve's reply told Lee that he had been waiting for just that question.

"He's out to destroy Varifoods. And he'll want your help. He'll say or do anything he has to to get it, even make love to you."

Lee felt insulted by the implication that she was just a pawn in a man's game. But then, maybe Steve had meant to insult her. Was he trying to arouse her suspicions, so that she would refuse to help Alex? If so, she had a sudden flash of insight that protest was not the best way to handle the security chief.

"I hear you, Steve. And don't worry. I'll be careful." Once again she tried to move around him to get to the door.

Once again he stepped deliberately into her path; this time his hand shot out and encircled her arm. His tone grew less formal. "What's your hurry?"

He moved closer. Lee could detect the unpleasant smell of cigarettes on his breath. She didn't like being this close to the security chief, didn't like it at all. Anger leaped up inside her.

"Look, our discussion is over. I told you, I'll be careful. Now let go of my arm. I'm cold and I want to go inside." She tried to pull her arm away, but he held on firmly, a slight smile curling the bottom of his lip. Even in the semidarkness, Lee could see it wasn't a pleasant smile. She was sorry she had ever wondered what one would look like on his face.

"Don't worry, I'll get you warm," he said.

As he moved even closer, Lee felt her initial anger yield to fear. She didn't like the look on Steve's face or the way his eyes were traveling over her body. She was acutely aware of the remoteness of this deck, of how easily the noises from the party would drown her screams. She repeated her demand with much more confidence than she felt.

"I said, take your hand off my arm."

Steve grabbed her other arm and tried to draw her to him. His grip was like cold steel, chilling her far more than the night air. Her heartbeat began to race again. Panic welled up inside her. She tried desperately to push him away, but he was too strong. No matter how much she strained against him, she was slowly being pulled toward his body. His next words stabbed at her like sharp knives.

"If you resist me, it will just be more fun."

Chapter Ten

A huge shadow came out of nowhere, grabbed Steve Gunn's shoulder and spun him around.

Alex's voice sounded like a roaring hot wind in the cool night. "The lady said, remove your hand."

The surprised security chief looked first in disbelief at the big man who was challenging him, then took a swing at Alex.

It was just what Alex was hoping the man would do. He was ready. He dodged the clumsy swing, happy for a chance to retaliate. His knuckles connected with Steve's jaw in an ugly crunch, tipping the man to one side. Before Steve could regain his balance, Alex punched him hard in the stomach and again in the face. Steve fell backward onto the deck with a heavy thud.

Alex watched until the dazed security chief picked himself up and staggered down the outside stairs of the deck, then he turned toward Lee.

She was wide-eyed and shaking. The fright in her eyes touched him. He felt an overwhelming need to assure her and reached out his hands. She stepped forward and placed her own—cold—hands in his. He pulled her to him, gently laying her head on his chest and wrapped his arms around her possessively.

As he stroked her soft hair, he could feel her body tremble, and her heart match beats with his own. It felt so good to hold her close, to touch her. He bent to kiss the top of her head and stopped stroking her hair when he realized that his own hand had begun to shake.

"Lee, it's all right. He's gone. It's over."

Her body was no longer shaking. She raised her head and looked into his face. Her eyes reflected the color of her deep violet dress; her long, blond hair flowed around her face like soft moonlight. He thought he could want for nothing more than to go on looking at her.

"Are you all right?" she asked.

He smiled into her eyes. "At the moment, never better."

She hadn't tried to move out of his arms, and he hadn't made any attempt to release her, he realized.

"He tried to hit you," Lee said. Her voice didn't quite have its full volume yet, Alex noted.

"He missed."

"I'm so glad. Things happened so fast, I couldn't follow your movements too well. Thank you. Thank you so much."

"It was my pleasure," he said.

"I've never been rescued before. It was nice," she said with a small smile. Her face seemed to be picking up color.

"I have a confession to make. I've never rescued anyone before. I have to admit I'm feeling rather pleased myself."

Her smile was steadier now. "Did you hit him hard?"

"Hard as I could," he said, smiling back.

"Good," she said, her own smile even broader. Then it disappeared, as another thought appeared to occur to her. "Did you hurt your hand?" She stepped back and out of his arms, reaching to capture his right hand.

Alex liked the feel of her exploring fingers. "Don't worry. I used to box in college. I know how to throw a punch."

She nodded; he sensed that her scrutiny had uncovered no scrapes or abrasions. "He was warning me not to trust you," she said, releasing Alex's hand. "Can you imagine? That sleaze bag telling me not to trust you?"

Alex could hear a more natural volume in her voice now. He was thankful both for it and the loyalty in her words.

But her words also reminded him of the seriousness of their situation. With her in his arms, he had momentarily forgotten everything else.

"How much does Steve Gunn know?" Alex asked.

She sighed. "He saw you put the yellow rose on Janet's grave. George, Ham and John also know you were a friend of Janet's. Of course, that makes them view your application for her job with suspicion. I just had a very uncomfortable session with Ham about that very subject."

Alex could see from the look on her face that the adjective "uncomfortable" was a gross understatement.

"How did it end?" he wanted to know.

"I told him I didn't take your application seriously. I think he believes we're lovers. I did my best to leave that impression."

Alex watched Lee shiver. He realized that she was becoming chilled from the night air now that she was out of his arms. Out of contact with the warm softness of her body, he was also feeling cold—a different kind of cold. He wanted to hold her again, but wasn't sure he'd ever want to go inside if he did.

"Well, maybe we'd best go in then and keep up the image," he said instead. "What's the party been like so far?"

"You haven't been inside?" Lee asked, obviously surprised.

"No. I saw you struggling with that ape as I was walking up the driveway. I came up the outside stairs—the ones Steve Gunn took down."

"Oh, I see. Well, I think you're right. We'd best get inside. We have a lot of mingling to do, and there are rumors going around about a new product line. If we can get any of the chemists aside, I think that might be a relevant topic of conversation. John Carstairs implied a link with Janet."

Alex knew his voice did not hide his surprise. "A new product line? Linked to Janet?"

"Sort of makes it a topic worth pursuing, doesn't it?" Lee suggested over her shoulder as they headed for the door that would lead directly into the main party room.

DENISE WILLIAMS had been looking around for Lee. She had to talk to her before it was too late. She had seen Lee talking with John earlier, but Steve had come and whisked her away before Denise could get to her. Then, just when she thought Lee might have gone home, she saw her enter the room with Alex, coming from the outside deck.

Denise watched them look at each other and frowned. The attraction was there, no doubt about it. That was really too bad, too bad for Lee, at least. Maybe it was already too late. As long as Lee stayed in his company, Denise knew that she had nothing to say to her. She turned and walked away.

"WELL, what can I tell you?" Pam inquired, after Alex had spent several minutes convincing her that Lee had also been a friend of Janet's and could be trusted. The three of them were standing behind a punch bowl in a corner of the large, red room, trying to look unobtrusive.

Lee was feeling so much better now that Alex was here. Vivid memories of his warm, comforting arms and the tenderness in his voice still surrounded her like a protecting cocoon. With some effort she concentrated on what they were attempting to accomplish.

"Was Janet working on a new product line?" Alex had just asked.

Pam shook her head. "No, I don't think so. She had been off on an extended maternity leave for eight months. I doubt George would have given her anything new or important so soon."

"Have you heard about this new line?" Alex asked.

Pam once again shook her head. "No, not specifically. But I had a feeling that something was going on. Denise, Steve and John had been popping in and out of the lab so much recently, the chemists were joking about requisitioning desks and chairs for the three of them."

"But you didn't know what they were doing?" Alex concluded.

"No. I don't think any of the chemists knew," Pam said. "Michael Ware asked me about it several times. And Tom, the new guy, asked George one day by mistake. Got really chewed out for being too inquisitive. Frankly, if any of the chemists were working on something special, there would have been signs, even if they didn't say anything. You know what I mean?"

"Like excitement?" Alex suggested.

"Yes. Exactly," Pam agreed. "The only excitement seemed to be coming from George's office."

"Was Janet excited?" Lee asked.

"No. Not really," Pam replied.

"What about overtime?" Lee inquired. "Did Janet ever stay late?"

"She left with the rest of us, between five-thirty and six. Except, I do remember something strange," Pam observed.

"What was that?" Lee wanted to know.

"Well, I remember asking her to come out for a drink with me one night last week, and she told me she couldn't, because she had to go back to work."

"And she didn't say why?" Lee asked.

"No. I just thought it was a repeat of a couple of years ago."

Pam suddenly looked uncomfortable. Both Lee and Alex could tell she regretted her words.

"She worked a lot of overtime two years ago," Pam added, as if to explain.

"She was working on an important project?" Alex wondered.

"I . . . guess so," Pam said reluctantly.

It was pretty obvious to Lee what Pam really thought. Before they could go any further, Lee knew she would have to get the chemist to say it.

"But you really thought she was having an affair?" Lee suggested.

The other woman apparently saw no point in avoiding the truth.

"Yes, I think so," she said.

"Do you know who her lover was?" Lee inquired.

"Not exactly," Pam said.

"But you have an idea?"

Pam nodded. "One night Michael Ware and I and the other chemist who used to work in the lab went out for a couple of drinks. It was about nine o'clock when we drove past the front of the building to drop Michael off near his car. We saw Janet coming out. She was with George."

"Could they have been just working late?" Lee asked.

"George works late, but never with one of us. He doesn't actually do the experiments. He coordinates what we do and analyzes our results."

"Could it have been just coincidence, the two of them coming out together?" Lee wondered. Had this occasion been the sole basis of the gossip Denise had passed on earlier?

"Maybe it was coincidence," Pam said. Her tone clearly told them that she thought it wasn't.

"But?" Lee prodded again.

"Well, I had noticed something different about Janet. For several months she seemed sort of edgy, distracted. And she asked me to cover for her on a couple of nights, to tell Mark that she had gone to a movie with me, if he asked where she was."

"So you suspected she was having an affair?" Lee concluded.

"I guess I realized that was probably what was happening."

"Did you cover for her, Pam?"

Pam shook her head. "I didn't have to. Mark never asked."

"Do you think he knew?"

"I don't know. But I do know Janet ended it," Pam added.

"How do you know that?" Lee asked.

"Well, we had a sort of strange conversation at lunch one day," Pam said. "She talked about how she had been taking Mark for granted, been doing some pretty stupid things. About how much he really meant to her. Then she confided that they had planned a weekend together at Lake Tahoe. She was going to go off the Pill and try to have another baby."

"Yes. She talked to me about wanting another child about a year and a half ago, too," Lee said.

"Well, she got her wish, of course. It was just about three months later when she told me she was pregnant," Pam said.

There was an undercurrent in Pam's voice that disturbed Lee.

"You think Janet's baby wasn't Mark's?" Lee guessed.

Pam nodded. She obviously suspected George. Suddenly Lee knew why Janet hadn't confided her most recent concern to this woman. Pam had not trusted Janet, and Janet must have sensed that mistrust.

Before Lee could pursue the matter any further, the band suddenly stopped and Ham's voice called for attention. She felt Alex stiffen as she tried to concentrate her attention on the announcement.

". . . new line will be revolutionary! We've been working on the secret process for the last six months. Three weeks ago we introduced a sample distribution in a small Iowa town.

"Now, you must understand that these Iowa townspeople have been growing their own food for more than a century. You can't fool them. They know what tastes good. And after only two weeks of eating our new product line, they selected it as superior in every way to our competitors."

Wild clapping followed Ham's remarks. He held up his hand.

"That's not the best part. The new product line can beat anything, even homemade. For example, these Iowa farmers judged our frozen corn sweeter than even their fresh corn right off the stalk!"

"Are you saying that they would grow corn to sell to us and then buy it back after our processing?" a voice from the crowd asked. Lee thought it might be John Carstairs.

Ham smiled with glowing benevolence. It was a smile that cloaked the room with goodwill, but it felt scratchy on Lee's skin.

"Yes, they'll buy it back from us, because they can't grow anything that tastes anywhere near as good as what we've got to offer—for any price."

"When will the new product line be out?" asked another voice from the crowd. Lee recognized that voice for certain. She looked over and saw Michael Ware.

"Monday of next week the processing formulas will be hand-carried to the various processing plants under the strictest security. They'll begin production immediately. We expect to distribute the first wave of new-line products within three weeks, coincident with a major marketing campaign."

Once again the big man's self-assurance brought a round of applause and cheers. But to Lee, Ham's words brought a feeling of deep foreboding.

As soon as he put down the microphone, signaling the end of his announcement, she turned to Alex—and heard her thoughts expressed in the words he whispered into her ear.

"This has to be it! This has to be what Janet was trying to warn us about," he said. "A product line good enough to stop Iowa farmers from eating their own food could be a revolution—a money-making revolution!"

"Yes, but what was Janet's concern?" she asked.

"Maybe the obvious. If Varifoods' processing was this superior to everyone else's, competition would be crushed. Varifoods would corner the market," he concluded.

Doubt still clouded Lee's mind.

"Alex, I don't think so. Superior products have inundated the market before. Other companies soon duplicate the formula. They're not burdened with recouping research costs, so they can offer the same product at a lower price than the company that introduced it. Within a relatively short period, sometimes just a few months, competition is restored. Economically, such improvements leave nothing to fear."

Alex nodded. "Yes, of course, you're right. I didn't think it through," he said. "If Janet was concerned about this new product line, it had to be because something was wrong in its chemical composition. But that seems like a dead end, too. My boss, Willy Hansen, told me the FDA's seen nothing from Varifoods."

"Which means?" Lee inquired.

"Which means that this 'new' product line is just a different blend of the same old ingredients. And the 'new' advertising is just a bunch of hype, as most advertising is. Unless..."

"Yes?" Lee prompted.

"I've got to get a sample and find a lab to test it in," Alex said. Lee could hear the urgency in his voice. He turned again to Pamela Heyer.

"Pam, are you sure Janet didn't say anything about this new line?" he asked.

The chemist frowned. "Like I told you before, it wouldn't have made sense for George to involve her. She had just come back to work and she was worried about something. She tried to hide it, but I know she was bothered. She left her cubicle in the lab for almost an hour last Friday morning. When she came back, I could tell she was upset."

"Did you ask her why?" Alex wanted to know.

Pam nodded. "She wouldn't tell me. I thought it was personal, so I backed off."

"Can you get me a sample of the new products?" he requested.

Lee watched the dark eyes dart around the room. No one seemed to be noticing their conversation. George Peck was nibbling on some woman's ear on the couch next to them. Her loud giggling was attracting most of the attention. Pam looked back at Alex.

"Ham said they'll be on the market in a few weeks. Can't you wait and get the samples you need then?"

Lee saw the fear in the woman's eyes and heard it in her voice. Alex had apparently heard it, too.

"Pam, it's okay. I was asking too much. You've already helped quite a bit with your information. It's enough. Besides, this new product line could have nothing at all to do with Janet."

The short, round woman closed her eyes as though attempting to summon strength, but the tone of her next words did not sound as though she had been successful.

"On Monday. I could try on Monday," she offered.

"No, forget it. I mean that. Really," Alex said.

It was at that moment that John Carstairs brushed past Alex's shoulder. Until then Lee had been so intent on the conversation that she hadn't noticed he was there. She leaned over to whisper into Alex's ear.

"I think John Carstairs is trying to overhear our conversation with Pam. Why don't you talk to her about the weather for a minute, while I go see Ham?'' she suggested. "I'll be right back."

Alex nodded and smiled, as though her whispering had been something very personal and pleasant. Then he leaned over and kissed her on the cheek, whispering, "More practice."

Lee felt the warmth rise to her face as she left him to find Ham Jarrett. It took her a few minutes to get through the crowd surrounding the company president. It was just as well. Even that brief contract with Alex had left her feeling breathless. But she had herself back in control by the time she approached the big man.

"Ham, this is certainly good news. Are you planning a formal press conference to announce the new line?"

Hamilton Jarrett looked at Lee as though she was an unwelcome intrusion.

"I'm not used to employees refusing my offer of a drink," he said, obviously still upset with her earlier departure and consequently not willing to address the new subject.

Lee smiled pleasantly. In a crowd of people, with Alex standing nearby, she felt a lot safer than she had when alone with the president. With security came boldness.

"But I'm sure you'll agree, it was natural after you questioned my integrity and loyalty to Varifoods," Lee said.

He studied her for a moment as though he was still unsure about something.

"All right, we need to schedule a press conference. Get together with Denise to work out the details. I'm flying out Monday afternoon for a status meeting with the board of directors of Trans World Inc. Have an appropriate statement on my desk early Monday, so that I can take it with me."

Ham then deliberately turned his back on Lee, as though he still needed to snub her. It mattered not at all to Lee. She had gotten what she'd come for. She smiled on her way back to Alex.

"So it was the prima donna's project, after all?" a voice said suddenly beside Lee. Lee stopped and turned.

"What are you talking about, Michael?" Lee asked. The Rasputin look-alike stroked his long, thin beard. "The new product line, of course! It wasn't Pam's, it wasn't Tom's, and it sure as hell wasn't mine! It had to be hers."

"You're saying that it was Janet's?" Lee's voice expressed her surprise, she knew.

"Don't tell me your little friend didn't tell you?" Michael challenged her. "Janet could be quite a little actress, couldn't she? Pretending to dislike George just like the rest of us, while she cuddled up with him behind our backs."

"You're wrong, Michael. About everything," Lee said as she turned and started to walk away.

"Well, if I am, whose project was it? Huh? You just tell me that!" Michael called after her.

Lee frowned. Whose project, indeed?

"What's up?" Alex asked as soon as she returned.

"Let's get out of here and go someplace we can talk," she proposed.

"Your place or mine?" he asked loudly—obviously for the benefit of the people around them.

"Now where have I heard that before?" she wondered aloud, with a small laugh. "Let's make it mine."

THEY WERE THERE a little over an hour later. Lee was fixing them a cheese omelet, since neither of them had eaten at the party. Alex had asked if he could wander around her house. The thought occurred to Lee that he might be checking to see if it was secure. She nodded and set about preparing their meal.

He joined her back in the kitchen, just as she was putting the omelets and some hot muffins onto the table.

"I'm surprised. A three-bedroom, two-bath house just for you?" he asked, sitting down.

Lee shrugged. "They don't exactly make new homes any smaller."

"You didn't consider a town house?"

Lee shook her head as she poured the coffee. "Too much like an apartment. The neighbors are still too close. You can hear their parties, their music, their children, their pets."

"Say no more. This apartment dweller shares your sympathies. At least with a house you have a little space between your life and the neighbors. I'm envious. This is nice. It fits you. You didn't believe what Pam said about Janet playing around, did you?"

Lee looked up, a little surprised at his sudden change of topic. "No," she said. "I don't know why Janet was working late two years ago, but I'm sure she wasn't playing around with George. Frankly, I understand why Janet didn't trust Pam, if Pam thought that about her. Janet would not have cheated on Mark. Molly is Mark's baby. I'm sure of it."

Alex smiled. He liked her faith. "Well, it's certain she's not George's."

Lee looked at him questioningly as she sat down. "I agree, of course, but you sound as though you know something I don't."

Alex nodded. "Genetics, my dear Ms. Lee, genetics. Janet had blue eyes and George has blue eyes. Molly's eyes are brown. It's not possible for two blue-eyed parents to give birth to a brown-eyed child."

"Really? But I know of two brown-eyed parents giving birth to a blue-eyed child," Lee said.

"Yes, genetically that's possible. You can have brown eyes and carry a recessive blue-eyed gene. If both parents have that recessive gene, then the child can get one recessive gene from each and end up with blue eyes," Alex said.

"But it doesn't work that way with two blue-eyed parents and a brown-eyed child?" Lee asked.

Alex shook his head. "No. Remember, blue-eyed genes are recessive. If a baby has blue eyes, he has only blue-eyed genes, one from each of his parents. If a baby gets even one brown-eyed gene, the baby will have brown eyes, because the brown-eyed gene is dominant. So you see, a blue-eyed parent only has blue-eyed genes. They don't have a brown-eyed gene to give to the baby. Therefore two blue-eyed parents cannot have a brown-eyed child."

Lee nodded in understanding. "And Mark has brown eyes. So Molly got her brown eyes from Mark!" she exclaimed.

"Or from a brown-eyed man, at least. No, don't look at me that way. I believe Mark's the father, too. I amend my statement. Molly is Mark's child."

Lee smiled. "Thank you. Now let's eat."

They finished their meal as the stereo played softly from the next room. He had meant what he said earlier. Her home was furnished comfortably. He couldn't say specifically what it was about her choice of drapes, carpet or couches, but everything blended to make him feel at home. He realized that he wanted to know more about her. Much more.

"Have you always been called by your last name?" he asked.

Her response took a while. He waited.

"The teachers in school would call roll that way. Sometimes they even forgot your first name."

"And you were glad when they forgot yours?" he prompted.

At first he wasn't sure she was going to answer. But then her head came up, and she stared at him with that direct look he'd seen before.

"Yes. I was glad to forget the name Bernard. And Bernie, and all the rest of its equally obnoxious derivatives."

The distaste in her voice made him chuckle. She didn't seem to take offense, but smiled into her raised coffee cup.

"Can't say I blame you," he said. "Bernard certainly doesn't fit. What's your middle name?"

"Allen. Not much better, is it?" she said.

He nodded and then repeated both names. "Bernard Allen. Strange how parents can be so insensitive. People forget how important a name can be, don't see past the first birthday."

"You sound as though you really understand," she said, wondering why.

"I should. My full name is Lake Erie Alexander."

"Lake Erie—as in one of the Great Lakes?" she asked.

"That's me. I was what is referred to as 'unplanned,' a late in life surprise for two distracted scientists. They picked a name for me by spinning a globe underneath a pointed finger. The globe stopped at Lake Erie, and that became the entry on my birth certificate."

The beginnings of a chuckle were born in her throat.

"Considering the possibilities, you were lucky," she observed dryly.

"I'll say. I remember trying the same trick when I was ten. If it had been my fickle finger deciding my fate, you'd be calling me Nouakchott."

"What?" Lee asked.

"Nouakchott is the capital of Mauritania on the west coast of the northern African continent, or at least it was when I was ten."

She laughed, unrestrainedly, joyously. It made him feel like laughing, too.

"So how did you get stuck with Bernard Allen?"

She had stopped laughing, but the words came out more easily, less hesitantly, less edited.

"I was a first child. My parents were sure I was going to be a boy. So in a bow to tradition, I was to be named after my father, Bernard Allen Lee. When my mother was on the way to the hospital to give birth, she and my father were involved in an automobile accident. My father died instantly. My mother was badly injured. But she hung on somehow until I was born."

They were tragic words, but she hadn't said them tragically. She had come to terms with the circumstances of her birth. Still, he wanted to put his arms around her then, to give and maybe even receive comfort for past losses.

"My father's brother took me in," Lee said, continuing her story. "Knowing my father's choice and being so caught up in the horror of his death, Uncle Joe couldn't bring himself to think up a new name for me. As you said, he couldn't think past my first birthday, what it would be like for me growing up."

Alex nodded. "Yes, it's amazing how inventive kids can be when they hear a different name. I went through a lot of years being told I was wet behind the ears, or all washed up. I guess the one that managed to stick the longest was Leaky. God, how I hated being called Leaky!"

"Yes, I can see it could be a drain on your spirits," Lee said.

Alex didn't miss her pun. He laughed happily. "All right, come clean. What did the kids call you?"

"Oh, anything and everything. But it got better about the age of ten, when I finally learned to laugh along with them. That laughter became a great release."

Alex didn't comment. He was seeing her growing up, being teased about her name, probably just as he had been. She had learned that fighting back did not stop the tormenting. Somehow she had found the strength to remove herself as the object of ridicule. That was a big lesson for a ten-year-old. He liked that little girl. And he liked the woman she had become. Very much.

Lee put down her coffee cup and leaned back. Alex could see that she had just decided something.

"Ham said the new processing technique was perfected during the last six months. Yet none of the chemists seems to have worked on it. Pam knows nothing about it. Neither does Michael. I only hired Tom Borden four months ago, so he couldn't have been involved. And Janet was on a maternity leave until almost three weeks ago. What is the answer?" she asked.

"We're missing a piece of the puzzle, that's the answer," Alex replied.

Lee nodded. "I'm going to go into work tomorrow, find the new product line file and get you that list of ingredients," she said. "And you're going to come with me. Now that we know what we're looking for, we'll go through every likely file until you see some formulas or new processing data that fit. Since we know the new line is about six months old, pinpointing the file should be much easier."

Alex nodded and leaned forward.

"Yes, tomorrow should be the perfect day. It's a company holiday for you. We should have the place to ourselves. We can take all day if necessary!"

Lee smiled back, obviously pleased with his concurrence.

Alex felt the forward momentum of their decision. He got up and took the dishes to the sink. He rolled up his sleeves and began to wash them, just as if he were at home. Lee got to her feet and wrapped an apron around his waist, feeling his warmth, trying not to linger too long over the task. She found herself a dish towel.

"If you stay here tonight, we can get up early and drive into San Francisco together," she suggested. "There's a couch that makes into a second bed in the guest room. There are sheets and blankets in the closet."

He looked at her as she picked up a dish, trying to read something more personal into the invitation. But she had turned her face away, intent on her task.

"Thanks, Lee. I'll take you up on the offer."

They finished the dishes, turned off the kitchen light and walked down the dim hallway to their respective bedrooms. He had every intention of being a perfect gentleman and living up to the trust she had demonstrated by inviting him to spend the night in her home. But he somehow forgot those good intentions when she looked into his eyes to say good-night.

Suddenly she was in his arms, and his lips were blending with the softness of hers. She tasted sweet and warm and willing, and he had no thoughts left for good intentions.

Lee had wanted this embrace, this kiss with this man, and all of it was exceeding her wildest expectations. She clung to him, thrilling to the feel of his powerful body, excited by the taste of his demanding mouth, indulging her desire for him until she realized what she was doing.

She had invited him to spend the night, and now she was inviting him into her bed, just as surely as if she had said the words.

But other words hadn't been said. Important words. She had promised herself that she would never love again without them. Then she remembered. This man lived and worked on the other side of the country. He couldn't say what she needed to hear. She pulled away.

"Just practicing. Good night," she somehow managed to say, turning to walk into her bedroom. As she closed the door behind her, she could still see him standing in the hallway, his expression unreadable in the semidarkness.

SHE NEVER KNEW what awakened her. A disturbance in the sounds of the crickets? The interrupted song of a frog? A broken twig? All she knew was that suddenly, in the black of night and under a heavy veil of dreams, she bolted upright in her bed and was instantly awake.

She knew where she was, and she knew something was wrong. Something was there—in the room with her— something evil. She felt its presence as she felt the mad rushing of blood through her veins. Then she heard the breathing, the soft scraping sound. It was coming from her window. Even in the blackness of the night, she saw the outline of the head and shoulders silhouetted against the glass. In absolute terror, she screamed.

Chapter Eleven

Whoever it was had not expected her to be awake and screaming. She saw the dark shape move quickly out of the window and away from her. As her own scream still echoed in her ears, she heard a shuffle, then the door to her bedroom swung open and the overhead light blazed like the sun into her unprepared eyes.

"Lee! What is it?" Alex asked. His hair was tousled, his chest bare. He wore the slacks he'd had on earlier that evening.

Lee pointed toward the window, not trusting her voice. Alex rushed to the sill and was out the open window in a flash. Minutes crawled by like hours. She felt she couldn't move and still sat straight up in bed, clutching the covers. Her heart was hammering in her chest.

When someone started to climb back into the room, she let out a little cry. Then she recognized Alex's disheveled hair and sighed.

He looked at her and tried to smile.

"Sorry. Didn't mean to scare you, but the front door is locked. Don't worry. Your intruder is gone. I heard a car engine start about a block away."

He locked the window and drew the drapes, then turned and came toward her.

"A car?" she repeated on a questioning note.

She must have looked as bad as she felt, because without further preamble he sat down on the bed and took her into his arms, cradling her against his bare chest.

"Could you see who it was?" he asked after a moment.

"No. Just a dark silhouette. But a big frame. Like a man's," she said.

"Thank God, you're safe. You've got a great scream. I know you started every dog in the vicinity barking. A few of the neighbors' lights went on. I think its vibration probably squeezed some grapes off the vines in Napa County."

The absurdity of the image made her laugh. Once again, in his arms everything seemed all right. Soon the beating of her heart had returned to normal—until the realization sank in that she was leaning against his broad and powerful bare chest.

She nuzzled up to him then, enjoying his clean scent and the excitement his body was bringing her. When he responded by holding her closer and kissing her hair, however, she came to her senses and reluctantly eased herself out of his arms.

She looked into his eyes, a little surprised by what she saw.

"Do you always wear your glasses to bed?" she asked.

One large hand swept his disheveled hair back from his forehead. "I couldn't sleep. I was reading when I heard you scream. Feeling okay?" he asked.

"Yes. Fine. Thank you. I guess it's time to pick up the phone and call the police," she said.

He was looking at her very warmly. Lee realized that in the bright lighting, her nightgown probably wasn't leaving a whole lot to the imagination.

"Unless you want to do some more practicing first?" he suggested.

Lee fought the desire to respond to his invitation. Instead she shook her head. "I don't want to practice anymore, Alex."

He was trying to catch her eye, but she avoided his gaze. After a moment he got off the bed and headed for the door.

"Of course not. I understand. I'll go call the police while you get dressed," he said just before closing the door behind him.

He was gone so quickly that Lee felt abandoned, yet she knew she had to fight these feelings for Alex. There was no future in them. They could only lead to hurt, her hurt. She shook her head sadly and got up to dress.

A little light romance was probably just a diversion for him. It could never be that for her.

IT WAS SIX IN THE MORNING by the time the police left. Lee poured Alex a second cup of coffee and one for herself.

"Well, they were polite, if not very encouraging," she said as she tried to restart the conversation with Alex. A new aloofness seemed to have enveloped her companion.

"They probably would have been more encouraging, if I hadn't smeared all the prints by going in and out of the open window," he observed. His regret was obvious.

Lee shook her head and came to his side. "Alex, you heard the officer say that the guy was probably wearing gloves. I very much doubt there were ever any fingerprints. You had a chance to catch him and you had to take it."

He sipped his coffee and looked at her.

His tone was even, polite, distant. "You really are very good at public relations. I don't think it would be possible to disbelieve anything you said. Perhaps we should leave for the office now. Will we be able to get in this early?"

She nodded sadly as she put their cups into the sink and went to get her coat and purse. When she came back, she noticed he had washed the cups and put them away. Somehow it made her feel even worse. He seemed to fit so well into her home.

They took her Fiero, and as they approached the 780 freeway, she asked about his wrecked rental car.

"Nothing was mechanically wrong with that Chrysler. They think the explosion was deliberately set."

Alex spoke quite matter-of-factly, but new fear wrapped itself around Lee. She tried to use her thinking process to overcome it. "How, Alex?"

"No obvious evidence remains, but it can be done. It's not difficult to make a time bomb."

"Time . . . bomb?" Lee looked at him in horror. Alex explained calmly, but his face was a mask.

"The fire started under the front seat of the car. There are lots of ways to do it. The easiest would be with a cardboard carton containing potassium chlorate and sugar. Just plug it with a cork stopper and pour a little sulfuric acid on the top of the cork—and in time the sulfuric acid will eat through. Once the sulfuric acid comes in contact with the chlorate-sugar mixture, it explodes in a chemical fire, very hot, very powerful.''

''Under the front seat?'' Lee knew she was repeating Alex's words like some demented parrot, but couldn't seem to help herself.

''Yes. Obviously, whoever it was wanted to be sure I was close to the little gift they left for me.''

''Oh, Alex! You could have been killed!''

His voice was still so calm, so deadly calm. ''That you can be sure was the point.''

''Why didn't you tell me this last night?'' she asked.

''You had a few other things on your mind, if you'll recall,'' he observed.

Yes, she had. But now Lee was trying to think through this latest outrage, trying to get past the overwhelming frustration of not knowing who was behind all these things. Then something occurred to her.

''Alex, what you're describing, this time bomb, could only have been made by someone with certain knowledge. Isn't that right?''

''Yes, a knowledge of explosives or—''

''Chemistry?'' she suggested.

''Yes. Chemistry,'' he said. ''I thought of the same thing. If Janet had gained access to one of the other chemist's experiments, the one on the new product line, for instance, she could have recognized something was wrong with it and told him to stop, or she'd tell the people who would make him stop.''

''Or her stop,'' Lee added.

''Yes. It could have been Pam. They were friendly enough that Pam might have showed Janet her experiment against the rules. And when Janet found out something was wrong...''

Alex hadn't finished his sentence, but he didn't have to. Lee knew he was about to say that Janet had been killed to keep her from revealing the truth about the experiment.

And now that same murderer had tried to kill both her and Alex. The rest of the trip into San Francisco was very quiet.

"WHAT DO YOU MEAN, I can't authorize Alex to come in with me?" Lee said to the security guard at the entrance to Varifoods.

"I'm sorry, Ms. Lee. They rewired our panels yesterday. No one can get into the administrative offices without a palm identification coding now."

Lee was shocked. "But this means I won't be able to interview prospective applicants anymore. It's crazy! Who made the changes?"

"The security chief, Ms. Lee. Like I said, the technicians came by yesterday and canceled our capacity to override the electronic eye, just like they did on the lab side a few days ago. Haven't been able to understand it myself."

Lee didn't say anything else. Instead she turned to Alex.

"I'm sorry, Alex. I'll have to go in alone, try and find it myself."

He nodded. "That's okay. I think it might be a good idea if I go see a certain chemist we both know. If she's innocent and really wants to help, maybe I can talk her into coming back with me and getting those samples from the lab today. If she's been playing games with us, now's the time for me to find out."

"But do you know where to get in touch with her?" Lee asked.

Alex nodded. "She gave me her address last night, when you left us to talk with Ham." Alex took a scrap of paper out of his pocket and referred to the address. "A condo out in Concord."

Lee handed Alex the keys to the Fiero. He looked at his watch.

"It's a little after seven. What do you say we meet at noon in the lobby of the Sheraton Palace?"

She nodded; his hand reached out for a moment to touch her arm in a reassuring gesture. Then he was gone.

She looked after his retreating figure, almost wishing that they were back to "practicing" again—and at the same time telling herself it was better this way. She put her palm print onto the security screen and passed through to attend to her urgent business.

THE FIRST THING Lee noticed when she walked into her office were a dozen long-stemmed, light pink roses in a vase that stood on the edge of her desk. A message in Marge's handwriting lay nearby. It explained that Alex had left the roses for her on Wednesday, when he had come by with lunch. It also said she had missed out on some very good lobster.

She extended a hand to touch the delicate petals. The flowers were part of the pretense she had agreed to, but they looked and felt real—just like her feelings for Alex. She sighed and circled her desk.

She signed on to her computer, and once in, went directly to the employee locator. It would be best to find out who was in the office this morning, in case someone decided to drop in on her. Apparently the only one who had made it in so far was George Peck. That was good. He was the one least likely to visit. It was time she went exploring.

Over an hour later she got up to make herself some instant coffee, shaking her head in frustration. She had not found either a new formula or anything that looked like a new processing procedure that had been begun in the last six months.

Since Janet's files were the only ones that could be eliminated from the search, she had tried using each of the other chemists' access codes to review the experiments they were working on. All to no avail. If Alex had been there, he could have read the files, helped to decipher the chemical language. But by herself it was proving a useless effort. There were just too many files.

She needed the file name. Without it, locating the right formulas would be close to impossible. They were there, she was sure—somewhere among the thousands of files—like the proverbial needle in the haystack.

Coffee cup in hand, she returned to her computer and stared at the screen. Some files had letter abbreviations, others numbers. Perhaps there was a code to the ones that dealt with the chemical formulas. How could she find out?

"You here, Lee?"

Lee just had time to hit the Clear key before Denise came within view of her monitor.

"Good morning," Lee said. "I was just about to wander over to your office to see if you had made it in yet. Thought you might want to inspire me."

From Denise's throat came a noise that sounded like the squawk of a drowning duck. She apparently was the worse for wear this morning.

"Don't count on me for inspiration today. And please don't try to get any coherent thoughts from this battered brain. You have no idea how much it hurts in my present state of dissociation."

"I take it you enjoyed yourself at the party last night?"

"Party? So that's what it was. I had this dream I had fallen into the garbage disposal."

Denise plopped heavily into a side chair near Lee's desk. Her eyes were two slits of crimson. Her thick makeup, normally applied with finesse, today looked as though it was the first effort of a young teenager.

"It's sort of a blank?" Lee asked.

"What's sort of a blank?" Denise inquired.

"Hmm. I can see it is. Do you remember anything? Ham's announcement of the new product line?"

"Softly, Lee. Softly. I'm right next to you, so you don't have to shout. Yes, now that you mention it, that sounds vaguely familiar."

"Well, Ham wanted you to fill me in on the new line, so that you and I could work on a press release, something that would associate his dynamic personality with the dynamic new taste. I need to be able to present something suitable to him by early Monday morning."

Denise seemed to be trying to focus on Lee's face—unsuccessfully. "How can you be so full of energy?" she asked.

"I left the party early last night, before you fell into the garbage disposal."

"I never would have taken you for a quitter."

"Last night I was, but not today. I really do have to talk with you about the new product line. I need the background on what type of foods have come under our new processing technique, and what this superior taste is all about, in order to decide how I can present it best."

"Say this is a joke."

"Will that make it any easier to do?"

The advertising manager's hands tried to hold up her eyelids.

"Oh, God, my head hurts. I have ten hours of work to do today, and I can't even keep my eyes open. And now you tell me we have to collaborate on a press release. Please, Lee, have a heart."

"There's a simple answer, Denise. Just tell me which file to access for the advertising program and background data, and I'll bring myself up-to-date on the new line."

Denise's yawn seemed to hurt. She uttered a groaning sound.

"Suppose it's okay now, after Ham's announcement and all. It's the HGJ file. But you'll need to use my access code. Yours won't let you in. Right now only Ham, George and I have clearance. Got a pencil?"

Lee shoved a pencil and paper underneath Denise's nose.

"How did you get to work?" Lee asked. "I hope you didn't drive in your present state."

"Drive? No way. I can't even walk. I took a cab. Besides, I can't find my Ford Bronco. It wasn't in my driveway this morning. And that reminds me. I've got to call the police and report it stolen."

"You might want to check with Ham's house first. I'm getting the feeling you may have been sent home in a taxi last night. Your truck is probably parked somewhere around his place."

"You think so? What a relief. I hate dealing with cops and insurance companies. Don't know which is worse. They both make you feel like a criminal. Now, what were we talking about?"

"You were about to write down your access code for me, so I can get into the HGJ file," Lee reminded her. "See the pencil in your hand?"

"Oh, yeah. Thanks. I'm not sure why I bothered to come in today. Unless I have a complete body transplant, I don't see much hope of getting any work done. Here's the code. God, I need a bottle of aspirin!"

"Will you settle for two pills?" Lee suggested, taking them from her purse.

Denise stretched out her hand to accept the offering.

"Got any water?"

Lee left her office for the bottled water dispenser down the hall. She was quick, but when she returned, she found Denise sitting in her chair, entering something into her computer. It might have been her imagination, but the advertising manager's eyes seemed less bloodshot and more alert than her stated condition should have allowed. She gave a small start when Lee entered the room.

"For God's sake, don't sneak up on me like that! Not in my present state of nerves!"

Lee put the paper cup of water on the desk in front of Denise.

"Make up your mind. Just a moment ago you were accusing me of being too loud, and now you think I'm too quiet. What do you really want?"

The question had a dual meaning that Denise did not miss.

"I was just checking the HGJ file to make sure it was up-to-date with the advertising focus. Actually, I don't see any real need for a press release. The advertising campaign should carry the products right into the consumers' homes."

"A press release is standard operating procedure for any new product launch—totally free publicity that can support your advertising campaign. How could you possibly not want to use one?"

Denise capitulated at once. "You're right. Don't listen to me. My brain has been ground up into little pieces. Let me at the aspirin."

Lee watched Denise wash down the pills. She did look pretty rotten. But the question was, had she intentionally made herself appear that way? Was this an act to get a look at what Lee had been checking in the computer? Was she purging the HGJ file of data she didn't want Lee to see? Or was she just doing as she said and checking the file update?

Suspicion was doing rotten things to Lee's insides. Her stomach was churning. She disliked not being able to trust what people said, not being able to assume they were honest and aboveboard.

"Have you tasted the new product line?" she asked.

Denise shook her head, then grimaced at the pain it seemed to cause her.

"When I asked to, George told me to get lost in his typically charming manner. But the Iowa test results are dynamite. I mean those people really went bonkers over the stuff."

"I don't suppose there are any samples around?" Lee inquired.

Denise looked at her, but the advertising manager's squint effectively hid any emotion in her eyes.

"Come on, Lee. This is George's little miracle we're talking about. Can you see that proprietary creep letting any free samples out of his kitchen?"

It wasn't a question that expected an answer. But it seemed strange to Lee that the advertising manager had not insisted on tasting the new product she was supposed to promote. Very strange. Of course, knowing George, it might indeed be the truth. Lee looked over at the woman, who was now sitting with her head in her hands, and felt somewhat contrite.

"Why don't you go home, Denise? If you've really got something urgent to do, tell me what it is, and I'll see how I can help. You need time to let your body work the party out of your system."

Denise lifted grateful eyes to Lee. "You're nice. Really nice. With everything else you have to do, you're offering to help me. No one else around this lousy place would. Thank you, Lee. But don't worry. I'll go lie down on a couch in my office for a few minutes and give the aspirin a little time. Be fine soon. Now, if I could just get out of this chair without my head falling off..."

Lee helped Denise leave her office and went back to her computer. As Denise had said, the HGJ file was on her screen. Everything the advertising manager had just told her could be true. Or she could be a very good actress.

Lee felt a headache of her own coming on. But before she even took an aspirin, she went back to the history update. Nothing had been deleted from the HGJ file, so at least part of her suspicions about Denise had been proved baseless. However, despite Denise's belief that only she, Ham and George had access codes, Lee knew that she herself could have brought up the file before this—if she had known its significance.

That was her biggest problem. She knew her way around computers well enough to gain access to anything she needed, but she *didn't* know what it was she needed.

She decided to go back to the HGJ file, and her fingers clicked off the request. It proved to be a fairly complete rundown of the Iowa taste-test results and the upcoming advertising campaign. But the very things Alex might need she couldn't find. The formulas for the various food and drink products were missing.

Five product categories had the new formulas: sliced ham-sandwich meat, frozen corn, several flavors of ice cream, a noncarbonated fruit punch and several flavors of packaged soup. They were the vanguard of the new process's uses, the beginning of its anticipated product-wide application.

She printed out the Iowa test results and the current products that made up the new line. It didn't seem like much, but at least it was a start. Then she got another idea. She activated the office intercom and punched out the lab's extension. George Peck's voice growled an acknowledgment.

"It's Lee. I'm putting together a press release for Ham. I'd like to come down to talk to you."

The intercom was quiet for a long moment, during which Lee would have given a lot to read George Peck's mind. When he finally spoke, his tone was abrupt.

"You know the way."

A few minutes later, Lee walked into the lab, carrying a second copy of her computer list of products. George Peck's office door was open. She entered and took a seat next to his desk without invitation.

His late night certainly hadn't improved George's looks. His face seemed thinner than ever, and the bags under his eyes were positively stuffed. Yet his sharp, focused look was still quick and penetrating.

"I need to take some of your time this morning to—" Lee began, but before she could go further, George interrupted.

"I understand your lover punched out Steve Gunn last night. I don't think his actions are going to improve your already tenuous position with Ham."

He wore his superior little smile, Lee noted.

"Anything Steve Gunn got, he deserved," she said.

George was watching her closely. "Probably," he said. "But that won't change things."

"This is not what I came to discuss," Lee reminded him.

George reached inside his desk and brought out a cigar, which he unwrapped, then lighted. He deliberately blew the smoke into Lee's face.

"George, I really wish you wouldn't smoke that thing while I'm here," she said in protest.

George smiled. "Yes, I know."

The fumes of the strong-smelling cigar were beginning to choke her. George leaned forward, bringing the dreadful odor of the smoldering weed even closer.

"Where is your lover today, anyhow? I thought you two were inseparable."

"He's visiting a mutual friend, George. Can we get to our business? What I need is—"

"You're wasting your time with Alexander, you know," George interrupted again.

Lee knew better than to go onto the defensive with the chief chemist. She was starting to realize that the man got his jollies from confrontation.

"Look, George, I'm not in the mood for this today. Why don't we just get down to business?"

George puffed away on his cigar, quickly filling the office with its foul smell, and obviously enjoying Lee's all too evident discomfort.

"Since you insist," he said, his irritating smile still quite evident.

She inhaled and made her statement with as much authority as she could muster. "I need the chemical formulations for the new line."

Her tone would have intimidated a security guard; the chief chemist didn't even blink.

"The hell you do. Our formulations are top secret. What are you trying to pull?"

He was instantly armed and attacking—and still smiling. But Lee was ready for George Peck. She had watched him in action against Denise. He was always catching the advertising manager off guard, but he would find Lee well prepared.

"No product can be sold today without a complete disclosure of its ingredients. And the public is demanding nutritional content, as well. Calories, carbohydrates, protein, fat, salt, cholesterol, artificial flavors, artificial colors, preservatives. They all have to be on the label."

"You think you're telling me something I don't know?"

"I'm telling you that this information is not available in the files on the new product line," Lee said. "The schematics on packaging just show the word Ingredients on the bottom of each container."

George waved a hand at her as though she were an annoying insect. "The packaging department will fill them in. They know what should be printed there, because they need to know. You do not."

"Oh, but I do. Ham will be holding a press conference in less than two weeks. He will introduce this new line as a processing miracle, one that has left foods in all categories tasting truly wonderful. It's the processing that's secret, not the ingredients. He could very well be quizzed about the wholesomeness of the ingredients."

Her last words finally wiped the smile off his face. Now he wore a quite different expression. Lee couldn't exactly make it out. His eyes were like two tunnels with the opposite ends blocked from an intentional avalanche.

"Why would he be?" George wanted to know.

"The public is demanding good nutrition, not just good taste. You can't be too blind to see that. We must be ready for such questions. There's no doubt they will be asked."

George looked at Lee uneasily. She could tell he had accepted her logic, but Lee also knew that his ego would never let him admit it. Not to her. Maybe not even to himself.

His tone was dismissive. "I'll think about it. Now get out of here."

Lee would not be dismissed.

"Are you trying to set Ham up as a fool, by not giving him the information he needs? Because if you are, I'll be happy to call and tell him. Then we'll see just how well you have him in the palm of your hand. You've got ten minutes to think about it, George. Then those lists of ingredients had better be on my desk."

Just for emphasis, Lee threw her computer copy of the new product line right in front of the chief chemist. It flew off his desk and onto his lap. She got a glimpse of his surprised and angry face as she turned and stalked out of the room.

Within ten minutes, Lee's office printer began to provide her with the new line's ingredients. The chief chemist obviously had decided to send her the information in this way, so that he wouldn't have to see her again. She didn't know if it would help, but she decided to call George to thank him. He didn't answer. He probably knew it was her. She gave up.

She glanced at the formulas, but they didn't mean much to her. So she rolled up the printout and wrapped it into her coat to smuggle out later.

For the next few hours, Lee busied herself in trying to clear out an ever-increasing In basket. When the phone rang, she was surprised to see it was eleven o'clock. She was also surprised that someone would be calling her at the office. Denise and George were surely the only two people who knew she was working today. And if they wanted to get a hold of her, they would have used the intercom. Who could be calling? She answered hesitantly.

"It's Alex. I'm sorry, but I had to call."

Lee could tell something was wrong. He sounded out of breath. She suddenly feared for him.

"Alex! Are you all right?"

"Yes. I'm fine. Don't worry. But I'm afraid I'm going to be late for our luncheon date."

"What is it? Why are you breathing so hard?" Lee asked.

"I've been chasing a green truck," he said.

"A green truck? What green truck?" she wanted to know.

"The one that just ran Pamela Heyer down," he told her.

Chapter Twelve

"You're sure she's all right?" Lee asked. She and Alex were making their way into the Garden Room of the Sheraton Palace for a late lunch.

Alex nodded as he held the chair for Lee. "Yes. She's in some pain from a bruised hip and cuts where she got scraped up as she hit the pavement, but the doctor said there's nothing broken. Her parents are with her at the Mount Diablo hospital now. She should be released soon. She gave me her home number."

"What happened?" Lee asked.

"Well, I didn't have her telephone number and I couldn't find it in the book, so I drove to her place in Concord and found she wasn't home. Her neighbors told me she was participating in a community jog at a nearby park. I had no choice but to sit on her front steps and wait. I had decided to give up and leave when I spotted her across the street and waved. At the same moment the green truck came screeching around the corner and headed directly at her."

"It deliberately headed for her?" Lee suggested.

"Yes, no doubt. Climbed up the sidewalk after her. Fortunately Pam saw it coming, jumped to get out of the way, and the fender of the truck just clipped her side. Frankly, she was lucky."

The significance of the truck's color dawned on Lee.

"A *green* truck, Alex?"

He nodded. "Dark green. Just like the paint on Janet's fender. I chased it for two blocks, trying to get a license number. Unfortunately, I never got close enough to make it out.''

Lee was trying to assimilate this new event. ''Well, at least this clears Pam of suspicion,'' she said.

''Yes. But it also raises another question,'' he pointed out.

''What?''

''Why was she attacked?'' Alex wanted to know.

Lee considered his question as the waiter took their order. By the time he left, she thought she had the answer.

''Maybe the murderer saw us talking with Pam last night at the party. The murderer would know she has access to the test kitchen. He could have figured if she was friendly to us, she might get a sample of the new product line. Maybe this attack on her was to keep us from getting our hands on it?''

Alex watched the worry lines dig deeper into her forehead and he wanted somehow to smooth them away.

''Very logical,'' he said, ''and my thoughts, too. But let's try to forget this business for a few minutes and enjoy lunch. You must be starved. I know I am. Neither of us had breakfast this morning.''

Lee nodded. She certainly wanted to forget the insanity that was hovering around them, even if it was only for a few minutes.

The Garden Room did indeed feel like a garden. Sunshine entered through two-story-high skylights and bathed the room in a soft glow. For some reason, Lee felt as though she had stepped back in time.

''This is lovely,'' she said as she looked around.

''I like it, too. This restaurant was an open courtyard in San Francisco's earlier days. Horse-drawn carriages used to rein up and let off their elegant patrons. Right where we're sitting, matter of fact,'' Alex said.

Lee pictured a pair of dappled gray horses with silver reins. Such pleasant fantasies seemed far removed from their present reality of exploding cars and predatory trucks. She shook her head.

''I'd like to think it was a less violent time, a more gracious world. But imagination is always an inaccurate guide, isn't it?'' she observed.

He stared at her, not speaking for a moment. The soft light from above enveloped her in its soft glow. She was so lovely. After that incredible kiss and embrace the night before, he did not doubt that she was attracted to him, but it was obvious that she didn't want to get involved in another romance without a future.

It was just as well. He didn't want that kind of involvement, either. Thank God, she had pushed him away! He wasn't emotionally geared for a superficial affair, and he couldn't afford to have anything else.

So why couldn't he just forget it and concentrate on the problems at hand? Because he hadn't really cared about a woman this way since Sally. And Sally had been dead five years. Such feelings just weren't so frequent that he could ignore them. They might never come again.

But on the other hand, what if he let himself love her, and something happened to her—something he was powerless to stop? No, he mustn't think about getting close to her—or about losing her. He mustn't think about anything but pursuing Janet's secret and her killer. Everything else had to be forgotten.

"Alex? Is everything all right?"

Alex unclasped his hands, as though reluctantly releasing a stray sunbeam that had tumbled from the ceiling.

"Yes. Everything's fine. I'm sorry. You asked me a question?"

Lee could see that nothing was fine. The sadness around his mouth was back in full force. Seeing it again made her forget what it was she had asked him.

"It doesn't matter. Here's lunch," she said.

They took their time, quietly enjoying the food; but after lunch it was back to business.

"Tell me what you've learned," he said.

Lee pulled out the computer printouts that she had smuggled out of the building. Alex took them and studied them over coffee.

"So what do they tell you?" she asked as soon as she saw he had finished his reading.

"Frankly, not much," he said. "Nothing here that isn't GRAS."

"GRAS?"

"Generally Recognized As Safe. Stuff that's been used for a lot of years without any known problems. I'm afraid that this isn't going to help much."

Lee was disappointed. "What will?"

"Some samples of the various products. And a lab. Somewhere I can do some tests."

"But if these ingredients aren't dangerous, what do you hope to find?" Lee asked.

"It's one of those situations where I won't know what I'm looking for until I see it."

"What if the improvement is truly in the processing?"

Alex shook his head. "I can't buy it. Labs have been experimenting with all types of processing techniques for more years than either you or I have been on this earth. You've got five different types of products here. Hot and cold. A revolutionary new process applicable to hot and cold just doesn't seem possible. Not something that could affect these divergent tastes."

"So you think it's something new?" Lee guessed.

"It's my gut reaction, but I don't know for certain. Varifoods hasn't applied for approval of a new additive. And they don't list one in these formulas. But what else could account for the flavor enhancement that Jarrett was bragging about? How else could these products be so improved?"

"I understand your reasoning," Lee said. "But if Varifoods has a new additive, are you saying they didn't try for approval because it's harmful?"

"Either that, or they didn't want to take the time. In order to prove the safety of an additive, a company has to carry out three kinds of toxicity studies," Alex said.

"What are they?" Lee asked:

"The first is an acute toxicity test. Rats are given a single, large dose of the additive. Then the effects are recorded. Next the same rats are fed diets with different concentrations of the additive for at least ninety days. Again with the results recorded."

"And the final test?" she probed.

"It involves long-term toxicity studies, finding out how the rats metabolize the additive and how it affects their fertility, reproduction, lactation, as well as the effects on their general physical well-being over a lifetime of consumption," Alex told her.

"How long does all this take?"

"Two years or more for the long-term toxicity study. Then it's generally years more before the FDA reviews the material and grants approval."

Lee's voice carried new energy; she could hear it as she spoke.

"That could be it, Alex! Hamilton Jarrett can't wait that long. He wants to make Varifoods number one this year. Maybe that was what Janet was going to tell us. Maybe there's an additive in this new product line that hasn't been tested."

"Or one that's been tested, and the powers that be at Varifoods didn't like what they found," Alex suggested. "You see, the Delaney Clause of the Food Additives Amendment passed in '58 forbids use of any substance that causes cancer in humans or animals."

"But wouldn't they be taking a big chance, if that's the case? I mean, if they actually knew the additive caused cancer?" Lee inquired.

"I hate to admit this to you, Lee, but actually they wouldn't be taking such a big chance at all."

"I don't understand," she said.

"Well, it works this way. Let's say Varifoods has developed an additive that causes cancer in their laboratory rats. If they release their studies to the FDA, they know we'll ban it. So they don't release the information. Instead, they just put it into their products and pretend nothing is new."

"But what happens when people start to get cancer?" Lee wanted to know.

"People get cancer every day. We're constantly exposed to carcinogenic agents in all parts of our environment. If you ask people who get cancer how they got it, with the exception of the cigarette smoking and lung cancer connection, they can't tell you. Neither can their doctors. It's an insidious disease, often creeping up on you over time."

"Are you saying that people who ingest the new cancer-causing additive won't know where their cancer came from?"

"That's exactly what I'm saying. The cancer may take years to develop. And by the time it does, so many other factors could encourage it to grow. Excess stress, a high-fat diet and a sedentary life-style might all contribute. There would be no way to trace the cause to a food source, much less to a specific product, even though the specific product was the original cause of the cancer."

"But in the case of food, isn't the FDA checking the products that come out? Making sure they're safe for human consumption?"

"No, Lee. You have a misconception of our role and the extent of our investigative arm. First, we don't test food that's on the market. Second, we don't even usually test additives that have been submitted to us for approval. Our role is limited to evaluating the manufacturer's submitted tests. We don't even perform our own tests to verify their information."

"You mean the decision as to what we eat is really in the hands of the food processors?"

"To a great extent, yes. Oh, every few years some university scientists discover that a supposedly safe substance, one that's been consumed for years, is really hazardous. Red dye #2 and Violet dye #1 were two such additives that were found to be dangerous only after years out on the market."

Lee felt a little sick. "I almost wish you hadn't told me. You're shattering a lot of my illusions of safety. Suppose you test the products from the new line. Suppose you do find a new additive, one that hasn't been submitted for approval to the FDA. What will you do?"

"I'll take the information to my boss, Willy. He knows what I'm doing here, Lee. He understands a new additive might be involved."

"He'll move on the information right away?" she asked.

"If he doesn't, I'll go to the director in the Center for Food and Safety and Applied Nutrition. And if the director doesn't act promptly enough, I'll go see the commissioner of Food and Drugs. I'll get someone to listen, to act."

"But how long will it take for them to act?" Lee demanded.

Alex looked uncomfortable. "I...don't know. But I'll do anything to keep a dangerous new additive from getting out," he said.

Lee could tell from his voice that Alex meant what he said, but she couldn't help thinking that no matter how much he tried, he would still be relying on the prompt action of others. If these others didn't act quickly, a harmful additive might indeed be released and consumed.

Lee had a sudden, overwhelming feeling that time was slipping away from them. Precious time. Alex's next words underlined his own sense of urgency.

"We've got to get a sample of those products."

"How? The only place that might have the sample is the lab kitchen. The only people who have access to it are the chemists. And now that Pam's been hurt..." She paused.

"What about the other two chemists?" Alex asked.

Lee shook her head. "Tom is new. He's afraid of his own shadow. He'd never have the guts to help us, particularly since it goes against company security."

"And Rasputin?"

"No, Michael Ware isn't the friendly type. He's already upset that he wasn't invited to work on the new line. If he's telling the truth, that is. And if he's not, then we certainly can't trust him."

Alex looked up at the people passing in front of them, as though he were looking for something. Lee realized that he was trying to answer some internal question of his own. When he turned back to her, she knew he had made up his mind.

"Is there anything urgent you have to take care of in the next couple of days?"

"No, why?" Lee asked.

"I need to go out of town and I want you with me."

"Where are you going?" she wanted to know.

"To the only place I can think of that has samples of Varifoods' new product line."

Lee caught on. "To Iowa! To the town where it was tested!"

"Exactly. We've got the names and addresses of the twenty-five families who got daily samples, so chances are good a few samples are still around. We should be able to pick up one or two. That's all I need to do a chemical analysis. Will you come?"

Lee smiled and reached out her hand, letting it rest on his arm. "Of course I'll come. We're a team, aren't we?"

Alex smiled back, unable to deny the pleasure her touch and assurance brought him.

THEY STOPPED at Benicia and back at Alex's hotel to pack a change of clothes for their overnight trip. The best flight arrangement they'd been able to manage was a late-evening departure, with two stops for connecting flights before landing in Des Moines the next morning.

It was a tiring trip. Lee kept falling asleep, only to be awakened for another plane change. She could see Alex was exhausted, too, and remembered that he probably hadn't slept at all the night before.

They both perked up, however, when they landed in Des Moines in bright sunshine. They rented a car and immediately took off, following their map to the small Iowa town that had been the site of Varifoods' taste test.

"We have twenty-five families to cover. I think we should split up the names and each interview half," Lee proposed.

"Sounds like an efficient plan," Alex agreed, looking over to smile at her. His smiles since they left California seemed less reserved. Whether they were really different, or whether her escalating feelings for him were making them appear so, Lee couldn't tell. She tried to concentrate on locating the addresses.

"Now if this map is correct, Main Street is our dividing line between east and west. The first thirteen families appear to be located on the the eastern side of town. I'll take them. You can concentrate on the twelve located more toward the west," Lee told him.

"We'll need a time and place to meet," Alex said, just as they entered the small town.

"What about that bar and grill over there? It looks to be the local gathering place," Lee suggested, as she tore the computer list of addresses in half to give Alex his section of names.

Alex pulled into a parking space in front of the bar and grill and switched off the engine.

"Okay. I'll meet you inside at two," he said. "Good luck."

"You, too," she said, wishing she had never said anything about not "practicing" anymore—and then reminding herself once again that she was being inconsistent.

They went their separate ways.

Lee looked at her list. The Stuart family was just a block away. She made her way to their door and knocked optimistically. The feeling didn't last long.

The large woman in the housedress listened to her request with barely restrained irritation. Lee could hear a crying child in the background. Perhaps she had come at a bad time.

"No, I don't have any of the samples left. Are you folks crazy? First you ask my family to participate in your taste test, and then you refuse to let us buy the products after the taste test is over. And now you're back asking if we have any of the free samples left. I thought you fools wanted to market your stuff!"

"The products are scheduled to be in the stores in less than a month's time, Mrs. Stuart. You'll be able to purchase them then," Lee told the woman.

"I don't want to purchase them in a month. I want them now. Hear that screaming? That's my little girl, Tabitha. She wants one of *your* ice-cream cones, not the one I've been trying to give her for the last twenty minutes. Unless you've got samples, lady, just get out of my face!"

ALEX ARRIVED at the bar and grill at one-thirty. He was more than tired, he was frustrated. He had not found a single Varifoods sample. Participants in the taste test had devoured them all, right down to the last piece of ham, the last package of soup mix, the last ice-cream cone.

And they all wanted more. All of them had gone on about how upset they were that the Varifoods representatives had driven away that Monday without leaving behind any products.

A lot of their irritation had been refocused on Alex as he searched for even one remaining sample. He couldn't understand why, nor why they were acting as though they had really gone wild over the stuff. It was insane. How could anything taste that good?

It was also puzzling how they described the products. The ice cream was sweeter, creamier, richer than the local dairy's. The ham was more tender and succulent than anything from the farmer down the road. The frozen corn tasted fresher and sweeter than ears picked fresh in the nearby fields. The packaged soup mixes were heartier than homemade soup. The fruit juices were fruitier than the familiar brands from the neighborhood store.

If just one flavor in the products had been enhanced, Alex would have been able to more clearly identify the difference as a new additive. But there was no one improved feature present in all of them. Each product had its own distinct taste, and each distinct taste had been enhanced. He shook his head. None of this made any sense.

He was thirsty, hungry and tired, in that order. He ordered a tomato juice as he sat down on a bar stool, and wondered if Lee was faring any better.

While watching her sleep on the plane the night before, he had wanted so much to take her into his arms and hold her. By now it had become impossible for him not to react to her presence, no matter how much he knew that this was the wrong thing to do.

"May I join you?"

The deep, raspy voice came from behind. Alex turned, started out of his memories, to see an older man with a face as wrinkled as a well-folded map. His green and gold suspenders tied his white shirt to his dark gray slacks like two package ribbons. A matching green and gold bow tie circled his neck like the faded wrapping to a well-worn gift, Alex thought. He looked more at home in the beginning of the century than at its end.

Alex had no idea why the older man had singled him out, but had no intention of discouraging the friendly gesture.

"Please sit down. My name's Alex. Let me buy you a drink," he said.

The older man settled on the stool next to Alex and put a half-full glass of milk onto the bar in front of him. There was a distinct odor about him. Alex could have sworn it was carbolic acid.

"No need to, son, I'm no freeloader. But I do appreciate the offer. Name's Ralph. Ralph Boynton. What brings you to our little town?"

The older man didn't look at Alex, but casually sipped his milk. Despite his slow and easy manner, however, Alex had the distinct impression that this wasn't a casual conversation.

"I'm looking for some of those Varifoods samples."

The other man didn't seem surprised. Alex had a feeling that he had known the answer when he asked the question. Perhaps that wasn't so unusual in a small town, where news traveled fast. Alex wondered how much else he knew.

"Had any luck?" Ralph Boynton asked.

"No. Seems the samples were just too good to sit around for long."

"You with Varifoods?" the older man inquired.

Alex tried to read his companion's face, but Boynton appeared impassive.

"No."

"Who you with, then?"

Alex could have lied, but there wasn't any clear reason to and sensed that this old man would know if he did.

"I'm a chemist from the FDA."

The other man scratched the light gray stubble on his chin.

"Why do you want that sample, son?"

Boynton's raspy voice had taken on a new note, in which Alex detected sharpened interest.

"I want to analyze it. To see if there's something wrong with these new products."

The older man's face now wore the slightest of smiles. He picked up his milk and finished it off with one gulp, then turned to Alex and swiveled off the bar stool.

"Come along. Something I want to show you."

He didn't even wait to see if Alex would follow, but just strolled out of the bar into the bright afternoon light and began heading down the street.

Alex took as big a gulp of his tomato juice as he could, and started off after the fast-disappearing Boynton. He was amazed at how quickly the older man walked. Keeping up with Ralph Boynton was a challenge. He wondered briefly if Boynton was really a twenty-year-old in disguise.

After about a block and a half, the older man stopped in front of a white clapboard house with an open porch. It looked as if it had been built in the thirties. Alex didn't miss the medical doctor's shingle hanging over the mailbox. Ralph Boynton, M.D., walked up the front steps and opened the door. Alex followed, listening to the bell being rung above him and wondering whom Boynton was summoning.

They walked to the rear of the house, and Dr. Boynton opened a door. A young woman in jeans was sprawled in a chair, reading a *True Romance* magazine. In the corner a younger boy, about thirteen, was sleeping on a cot.

"Donna, how is Leroy this afternoon?"

The young woman put down her magazine and turned to face them. Alex guessed she was in her late teens. Her complexion was marred by a bad case of acne.

"Oh, he's a lot better, Doc, almost back to normal. Except he's been sleeping a lot."

"Donna, this is Alex. I want you to tell him about Leroy. Why you brought him to me."

Her eyes traveled over Alex. She looked back at the doctor who nodded in further assurance.

"Well, Leroy started acting real irritable. I mean shaking and crying and depressed. I thought he was coming down with mono again."

"When did this start, Donna?" the doctor asked.

"Last Monday. When he wouldn't eat the hot dogs I cooked for him."

"And why had Leroy been eating before that, Donna?"

"Why, all that free stuff from those food people."

"The Varifoods people?" Alex asked.

"Yeah, them," she said.

"Thank you, Donna," the doctor said. "Now, you keep watching him, and I'll be back in a few minutes."

Dr. Boynton led Alex from the back room and closed the door. They both went into the front room, which was obviously Dr. Boynton's office. He took a seat behind the battered, but dust-free oak desk with its neatly arranged stacks of paper. Alex followed suit and seated himself opposite the doctor on a wooden chair that creaked beneath his weight.

"You understand what you just heard, son?"

Alex was trying to piece together the information. "This boy, Leroy, went into some kind of a depression when he couldn't have the Varifoods products?"

The doctor shook his head. "I guess I'll have to spell it out for you. Donna and Leroy were part of the original twenty-five families selected for Varifoods' tasting test. You know how that test was run?"

Alex nodded. "I've read the test parameters. Each family chosen had four members, and each had been using products that were competitive with the Varifoods brands. Every morning for two weeks, a representative from Varifoods visited each family and provided one sample serving of that day's products for each member of the family. Then each member was to fill out an opinion sheet."

"You got it basically right. But there was one thing those Varifoods people didn't know."

"What was that?" Alex asked.

"Well, Donna and Leroy's parents have been out of state these last two weeks. They've been visiting a dying relative. Donna was left here to care for Leroy. And when four free food samples kept coming every day, well, giving the extra to Leroy was a whole lot easier than fixing meals."

"So the boy got three servings a day instead of one?" Alex asked.

"Actually he got four. Donna's on a special diet for her acne, teenagers being real particular how they look. She didn't eat any of the free samples. After the first week, she noticed that her brother wasn't eating anything but the free samples. He ignored everything else she fixed."

"And when the free samples stopped, he got irritable?" Alex guessed.

"Not just irritable. When Donna brought him to me, he was exhausted, sleepy, depressed, no energy, shaking like a leaf. And he was crying and begging me for some more Varifoods samples."

"Didn't his sister say something about mono?"

Doc Boynton nodded.

"Leroy got mononucleosis, a glandular fever, about a month ago. He had a high temperature, headache, sore throat, weakness, fatigue. I've had him out of school recuperating. Donna said the Varifoods test products were the first thing he has wanted to eat. And now they're the only things he wants to eat."

A small light flashed on in Alex's head.

"Are you saying this boy is suffering withdrawal symptoms from the food? As he would from a drug?" Alex probed.

Doc Boynton's sharp eyes belied his mellow manner.

"Now you're catching on, son."

Alex couldn't believe what he was hearing. Yet it explained why the other participants in the taste test had become so hostile since their supply was cut off. They were going through mild withdrawal. But for a youngster of lower body weight, one who had received four times the normal dosage, the effect could be much more serious.

"You're sure Leroy wasn't experiencing renewed symptoms of the mononucleosis?" Alex asked.

"I'm sure. Kids who get mono lose their appetite, just like Leroy did about a month ago. But now I'd venture to say he'd eat all the Varifoods products he could get his hands on."

"Did you take a sample of the boy's blood when he first came in?" Alex inquired.

The doctor smiled.

"Now my faith in you is renewed. Yes, I've got a blood sample, actually two. One is from a little over a week ago. I took it so I could check for the atypical lymphocytes from the mono, see if they had cleared up and if Leroy was free of the disease. The second sample is from a few days ago, when the boy started demonstrating those withdrawal symptoms. I put both samples in the refrigerator when my station wagon broke down, and I couldn't make it into Des Moines for an analysis."

"So you have a sample of Leroy's blood from when he was consuming products and when he had stopped?" Alex asked.

"Right. I don't test any blood here. I'm not equipped with any of those fancy devices. You're lucky my car broke down."

Doc Boynton headed for his small refrigerator to get the blood samples. Alex realized he would need some kind of a cooling unit to transport them. He was trying to think of the most appropriate when he felt Ralph Boynton's sharp eyes on him again.

"I don't mind telling you that I haven't slept much since Donna brought Leroy in. You understand, I've always had faith in my government, but these are crazy times we live in."

"Yes, they are. I appreciate your information more than I can say," Alex told the doctor.

"You are going to stop this Varifoods Company, aren't you, son? This stuff, whatever it is, can't be allowed in the stores. It could give a new meaning to the phrase 'junk food'—the food from which junkies are made."

Chapter Thirteen

"Willy, I said the new Varifoods product line is addictive. Didn't you hear me?" Alex demanded.

"Yes, I heard you. I just don't understand you. Are you saying that the company is putting drugs in its food?" Willy asked.

"I don't know what they're putting in the stuff. All I know is that I'm calling from a pay phone in a small Iowa town, where families are going into heavy withdrawal when they're cut off from their supply of Varifoods. You understand? Withdrawal."

"That's a pretty wild statement, Alex. What facts do you have to back it up?" Willy wanted to know.

Alex tried to breathe deeply, remain calm. "Look, Willy. Varifoods' president claims they've discovered a new process that enhances the flavor in foods of all kinds—hot, cold, sweet, salty."

"'A new process' is a pretty ambiguous term. Improvements you're describing are much more likely formula changes," Willy pointed out.

"Yes. Exactly what I thought. But I've looked over a list of ingredients in the products. There's nothing new, and yet consumers of the samples raved about them, and that's not an overstatement."

"Raving about them and being addicted to them is quite different. Have you done a chemical analysis?" Willy asked.

"No. I'm having trouble locating a sample. But—" Alex began.

"But nothing, Alex. Without a chemical analysis, you don't know what you've got."

"For God's sake, Willy, listen. Something's wrong with these products. I've got a doctor here who's treating a boy with all the classic symptoms of drug withdrawal. He was a participant in the test, a participant who got a lot more of the samples than the others."

"Are you sure this kid isn't into drugs?"

"Willy, I'm sure. He's not the only one who's reacting to the product intake. Every family member I talked to today who participated in the taste test looked and acted as though they were covered with itching powder. I don't know what's in this stuff, but I know it's addictive."

Alex heard Willy exhale. "All right, Alex. Start the testing. Generate a case for me that proves this new line is harmful, and I'll start the process to take it off the market."

"Willy, if we go according to the book on this, it will take months. We don't have that kind of time! These products will be out on the market in just a few weeks."

"What are you suggesting I do?" Willy asked.

"I want you to get some kind of restraining order. I want you to stop Varifoods putting these products in the hands of consumers."

"Alex, that just isn't possible. I have absolutely no proof that there's anything wrong with this food. Have you forgotten how powerful their parent company is? Trans World would eat me alive if I tried to disrupt their subsidiary's introduction of a new line. I need hard evidence. That means a fully developed case with properly conducted experiments from independent labs."

"You'll do nothing now? Even though your inaction could mean the human suffering of countless people?" Alex asked provocatively.

"Damn you, Alex! Stop trying to lay a guilt trip on me. If there's something wrong with this food, I'll take the proper measures to have it corrected. I repeat, the proper measures, not some irresponsible action that can only make us look bad."

"Willy, I'll go over your head if I have to," Alex told his boss.

"And if you try, it won't do any good and I'll have your job. Once and for all, I'm not going to jeopardize my career for one of your crusades. Are you reading me?"

"Loud and clear," Alex said as he slammed down the telephone. He stood there for a moment, squinting in the sunlight as he leaned against the pay phone in front of the bar and grill.

He should have known what Willy was going to say. After all the years and all his experience with the man, he should have known. Trying to go over his head wouldn't work, either. Those people wouldn't risk their comfortable jobs. He had been fooling himself.

He looked up to see Lee just crossing the street on the way to their rendezvous. He watched her walking toward him, the sunlight swimming through her light hair. He could see that she was empty-handed. So she too had failed to collect any samples.

At that moment he just wished that he could take her away and forget this madness. If only he had met her under different circumstances. If only she wasn't the target of some murderous creep. If only he didn't feel so damn helpless.

He tried to exhale his frustration as he straightened to greet her. Now it was up to them, but he mustn't let her know. He had to encourage her in the belief that everything would come out all right. One of them had to go on believing.

"ADDICTIVE FOOD? That's extraordinary! If I hadn't talked to all those angry people today, I wouldn't have believed it. But it all fits," Lee said, as they finished a quick lunch. "So, where to now?"

"Back to the airport. I've got to find a lab quickly," Alex told her.

"So you have the blood samples in that ice chest?" Lee asked as they got up to pay their bill.

"Yes. It's the only thing I could find. What would you say to catching a flight east instead of west?"

"What do you mean?" Lee asked.

"Well, we could go back to my lab at the FDA to analyze this blood. You—correction—we would be a lot safer there."

Lee looked at Alex. In some indefinable way he seemed different. Maybe he was just tired. She sure was.

Lee shook her head. "Finding out what's in the new product line is only half our problem. The other half is finding out who's behind it. And that answer is back in San Francisco."

Alex nodded, but the accompanying smile was strained. "Right, of course. If we hurry, we can make a late-afternoon flight out and be back in California early tomorrow. Genustech has a good lab there."

"Genustech?" Lee inquired.

"It's a biotech company in South San Francisco. They've got the latest lab equipment. As a matter of fact, I wish we had some of their stuff at the FDA. A friend of mine from graduate school works there. Since tomorrow's Sunday, the lab will be deserted, so I'm sure he'll let me run these blood samples."

They left the bar and grill and drove back toward the airport. Lee was still trying to absorb the import of what they had discovered.

"This new product line seems like something out of *The Twilight Zone*, or maybe I should say *Friday the Thirteenth*. Do you think Janet's secret was this addictive factor?"

"What else?" Alex said. "Although I admit, even I am having problems believing Varifoods would deliberately put out products that are physically addicting. This isn't something that can be hidden for very long. It's not like a carcinogen, producing a cancer that doesn't show up until years later. Leroy was addicted after four doses a day for one week."

"So you're saying that this food addiction is going to be traceable?" Lee asked.

"Not at first, of course. The idea sounds so absurd that it will take a while to convince people. But sooner or later, someone is going to figure out the connection between the products and the symptoms that follow. Like Doc Boynton did."

Lee heard an uncharacteristic weariness in Alex's voice and grew quiet. What was it? Just fatigue? Probably. But she decided it would be a good idea to give him a rest from talking. The rest of the drive to Des Moines passed in silence.

When they reached the airport, they boarded a flight that had two stops to make before they would change planes for the last leg into San Francisco. By the time Lee was fastening her seat belt on the second plane, she was sure she never wanted to fly again, much less view another film on flight safety. She felt awfully tired.

The next thing she knew, she was lying in Alex's arms, and the aircraft was being buffeted by strong turbulence. She sat straight up, feeling embarrassed for having fallen onto him while she slept.

"I'm sorry. You should have pushed me away," she said, looking into those steady brown eyes in the dim interior light of the plane.

His voice was gentle. "I'd never do that," he said. Lee got the funny feeling he meant that in a deeper way. Maybe it was just wishful thinking.

But some things weren't. She remembered the times he had stroked her hair as he held her; how incredibly tender his touch had been! It seemed the right time to get the answer to some questions that had been keeping her company.

"What happened to your wife, Alex?" Lee began.

At first she thought he hadn't heard her. He stared into the darkness of the cabin as though he had seen something important there. Then he started to speak, and the sadness returned to his mouth. As she listened to his words, Lee thought how much she wanted to kiss that sorrow away.

"Sally was two years younger than Janet and I. We were married the day I finished graduate school. She was a promising investigative reporter by then, eager to expose the wrongs of society. I was the young chemist, sure to invent new and wonderful combinations to benefit humankind. We had so many hopes, so many dreams."

The plane dipped and rocked as the pilot fought with erratic air currents. Lee waited, knowing that Alex would go on when he was ready.

"Sally called me one afternoon. Her editor wanted her to cover a political dinner at one of the big hotels. She asked me to join her, had even bought an extra dinner ticket. I told her I couldn't get away, that I'd be working late, but I'd try to come by later. So she went alone."

Alex had stopped again. Lee wanted to tell him that he didn't have to go on, but she sensed how much he needed to share his pain.

"The senator being honored was targeted by some psycho who showed up at the dinner, pulled a gun and shot at the senator, hitting Sally instead. I arrived at the hotel less than a minute later. It was too late. She died on the way to the hospital."

"Alex, I'm so sorry."

"If I had gotten there even a minute earlier, Sally might still be alive. Just like if I had only caught the next plane out when Janet called, she might never have died in that tunnel."

Lee shook her head in disbelief. "For heaven's sake, Alex. You're not blaming yourself for their deaths? You're too levelheaded for that. I can't believe you would accept such impractical guilt."

Alex almost smiled. "Impractical guilt? That's an interesting blend of words. But no, it's not guilt that I've been living with, Lee. It's a sense of helplessness."

Alex's words surprised Lee. "Helplessness?"

"I couldn't help my dying wife as she lay in my arms. I couldn't even take revenge on the mental deficient who stood by, babbling about how he had been trying to shoot the demons out of the senator. And then Janet called, and once again I couldn't help."

"Even Superman couldn't foretell the future, Alex. And neither could I, or I would have been home when Janet tried to reach me. Besides, you are helping. We're both committed to finding the answer." She put her hand into his.

He looked at her hand, then slowly raised his eyes to her. His mouth still seemed sad.

"Yes, I'm committed to finding Janet's killer. But understand, Lee, my commitments to people are a thing of the past."

He was telling her precisely what she didn't want to hear. He must have read it on her face, because he drew his hand away. She told herself she should be grateful for his honesty. He had understood that she needed a man who would care deeply enough to commit himself. He was telling her he was not that man.

Yes, she should be grateful, but all she felt was sadness. Incredible sadness.

They landed a little after four in the morning, Pacific time. After three nights without any substantial sleep, she felt like a walking zombie. As she looked at her companion, she realized he wasn't in much better shape.

"We can't drive all the way to Benicia," she said.

He nodded. "It's not safe, either. Whoever is behind this business knows where you live. Let's go to my hotel. We can get you a room and both get some sleep."

It was a good plan, but when they walked into the lobby of the Sheraton Palace, the desk clerk advised them that there were no rooms to be had.

Alex looked at Lee and tried to smile.

"We'll call around and find you a place at another hotel. Then I'll drive you over and get you settled," he said.

"Sir, we have a lot of conventions in town this weekend," the desk clerk said. "Unless the lady has made a reservation, I very much doubt she will find accommodations. Would you like me to check with some Oakland hotels?"

Lee shook her head wearily. "Alex, Oakland's too far. I'm dead on my feet."

He looked at her a minute more. "Lee, my room has just one king-size bed."

"It's all right, Alex. I won't attack you. Girl Scout's honor."

He found a smile somewhere as he picked up the ice chest and turned back to the desk clerk.

"Do you know where I might refrigerate some medical samples for a few hours?"

"Yes, sir. I'm sure we can make some suitable arrangements. Follow me."

Alex went off with the desk clerk, while a bellhop showed her to the room and carried their luggage.

She was in her nightgown and fast asleep before Alex used his key to open the door. He watched her sleeping as he undressed in the semidarkness. A long, blond strand of hair had fallen across her cheek. He bent and gently swept it back and found himself studying the soft curve of her cheek.

He shook his head. This was a crazy arrangement. He should have thought of another way. Tired though he was, it was still almost an hour before he could fall asleep beside her.

LEE AWAKENED to see something dark and furry in front of her eyes. Coming out of the depths of sleep, she stared, her mind fuzzy as she struggled to identify the strange object. Then, in a rude intrusion of consciousness, she realized it was the hair on Alex's bare forearm, and memory returned.

She couldn't tell what time it was, but a strong light was peeking through the slit between the hotel room's drapes. She was lying on her right side, and Alex's arm was draped over her left shoulder and just below her breasts. She could tell from the rhythmic breathing behind her ear that he was still asleep.

She remembered thinking that there was nothing remotely compromising about sharing a bed, considering how tired they both had been. But in the strong light of day and feeling more rested, Lee began to feel differently.

She yawned involuntarily and watched as the expelled air tickled the hairs along his arm. It made her smile. She deliberately blew on the hairs this time. Finally after a firm nudge, Alex made a slight grunting sound and rolled onto his back, releasing her.

Lee rolled carefully onto her left side and studied him as he slept. The bottom half of his face was covered with dark stubble, relieved only by the flesh of his slightly parted lips. His hair was tousled. His dark eyelashes were long and thick and swept across his cheeks. Somehow, a captive to sleep and without his glasses, he seemed defenseless—and absolutely irresistible.

She had never met anyone who could touch her so deeply with the strength of his emotions, with the warmth in his eyes and the gentle touch of his hands. She had experienced his anger, his sadness, his bravery, his determination, his tenderness. Now, as she observed him lying there, she felt so much love for him that nothing else mattered.

Somewhere an irritating thought was trying to remind her of the hopelessness of a future with this man, but right now her feelings left no room for conflicting thoughts. She pushed them aside.

Slowly her hand came up to touch his face, to trace the line of his square jaw. When her fingers touched his lips, his eyes opened, he looked at her and blinked.

"Good morning, Alex," she said softly as her hand traveled down his neck and began to feel its way across his massive chest.

"Lee?"

"You were expecting someone else?" she inquired teasingly, moving closer to kiss him beneath his right ear.

"Lee, what are you doing?" Alex asked, turning at the feel of her lips, now fully awake.

"Well, if you have to ask, I'll have to improve," she told him, smiling, as her right hand began to explore the muscles of his back. "Perhaps you have a suggestion or two?"

His left hand reached out and imprisoned hers. The look in his steady brown eyes was now very warm. "I know I'm crazy for asking, but do you understand what I said on the plane?" he asked. "You're not going to have second thoughts about this in the morning?"

She smiled. "It is morning, and we'll talk about second thoughts after the first are attended to. Besides, I seem to remember your saying that you would never push me away."

He smiled broadly, released her hand and settled his arm around her body. "Humph. I seem to remember somebody giving me her Girl Scout's honor that she wasn't going to attack me."

Lee laughed and moved closer at the urging of his hands.

"I have a confession to make," she said, feeling more and more breathless as he began to kiss her neck and shoulders.

"And what's that?" he wanted to know, his voice huskier.

"I never was a Girl Scout," she said through a sigh of pleasure.

His laugh was deep and happy. They didn't speak again for a long time. It was a long, satisfying, fulfilling time in which their bodies blended as one.

When at last they lay quiet, he held her to his side, thinking how well she fitted the contours of his body and filled his heart. It was too late to worry about the unsuitability of this love affair. He was right in the middle of it and enjoying it far too well. But of course, it had no future.

"Being with you like this means so much to me, Alex."

He looked at her lovely face; her words tugged at his heart. "I have to admit that with you in my arms, Lee, I feel renewed, as though together we can tackle anybody, accomplish anything. It's a great feeling."

She sighed, happy at his words and yet also sad, because she knew they were the nearest thing to a declaration of love that she was ever likely to hear from him.

"I'VE BEEN THINKING about the most likely suspects, Alex, and I think we have three: George Peck, Michael Ware and John Carstairs."

Alex swallowed some French toast before he answered, giving the waitress in the hotel coffee shop time to move along. Although he hadn't completely caught up on sleep, he felt much better after being awakened in the totally unexpected and delicious way Lee had chosen. And he felt hungry, as though his appetite for everything had increased a hundredfold.

"What about Steve Gunn, Hamilton Jarrett or Denise Williams?" he asked.

"It wouldn't take much to place Steve at the top of the list, but none of those three saw us talking with Pam."

"Can we be sure? Even if they didn't see us themselves, someone else could have told them. Can we even be sure that's why Pam was attacked?" Alex probed.

Lee sighed. "You're right, of course. I'd just like to start eliminating suspects. It's awful, not knowing whom to trust. If we only knew which chemist really worked on the products."

"Couldn't it have been George Peck alone?" Alex suggested.

Lee shook her head. "Remember what Pam said? He's never done original research. He supervises and evaluates the work of the chemists reporting to him. No, one of them had to have originated whatever is making this new product line taste so good and be so deadly."

"What about the chemist who left?" Alex asked.

"No. Forget him. In his exit interview he complained he was working on very routine stuff. It's one of the reasons he left when he got a better offer," Lee told him.

Alex nodded in understanding. "Well, at least we have these now," he said as he patted his ice chest. "We've got to get these blood samples tested as soon as possible. Right after breakfast."

Lee looked at him, seeing that the brown curls on his forehead were still damp from his shower. His eyes were such a warm, wonderful brown. Looking into them could make her forget everything else. With some reluctance, she glanced at her watch. "It's already noon. Half the day is gone. Will you need me at the lab?"

"Until this thing is over, I'm not letting you out of my sight," Alex said.

He had said it possessively, as though he had the right to assume a proprietary air. If he had been anyone else, Lee would have resented it. But he wasn't anyone else. He was the man she loved and he wanted to protect her. Although she tried to remind herself that he was resisting commitment and that they lived on opposite coasts, her heart wouldn't accept the fact of their eventual separation.

"Have you called your friend at Genustech yet?"

Alex nodded. "While you were showering. Everything is set."

"Who is he?" she asked as she sipped her coffee.

"We were beaker squeakers together in grad school. He's fixed everything, so we'll have no trouble getting in."

"Beaker squeakers?" Lee asked with a smile.

"Why, yes. Didn't you know that's one of our scientific expressions? We always use it to help us concentrate on the big picture."

Alex's comment had been made lightly, teasingly. But his use of the jargon made her recall something Ham had said in their meeting last Monday. She wondered briefly just how much of the "big picture" gazing Ham had done with the new product line. Had he really managed to rationalize the introduction of an addictive food?

"Lee? What is it? What's wrong?" Alex inquired.

She looked at his nice face. "This whole business has me thinking the only way to be truly safe is to buy a farm somewhere and grow my own food," Lee said.

Alex didn't miss the unhappiness that clouded her eyes. He nodded his understanding and reached over to touch her arm.

"When I first became aware of all the nitrates and hormones that get into our food, the thought crossed my mind, too. I even went so far as to visit a couple of small farms that were for sale back East," Alex told her.

"Oh really?" Lee's interest was piqued. "What made you change your mind?"

"I got a whiff of the cows. Ugh! After them, facing almost anything else seemed preferable."

Lee's laugh brought a smile to his face. He indulged himself for a moment by just looking at her, marveling at the whiteness of her skin, the flashes of turquoise in her eyes reflecting off the blouse she wore.

He had needed to change the mood of their conversation and to feel the happiness her laughter gave him. Too much about their situation could be depressing.

Lee didn't miss the crease between Alex's dark eyebrows.

"What is it?" she asked.

She saw too much, he realized and tried to smile again. "We've got to stop Varifoods from putting this new line out before it's too late."

"You can do it, Alex. Just as soon as you show the FDA what it is. Meeting you has made me aware of a lot more problems in the world. But it's also brought the feeling that they can be surmounted.''

He was touched by her words and by her belief in him. He wanted to live up to that trust. He almost told her then about Willy and how precarious their position had become without the backing of the FDA. But he found he couldn't. He couldn't give her reason to doubt him just now. He needed her belief too much.

"Come on. Let's go visit Genustech," he proposed.

"Right," she said, and they rose to their feet. "Do you suppose they'd let me use the phone to call Pam?"

"I'm sure it wouldn't be a problem. But why do you want to call Pam?" Alex asked.

"Something just occurred to me that I want to check out."

After talking with Pam for a few minutes, Lee realized that the chemist had no suspicions that the driver who had hit her and run was probably the same one who had killed Janet Homer. Pam considered both events unrelated incidents.

Lee thought it was just as well. Fear might inhibit Pam's recovery. She moved to another subject.

"Pam, there were some things I neglected to ask you the other night. Would you mind going over them now?"

"No, of course not. Go ahead, ask," the other woman replied.

"You've told me that the chemists are not allowed to discuss their projects, even with one another. Only George has the complete picture. Why is that?" Lee asked.

"George told us that chemists have been known to develop a promising new formula and then sell themselves, along with the formula, to another company. So at Varifoods, only the chief chemist knows the complete experimental design. Generally, individual chemists are aware of only one piece. That way, none of us can develop something on our own and leave with it."

"And you have no idea what Janet was working on?" Lee went on.

The other end of the phone grew very quiet. Lee waited.

"Not really."

"But you heard something?" Lee asked.

"Well, I didn't say anything to Alex, because I couldn't be sure. But the more I think about it…" Pam paused again.

"Yes?" Lee prompted.

"The first day Janet came back from her maternity leave, about three weeks ago now, she and I went for coffee. I asked her then how she felt to be back. She told me she wasn't sure, something about how so much had happened on her project in the time she was gone that she felt smothered with information. She said something about how it might take her weeks before she even understood it again. And then something about how originally it had been her pet project."

"She never told you what it was?" Lee probed.

"No. I've told you, that's against the rules. We all stuck to the rules. But it struck me as odd, her saying that it had been her pet project."

"Why was that?" Lee asked.

"Well, it suggested that Janet had talked George into an experimental design of her own, instead of just accepting a list of parameters and being told to find specific answers. That doesn't sound like George at all."

"Can you remember back before she went on leave? Did she ever hint to you what she had started?"

"No. Sorry."

"Did you and Janet meet at Varifoods?"

"No. We actually met in graduate school. We both got our Ph.D.'s in microbiology from MIT. After graduation we had several offers, but Varifoods' included moving us to California, land of sunshine. They won hands down. I was doubly happy because my parents live in the Bay Area."

Lee's mind was replaying her conversation with Janet. She remembered the degree from MIT. Suddenly she had a thought.

"Do you remember by any chance the subject of her thesis?"

"Hmm. Let me see. It's been a few years. As I recall, hers was a real theoretical piece on computer-simulated molecular genetics."

"Come again?" Lee asked.

"Sorry. I'm not sure how well I can explain it in lay terms, but think of it as improving on the design of a chair. Can you see one where you are?"

Lee looked around and found a chair to stare at. "Yes. Go ahead."

"Well, you'll notice it has various components: a back, a seat, four legs. And it works that way. But let's say you want to experiment. You want to see what it would look like with just three legs or maybe five. A computer can simulate the new look. It can display it on your monitor three-dimensionally. And if properly programmed, the computer can also tell you if the new design is feasible from an engineering point of view."

"In other words, if you can sit on it and it won't fall apart," Lee said.

"Right."

"I understand the concept. I've dealt with computer modeling before. But are you saying that changes in molecular genetics can be studied the same way?"

"Can and are all the time. You just ask the proper program, 'What would happen if?' and the computer projects the end result. Computers are becoming the hands-on experimenters in science."

"And you use them this way to come up with new food tastes?"

"Not really. A computer can't taste for a human being, not yet, anyway. But they can come up with new combinations. Aspartame, for example, is a combination of two different amino acids: L-aspartic acid and L-phenylalanine, a combination that produces a taste one hundred eighty times sweeter than sugar."

"What everyone calls NutraSweet?" Lee asked.

"Yes, that's its trade name. NutraSweet was a real breakthrough. Metabolizes as protein, not as a carbohydrate. Great for dieters and consequently making a mint. Wish I'd discovered it."

"Did Janet's thesis concern such combinations?"

"No, I only used aspartame as an example of a chemical advance in the food industry. As I recall, hers was more a theoretical piece on what would happen if a molecule could be genetically altered, a chemically induced mutation and its effect on the nourishment and reproductive status of a cell.''

"You've lost me," Lee said. "Is this anything that might have application to the food processing industry? Something that Janet might have tried to apply at Varifoods?"

Pam's voice was beginning to sound tired. "I don't know. It's been so long. You'd have to read her doctoral dissertation. You could probably get a copy from Mark. I'm sure Janet kept one copy in her files. Is it important?"

Lee was sure the dissertation would be way over her head. But it wouldn't be over Alex's. She thought about Pam's question.

"Important? Yes, I think so. As a matter of fact, it may hold the answers to everything," she said.

Chapter Fourteen

"It's there, all right. The electrochemical trace analysis has identified it. Less than one part per million. Pretty potent to be so effective at that small a concentration."

"What is it, Alex? What is it you've found?" Lee asked as she walked up to him in the lab after finishing her call to Pam.

Alex smiled up at her. He had obviously been talking to himself, since he hadn't realized she had returned.

"Quite honestly, I don't know. It has a molecular structure that shouldn't even exist! As a matter of fact, I'm not even sure how it is existing!" he said as he once again concentrated on his data.

For the next fifteen minutes Lee just waited for Alex to complete his review. Her news would wait. She could feel the excitement that he was generating. He was on a voyage of scientific discovery. And like a true scientist, he seemed to have forgotten everything else around him.

"I can't believe it! This computer model projects that it would assimilate into the tissues of the brain and become part of the hypothalamus!" he exclaimed finally.

"Alex, what does it mean? What are you telling me?"

He blinked at her, remembering again who she was and where he was. Then he smiled his happy smile and drew her to his side with one warm, strong arm.

"The hypothalamus is a place in our brain where we feel and taste and smell things. Remember how those people in the taste test went on about how good the new Varifoods products tasted?"

"You think this new substance is acting as a flavor enhancer in the brain?" Lee asked.

"Absolutely. It's increasing the brain's awareness of flavor by exciting the centers for taste. No matter what food it's added to, it will magnify that food's natural texture and taste. Creamy, sweet, nutty, rich, it doesn't matter. Anything would taste better—much, much better. I can also see how it would be addictive. The abnormal excitation of the brain tissues wears off, slowing down the entire surrounding tissue of the hypothalamus."

"So, in other words," Lee concluded, "someone eating the new product would crave more of it within a short period of time? To excite the cells again?"

"That's it, although it would take a lot more experimentation to identify the precise time involved with people of different body weights and metabolisms."

"Are you going to do that now?" Lee asked.

"No. We have neither the time nor a large enough sample of the material. Now I've got to put this new substance through the Ames test."

"What is the Ames test?" she wanted to know.

"It will detect cancer-causing properties. It measures a chemical's tendency to cause mutations in bacteria. Because bacteria reproduce so much more rapidly than animals, lifetime effects of a chemical can be studied much more quickly. Come on, you can help."

Lee assisted Alex in setting up two samples for the test, each containing the necessary ingredients. The only difference was that one held the mysterious additive and the other, the control, did not. Feeling very happy and contented that he had wanted to include her, she was soon caught up in the experiment, too. The hours went by unnoticed.

"If I wasn't seeing this, I wouldn't be believing it," he said finally, studying the figures from the last microscopic slide.

Lee looked at Alex when she heard the unusual tone in his voice. As she studied his face, she realized it had gone white. She had a sudden sinking feeling.

"Tell me what you see," she said.

He didn't speak for a moment, but just kept gazing at the data before him. Then he gave her a look of genuine concern.

"I've compared the number of mutant bacteria that have formed as a result of using this new substance to the mutants formed in the control. Whatever it is, this new substance accelerates the mutations by five hundred percent."

"And, mutations correlate closely with the ability to cause cancer?" she asked.

"Yes, Lee. Very closely. This substance is the most potent carcinogen I've ever seen."

"How long would it take to give the cancer a foothold?" Lee inquired.

"No way to tell."

"The Iowa people? Could they already have cancer?" Lee asked.

Alex seemed to finally understand her concern; he looked at her and shook his head. "No. The body has some pretty good defenses against occasional influxes of carcinogens, even at this high a dosage. It's prolonged or massive doses that break down the immune system and get the cancer rolling. Even Leroy probably hasn't had enough."

"So if we can stop it now, they probably won't get cancer?" Lee surmised.

Alex wasn't listening anymore. He was rechecking the data before him.

"I'd lay odds that this one is fast growing. Really fast. Once it gets a foothold, it might take only months to spread throughout the brain."

"The brain?" Lee repeated.

"Yes, Lee, the brain. It's the site of the chemical's absorption. This new substance crosses the blood-brain barrier easily, because it mimics the structure of the hypothalamus tissue. And once the cancer got a hold in the brain, it would be inoperable. It would be terminal."

Lee was trying to take in everything Alex was saying. The idea of an addictive food was frightening enough, but this! A swiftly forming cancer of the brain!

"Nobody at Varifoods could have known this and still gone ahead with the new line. They couldn't have!" she exclaimed.

Alex put his arms around her, as much for his own sake as hers.

"They must have run the Ames test, Lee. Manufacturers routinely screen any newly synthesized chemical that way. It quickly lets them know whether a substance is worth pursuing—or should be quickly dropped because of its cancerous properties."

"So they knew this ingredient was an addictive carcinogen! It seems inhuman!" Lee declared.

"I'm not disagreeing with you about their criminal responsibility in this matter. Obviously, they're after the quick bucks they can make with the flavor enhancer. But they may not have known about the addictive factor. If Doc Boynton hadn't told me about Leroy, I wouldn't have known, wouldn't have looked for that possibility."

"No. I can't believe it. It's just not possible!" Lee protested.

"I wish I could be as certain as you. But they killed Janet and have gone after you, Pam and me. They're desperate. These are high stakes they're playing for."

Lee was shocked and sickened by what they had discovered. She looked squarely at Alex and saw the deep frown on his face. Something was still puzzling him.

"Alex, what is it?"

"This doesn't make a whole lot of sense. I can't shake the feeling that I'm missing something here."

"What do you mean?"

"Let me present the situation to you, and you tell me how you would react. Okay?" Alex suggested.

"All right," Lee replied.

Alex let her go and began to walk around the room, as though the movement might help his thinking process.

"You're Varifoods. You've got a new, fantastic flavor enhancer. You know it causes cancer, but maybe you don't know it's addictive. You put it in your product line and distribute it to your retailers with a major advertising campaign. What can you expect?"

Alex had paused to face her. Lee didn't have to think long.

"Consumer acceptance. And off-the-chart demand curve. Fantastic profits," she said.

"What about the competition? Don't you think they might take some action, when their share of the market starts to drop so dramatically?"

It now became clear what Alex was getting at.

"But of course! They would take Varifoods' products, analyze them to identify the new flavor enhancer, and report it to the FDA as soon as they ran the Ames test!"

Alex nodded. "Makes you wonder, doesn't it?"

Lee shook her head. "Then why is Varifoods doing this? Why is it using this additive in its food knowing that it will soon be found out? They have to know this would ruin the company."

"That's what puzzling me," Alex said.

"Yes." Lee nodded. "We have to be missing something here. I know these people. Hamilton Jarrett is no fool. He wouldn't do this to Varifoods, to himself. He'd be signing his own corporate death warrant. And, he's not the suicidal type."

"Yes. Even huge, short-term profits couldn't make up for the eventual wave of lawsuits from victims of the additive," Alex said.

"Well, whatever their reason for pursuing this, at least you've found out the truth about the additive. Now you can go back to the FDA. You've got the proof to stop them," Lee told him.

Alex was too quiet. Lee felt the hesitation. There was something he wasn't telling her. She took two steps and put both hands on his arms.

"Alex? You are going to your boss at the FDA with this information, aren't you?"

"It's still too soon, Lee. I . . . need to find out how this chemical was created. I tried duplicating its molecular structure with the computer. I can't. It's been genetically engineered. How, I have no idea. I need the original data, the original program. I must have it."

He withdrew his arms, and Lee felt a sudden chill. She hoped it was just from losing contact with his warmth.

"I think I know where you can find it. I think it was Janet's program," Lee told him.

Alex turned to face her fully as her words sank in. "Janet's? No, Lee. You must be wrong."

Lee told him then about her telephone conversation with Pam. About Janet's references to her "pet project."

"You see, Alex, after hearing Michael Ware go on about how the new line had to have been Janet's project, I got to thinking. If the other chemists were telling the truth when they said it wasn't theirs, Janet was the only one left. That would explain why she was the only one who knew something was wrong."

"Assuming our Rasputin look-alike is telling the truth," Alex said.

"Yes, assuming that. I also asked myself if the project was Janet's, how could it have gone wrong?"

"And you decided..." Alex asked.

"I'm not sure, Alex. But if Janet started some experimentation before she went on maternity leave, and if that experiment had somehow been altered to yield this new additive, it would explain why none of the other chemists seemed to be involved in the new product line."

"I see. And you think she might have lost control over her original design?" Alex probed.

"Yes," Lee said. "All Ham's talk about perfecting the new process over the last six months might just have been a smoke screen, a way for him to take full credit for the new flavor enhancer, since it was developed during his tenure as company president."

Alex nodded. "And if what you're saying is true, then Hamilton Jarrett is behind all this. He killed Janet when she threatened to expose the harmful side effects of the additive."

Lee nodded. "Yes, you have a good point. Hamilton Jarrett may have been in on Janet's murder, but he's not a chemist. And it would have taken a chemist to understand the dangers in the new additive, wouldn't it?"

"She could have explained it to him, Lee, and he could have refused to withdraw it. But that brings us back to the same old problem, doesn't it? Why would Hamilton Jarrett put out this new flavor enhancer, knowing it would be discovered and eventually ruin him?"

Lee shook her head. "Alex, why is it the more we learn, the less sense it seems to make?"

He shook his head. "I believe in reason. There has to be a reason behind it all."

Lee sighed. "Maybe I'm wrong. Maybe it wasn't Janet's project at all," she said.

"I guess there's only one way to find out," Alex told her. "We've got to pay Mark a visit, and see if he has a copy of Janet's thesis somewhere around the house. I've got to have a look at it."

Lee glanced at her watch. "Alex, it's six-thirty!" she exclaimed, surprised.

"No wonder I'm hungry again. You must be, too," he said, bending quickly to kiss her cheek. "I promise I'll get us some dinner after we see Mark. Come on. Let's go call him and tell him we're on our way."

DENISE WILLIAMS paced up and down the Varifoods lobby, waiting for Steve Gunn to return. When he finally came out of the elevator, she immediately walked up to him.

"Well? Has she been back in the building?" Denise asked.

"Not since Friday morning," Steve answered.

"Maybe we've been wrong. Maybe she won't go along with Alexander," Denise said.

Steve shook his head. "I'm betting she will. I've entered a new code in the computer. The next time her palm print registers on the green security screen, it will generate a message to the guard on duty to call me right away. I'll call you, and we can catch her in the act."

"Maybe she won't be back until Monday morning," Denise suggested.

"Yeah, sure," Steve said. "I bet you still believe in the tooth fairy and Santa Claus, too."

ALEX DROVE Lee's Fiero as they took the Bay Bridge toward the East Bay and the city of Lafayette. Neither talked much, both preoccupied with the numbing horror and the perplexities of their discovery.

Lee was brought back to the present, however, when she looked up to see the Caldecott Tunnel looming ahead. As they entered the darkened hole, she realized she was holding her breath. A vague shadow seemed to have entered the car. Then Alex spoke beside her; had he read her thoughts?

"It's eerie, isn't it? Knowing she died here? It makes me feel as though I'm driving over her grave. They haven't repainted the part where it happened yet. It's still blackened from the fire, like the inside of a tomb."

Lee shivered. Suddenly she felt his hand resting across hers.

"I'm sorry. That's a stupid thing for me to say to you, particularly after that creep attacked you in the same way. It's just that sometimes I want to avenge her death so much, I can taste it. Can you understand?"

Again Lee recalled Janet's smiling face, then the faces of her motherless children: Mark Junior and little Molly with the big brown eyes. "Yes," she said. "I can understand."

"YOU FOUND the thesis so quickly?" Lee exclaimed as the slim man handed over the thick, bound volume to Alex.

"Yes. It was right on the bookshelf. I remembered Jan used to come home after work sometimes and just curl up for an hour or two, reading it over."

"Was this recently?" Lee asked.

"Yes. Before she went on maternity leave, and since she returned," Mark told them.

"Do you have any idea why she was reading it?" Alex probed.

"I didn't question her. However, I think I know," her husband said. "It reminded her of the good times."

"Good times?" Lee asked.

"When you're young and everything is possible."

Mark's words were vague. Lee got the impression that his thoughts were drifting away.

"I don't understand," she said.

Mark turned back to his guests and motioned them to sit down. He took a seat across from them.

"I guess it all started when we met. She had just gone to work at Varifoods. I had just begun teaching over at Berkeley. One day we found ourselves sitting together on a BART train, heading into the City. It was delayed at one of the BART stations for twenty minutes while they cleared a stalled train off the the tracks."

Mark paused. He was fidgeting in his chair. Lee knew he was reliving a memory. His face said so. And it also said that it was a memory filled with pain as well as pleasure.

"You struck up a conversation?" she prompted.

Mark nodded, got up and began walking slowly around the room, looking at everything, but obviously seeing only the past.

"She was upset, unhappy. I thought it was because of the delay. But when I started talking to her, she explained she was angry because her boss wasn't giving her any room for creativity, any chance to try some of her ideas. She was disillusioned with the business world after the comparative freedom of academia."

"Did she talk to you about what she had pursued in college?"

"Only in general terms. Said she had hoped to apply her graduate studies, but that there seemed no opportunity to do so."

"Did she mention how she hoped to apply them?" Lee asked.

"No. I told her my field was history. She didn't try to explain what I guess she knew I couldn't understand. She was just unburdening herself to a sympathetic ear, lamenting the lack of freedom that came with the acceptance of a paycheck."

"So you think she reread her thesis sometimes just for the pleasure of knowing at least once she had had creative freedom?" Alex asked.

"It's what I thought, but I could be wrong. Jan had a very demanding job. She worked a lot of overtime over the last couple of years. She was tired when she got home. She didn't like to talk about her work, and she wasn't supposed to."

"She never gave you any reason for the overtime?" Lee inquired.

Mark shook his head. "It was a sore spot with me. I didn't care what the reason was. I wanted her home with me and the kids. I pushed too hard. Maybe that's why she didn't listen."

Mark seemed so sad that Lee didn't have the heart to ask any more questions. But Alex pressed for the answer to just one more.

"Please, Mark. Think. Did Janet ever explain why she had to stay at work? Even a casual comment about something that interested her? Or maybe an opportunity opening up for some original research?"

Mark shook his head. "We just didn't talk about business when we were together. Partly because neither of us knew much about the other's work. And partly because, well, we tried to use the time to focus on each other. As it turned out, we didn't get that ... much time."

Mark had stopped by the piano and picked up a picture of Janet that had been sitting there. He stared at the image of his dead wife. Alex motioned to Lee and they quietly let themselves out.

THEY WAITED until they had driven back into San Francisco before stopping to eat. Dinner was a silent meal. Alex read Janet's thesis, and Lee tried to concentrate on enjoying her food, but found she couldn't help thinking about what might be in it. Had other food manufacturers been experimenting with new substances? Dangerous ones? She pushed her plate away and wondered whether she would ever be able to enjoy a meal again.

Or her job? If Varifoods truly intended to release a dangerous food additive, Lee knew she couldn't be associated with the firm. She couldn't dedicate her energy to a company that would totally disregard the health and safety of the consumer. She would have to look for another job.

It was an unwelcome thought. She had been with Varifoods since earning her M.B.A. Nine years. They had been a good company in those nine years, an ethical business. At least, she had thought so until now. Damn. She would have to find a company with some ethics.

But could she find one? So much of what she had read recently pointed to the fact that few business people saw beyond the short-term profit. And now Varifoods seemed to have joined the race.

Was the world really going insane? Or was it her?

She gazed over at Alex, realizing he had put down Janet's thesis and was looking into space, drinking his after-dinner coffee. He scratched his ear. It was such an unconscious, normal, everyday act and yet it fascinated her. He could make this overturned world seem right to her again. He was the one person who could make a difference.

"Alex?"

He came back from wherever his mind had journeyed and looked at her with his steady, serious brown eyes.

"Jan truly was a brilliant woman," he said. "A top-rate scientist. If she had only known what she was creating..."

"You know how it was done? It's in Janet's paper?" she asked.

Alex adjusted his glasses and nodded.

"This explains the theory behind the chemically induced mutation and how it mimics the brain cells. She also explored her idea of enhancing pleasure in the hypothalamus, the pleasure center in the brain I told you about. But the method she found to mutate the molecules isn't described here. She did write that it would be so intricate, so multiphased, so technically involved that only a sophisticated computer could accomplish it."

"So she programmed the one at Varifoods," Lee said.

Alex nodded. They had obviously both been thinking the same thing.

"With the updated chemical data constantly being fed into the computer and with a lot of time and constant monitoring, the odds were still against achieving the right genetic code," he told her.

"But it happened. How do you explain the fact that it somehow happened?" Lee asked.

Alex shook his head. "I can't, except that maybe it was a fluke, an accidental chemical reaction that proved to work. The substance I saw didn't seem able to exist outside the body. I could have sworn it couldn't exist in the food medium, either. Yet it does. And since it does, it can't be conforming to known chemical laws. Or shall I say that our chemical laws have just been invalidated? It's absolutely fascinating."

Lee knew that he was the scientist in action now. For the moment he had forgotten that this was a substance that could kill. All he saw was its significance as a scientific curiosity.

"Alex, if you couldn't reproduce it, how is it being reproduced?"

"By extrapolation from the original program. Without the original program, without all the variables that have been assimilated, reworked in a precise order and allowed to mature in time, the substance can't exist."

"So it's all done by computer," Lee concluded. She was reflecting on that fact and the possibilities it opened up when Alex's urgent tone recaptured her attention.

"Lee, we have to get that program. Tonight. Tomorrow it will be distributed to the processing plants. We have to stop it. We have to go to Varifoods. You have to get me in somehow. I must get that original data!"

Lee shook her head. "There's no way I can get you in. We've gone over the security system. If anyone unauthorized tries to enter, the alarms go off automatically. The police would be there in minutes, and that wouldn't give us nearly enough time to find the right file. We'd just end up in jail."

"Why can't you fake my palm print in some way? Or program it in so that it accepts me?"

"No, I can't. Verification of a palm print of a new employee is the one thing that takes place at the corporate headquarters of Trans World. I don't have the software that would be necessary to introduce your print into the system. I might be able to write a workable program, but we just don't have that kind of time."

Alex's face showed all the frustration he felt, and Lee winced.

"Let's get out of here. Take a walk. I've got to think," he said.

They walked for several blocks. Lee kept waiting for her companion to come up with a brilliant idea for getting hold of the computer file. But all the time she realized there was only one way. She finally took a deep breath and said what she knew was on both their minds.

"I'll go in alone. I'll get it."

"I can't let you," he said without hesitation.

She took his hand into hers.

"It's the only way. We both know it. Besides, it's Sunday night and no one else will be around. I'll be safe."

"But you told me you looked for files before without success, because you didn't know the file name. Why do you think you can find this program file now? You still don't know the file name."

"True. But I do know my way around the computer. And I've been thinking. Since we now know this was Janet's file, all I have to do is use her access code, and I'll have cut down the search considerably."

"Can you find Janet's access code?" Alex queried.

"Access codes, like everything else, have labels within the software. They had to be programmed in and properly identified. I'll be able to find the one that was Janet's."

He protested for the next thirty minutes, but she wore him down, primarily because she was right. There was no other way. It was getting late. Finally they returned to the car and he drove them to the Varifoods building, parking on a side street about a block away.

It was after ten. Market Street was dark and windy. They walked silently to the entrance. Lee averted her face, to avoid the cloud of dust that was blowing in swirls around them.

Just before they turned the corner and became exposed to the interior lights of the building, Alex reached out for her. In a darkened crevice of the building's side, he pulled her to him, holding her close, safe within his encircling arms. She felt the beat of his heart, warm and strong.

Lee said nothing. She just held him close and drew strength from his body.

"You can still change your mind." His voice was a tentative whisper in her ear.

The thought was tempting. Every step closer to the building had reminded her that a killer was loose. The last thing she wanted to do was go inside. But she had no choice.

"From the moment we knew the danger there's been no other way," she said. "I must go."

He held her away from himself, searching her face in the darkness. "I'll give you an hour. If you're not out by then, I'm coming in, alarms or no alarms. Understand?"

She looked at her wristwatch. "All right. It's almost ten-thirty. I'll be out by eleven-thirty."

His voice was gentle, his face dark and shadowed. "You'll be careful?"

She nodded her head.

Then he bent to kiss her warmly and wildly, as though in desperation, as though it might be their last embrace. When the unwelcome thought penetrated her numbed brain, she clung to him fearfully, wanting never to let him go. But at last she did, because she knew she must.

Chapter Fifteen

Somehow Lee opened the glass door and approached the electronic eye next to the guard's desk. Somehow she smiled at the uniformed man as she put her hand onto the glowing green screen.

"Good evening, Ms. Lee."

"Good evening," she said as she walked through.

Had Lee imagined it, or had a frown crossed the guard's face when he read the information about her on his screen? She felt stiff and unnatural as she headed toward the elevators.

On the way up to her floor, she tried to shake the uneasiness and think about what she had to do. There was no time to waste. Her work must be efficient. As soon as the elevator doors opened, she ran to her office. She had the computer warming up before the fluorescent lights had had a chance to finish flickering on.

She located the access codes and began reading down the labeling column searching for Janet's name. There were more than two hundred names, but Janet's wasn't among them. This couldn't be! Her eyes darted back and forth as she checked and rechecked. But it was no use. Janet didn't have an access code!

Disappointment welled up inside her. She tried to fight it, to push it down so that it wouldn't drown her thoughts. She must think straight. Why didn't Janet have an access code? No. That was the wrong question. The right question was why didn't Janet have an access code *now*? There was only one answer. It had been deleted.

Of course! She remembered that when she reviewed the computer data on Tuesday she had found that in addition to the change in the security system, an access code had been deleted. It had to be Janet's code. Why hadn't she realized that before?

She wasted no more time in self-recrimination, but went back to the history data and brought up the missing code. Recovering the deleted data was a trick she had learned a year before, while playing with the computer.

She was smiling as she noted Janet's access code on her desk pad. Then she reactivated the code and signed in under it. When the hundreds of files appeared on the screen, however, her heart sank once again.

She looked at her watch. Already ten minutes had gone by! She simply had no time to methodically go through each one of these files, looking for the one on the new additive. She wouldn't even be able to make it through the first fifty. And if the right file wasn't among the first fifty....

She fought down the time pressure that was threatening her logical pursuit and concentrated on thinking and feeling calm.

The files were in alphabetical order, each labeled with a four-letter code. Most of the letters spelled words. Lee searched for the obvious solution first. MARK? Yes, there was a MARK file. She accessed it. No. It was a formula for a hearty bread, developed four years before, called Staff of Life. Lee saw the connection. Janet had thought of her husband as her "staff of life."

What association would she have used to name the research on her new additive? MASK? QUIP? SNAG? STAR? She accessed each of the possible candidates, but none held data on the new additive. As she moved the cursor down the screen, the file names began to blur in front of her eyes.

This was useless. She had to think about Janet, think back to her position in the lab. Lee closed her eyes and tried to put herself into the dead chemist's place. She tried to imagine how she might have thought a couple of years ago.

She visualized Janet's smile, the smile that had shown her zest for life. Now she had reason to smile. She was finally being given a chance to do some original research, to pursue experiments of her own design. After years of following others' directions, she would be able to choose her own.

And she was pregnant, happily anticipating the birth of her second child. Then in a flash of insight, Lee knew what the name of the file would be. She opened her eyes and checked the column listings. It bounced out at her as though it had been anxiously waiting: BABY.

It was exactly how Janet would have thought about her original research. She would be giving birth to another baby—a scientific one.

Quickly Lee pressed the keys to access the information. It seemed like an eternity before the computer responded, displaying on the screen the first page of a voluminous file. She read the experimental parameters, understanding just enough to convince herself that she had found the right file.

Relief swept over her. She wouldn't have time to print everything, so she tried to concentrate on the original design parameters and modifications. Once she had identified them, she pressed the Print key. She waited, but nothing happened. She pressed the Print key again. Still nothing.

Then she realized what was wrong. The program had a print barrier, a fail-safe mechanism. Even if someone gained access to it, they were prevented from printing it out. Quickly she signed out of the file and went back to the programming data to find the instructions for the print barrier.

The experimental data weren't protected and could be printed out at will. That must have been what Janet had printed the night she died: the results of some experiment demonstrating the hazards of the new additive.

Lee refocused her attention on the program. She rewrote it to allow the printing of the entire file, not just the experimental parameters and test results. Next she returned to the file, identified the material she needed and pressed the Print key again. She sighed in relief as she heard the printer start up, then went over to close the top of its container so that the noise would be muffled.

Since the computer had already transmitted the data to be printed to the printer's buffer, she was now free to return to the computer program and make her changes.

She thought of Janet. She could imagine the sunny-blond head nodding in approval of what Lee was about to do. There was no time for hesitation; she had thought it all out beforehand. Too much was at stake. She began to initiate her own programming.

When she was ready to press the Execute button, she looked up—and jumped in surprise, belatedly realizing that she'd been so intent on what she was doing that she hadn't heard the quiet footsteps coming down the hall or seen the shapes forming inside the door to her office.

"Denise! Steve! You startled me. What are you doing here?"

Denise's chestnut curls bounced as she shook her head. The advertising manager's tone was accusing. "No, Lee. The question is what are *you* doing here?"

"I'm working on the press release for Ham, of course." Lee hoped she sounded convincing. "He needs it by tomorrow morning."

Denise moved over to Lee's computer monitor. Her tone grew skeptical. "This late, Lee?" Lee just had time to press the Clear button before Denise had a chance to view the screen.

Now Denise's voice was harsh, her tone upset. "What was it, Lee? What are you really doing?"

"I told you. Now I think you'd best tell me what you're doing," Lee retorted.

"Check the printer, Steve. See what's she got coming out," Denise said, ignoring Lee's question.

Lee watched Steve step around the other woman. His cheek was cut and bruised—an uncomfortable reminder of his encounter with Alex. And then she realized he wasn't moving toward the printer. He was glaring at her. Denise turned back to him.

"Steve, I said check the printer. We have to be sure."

The security chief reluctantly turned and removed the printer's cover. He tore off the printed pages and brought them to Denise. The noisy clicking of the uncovered printer filled the office. Denise sat down in one of Lee's side chairs. She took the sheets and began to read.

"Damn! I can't understand a thing here. It's all chemical formulas. But this has to be it. Janet's name is in the designer block." Denise looked back at Lee.

"You want to try again, Lee? Tell us what you're doing here?" she asked.

Lee didn't know how deeply the two of them were involved with the deadly additive, but they obviously knew it had been Janet's creation. That was enough to caution Lee not to say anything.

She tried to keep her voice even. "I don't know what you're talking about."

Denise shook her head. Lee looked at Steve's face, thinking it almost placid until she saw the jabbing twitch in his jaw. Her eyes traveled down to the balled fists at his side. She tried to calm the sudden lurch in her stomach.

"Lee, it won't work," Denise said. "We know about Janet and Alex. And we know you're helping Alex now. You must understand, I can't let you do it. I can't let you ruin Varifoods."

Ruin Varifoods? A sudden thought occurred to Lee. Maybe they didn't know the truth about the additive. Maybe once they understood that releasing this additive would mean the end of their company, they might see that she and Alex were trying to do the right thing. Lee looked at Denise with new resolve.

"Denise, I am helping Alex. But you must understand, it's because I must. Varifoods' new additive is a dangerous carcinogen. When that's discovered, it will ruin us."

Denise looked at Lee and shook her head. "New additive? What new additive? We have no new additive. We have a dynamite new process. You don't believe what you're saying, do you?"

Lee reached over and grasped Denise's arm. "Yes, I do. You must believe it, too. You've admitted you don't understand the formulas in those printouts. But Janet did. That's why she tried to warn me about it before she died. She tried to warn Alex, too. She tried to get the FDA involved."

"The FDA? Who works for the FDA?" Steve asked.

Denise shook her head again and turned to Steve. "Alexander claims to, but it doesn't matter now. You can see Lee didn't understand. I told you and Ham that she would never betray the company. She's been duped. Just as Janet was duped."

Lee frowned at her. "What are you talking about? What do you mean, 'Janet was duped'?"

"I mean that Alexander told her he worked for the FDA, too. It wasn't until recently that we found out the truth," the other woman said.

Denise pulled some folded sheets of paper out of her pocket and handed them to Lee.

Lee read what appeared to be a confidential report from a Tyberry Foods personnel file. Its subject was the job duties of one L. E. Alexander, industrial spy. His assignment: Varifoods' secret processing technique for a new food line.

Lee shook her head. "No. That's not possible. Alex does work for the FDA. I'll prove it to you," she said.

"How?" Denise asked.

"We can call them. His boss's name is Willy something. I've forgotten his last name, but I think it starts with an *H*...."

"Hansen? Willy Hansen? I know, Lee. You can't call them now. It's Sunday night. I called the FDA last Wednesday, when I saw Alex trying to get into your office. They have a Willy Hansen, all right. I spoke to him. And you know what he told me? He told me that nobody by the name of L. E. Alexander works for the FDA."

Lee looked at Denise. The advertising manager was calm, leaning back in her chair, the look on her face one of concern and worry. Lee could tell that Denise believed everything she was saying, even if Lee didn't.

"There's an explanation. I know it," Lee said as she returned the sheets to Denise.

Denise shook her head again. "The explanation is that you've been very cleverly taken in, Lee. Steve was able to get this report from his own spy at Tyberry. It was so buried it didn't come across the network until Friday afternoon. Apparently, since Alexander is one of Tyberry's top spies, they covered his file with extra secrecy. We were warned earlier that a specialist was involved in stealing the new process. Friday afternoon we learned who that specialist was.''

Lee's stomach began to churn. This wasn't true.

Steve's voice shot out nastily, "And you wouldn't listen to me!"

Lee looked up at the security chief. His black eyes were like hot coals in the overheated furnace of his face. If looks could cook, she would have been done to a crisp. Lee felt very irritated.

"You're not fooling me with this pompous act, Gunn. There's nothing you could say I would believe. You were the one who attacked me!"

Denise looked at Steve's face and then back to Lee. "Steve attacked you?" she asked. The news seemed to be an unwelcome surprise to the advertising manager.

Lee nodded. "I can see he didn't fill you in on all the details of his recent assignment. How do you think he got his face bashed in?"

"He said Alexander caught him following the two of you. He told me Alexander attacked him," Denise said.

Lee shook her head. "Alex caught him trying to attack me. He lied about that, Denise, so how do you know he's not lying about everything else?"

Denise turned back to the man who was now standing quietly. "Well, Steve? Did you attack Lee?" she asked.

The security chief didn't say anything. He didn't have to. Uneasy guilt was written all over his face. "You imbecile," Denise commented. She turned back to Lee.

"Everything makes a lot more sense to me now. At first I couldn't understand how someone as intelligent as you could be duped by this Tyberry spy, despite his cover. But that idiot behind me gave Alexander a perfect opportunity to come to your rescue. I can see how your loyalties got confused. But you've got to unconfuse them now. You've got to understand whose side you're on. These reports are the real thing. I was in Steve's office when they came through.''

Lee felt uneasy at the confident tone in Denise's voice.

"How can you be so sure?" she asked.

"Look, Lee. Just as soon as this new product line was developed, Ham pulled me out of Trans World to spearhead the marketing campaign. We knew Tyberry would make an attempt to steal it. We have our own computer tie-in to Tyberry, manned by our spy over there. It verified what we knew about John Carstairs, of course, but..."

"John Carstairs?" Lee asked in surprise.

"Yes, Lee. He's been secretly working for Tyberry since he joined Varifoods three years ago. They planted him right after we were acquired by Trans World. Even the old security chief knew. That's why when Ham took over, he moved John Carstairs and his people away from the lab."

As Lee thought about it, it did make sense. John was the curious one, always asking questions and willing to give information to get some.

"But if you knew John was a spy, why wasn't he fired?" she asked.

"That would be stupid. If we got rid of him, Tyberry would just send in someone else, and we'd lose valuable time in trying to identify the new spy. This way we already knew. And he has his uses. He helps us weed out the disloyal. We know people who will talk with John are security risks. He was the one who introduced Alexander to Janet a couple of years ago."

Lee shook her head. "No, Denise. Alex was married to Janet's sister, Sally. Janet and he knew each other since college."

Denise shook her head. "He told you that, of course. Just like he told you he worked for the FDA. The only trouble is, Janet didn't have a sister, and Alexander never worked for the FDA."

"You're wrong, Denise."

"Am I, Lee? Think about it. Did anyone else corroborate anything he told you? Anything?"

Lee was thinking and she didn't like her thoughts. No one else had mentioned Janet's sister. Not even Janet. Nor had anyone else vouched for Alex's claim that he worked for the FDA. As a matter of fact, Alex had given every indication that the FDA shouldn't be contacted to verify his employment status. Lee tried to shake her doubts aside.

"I believe him," she said.

Denise leaned forward in her chair.

"Just like you believed his lies about the dangers of this new product line? You told me a moment ago that I didn't know anything about chemical analysis. What do you know about it? How many of his claims can you verify?"

Lee thought back to Iowa. Could Alex have lied about his conversation with Doc Boynton? Had the ice chest contained nothing but ice? Had this afternoon in the Genustech Lab all been part of an elaborate ruse designed to fool her?

Denise gently took a hold of her arm. "Don't you see he's made all this up? Wake up, Lee! If this new process is really so dangerous, why would Ham be going ahead with it? Why would he put it on the market?"

That was the very same question she and Alex had wrestled with. But now it was taking on a different significance. Had he brought it up to allay her suspicions? Had he tried to cover the hole in his logic by filling her with confusion?

Denise seemed to read the doubt on her face. "Lee, ask yourself this question. If this process was so dangerous, why didn't he just tell you to destroy it? Why did he want you to give him the secret to the new processing? That's who this printout is for, isn't it? Well, isn't it?"

Lee felt more and more confused. Denise couldn't be right. If she could just think this through, she'd be able to find the words to convince her. But her own concerns continued to surface, continued to add to her confusion. Why hadn't Alex called his boss once he found what the additive could do? He had the blood samples. Why did he need Janet's original research?

"Lee, I asked you if you were taking this research data to Alex?" Denise repeated.

"Yes, Denise. But you don't understand. Janet wrote me a letter. She told me something was wrong. She was trying to warn me about something. Something to do with the new line!"

Denise reached into her pocket and pulled out a white envelope. She removed a letter from it and handed it to Lee.

"You said Janet tried to warn you. Well, you weren't the only one Janet tried to warn. Read this."

Lee took the typed sheet from Denise's hand. It was dated the Friday of Janet's death.

Denise,

I've got to tell someone and I can't find anyone who will listen. Lee is out of town and George is too busy.

A spy for Tyberry Foods has been trying to steal my new processing technique. We met a couple of years ago at Lake Tahoe and we had a brief affair. I know it was wrong, but Mark and I were having problems. The only reason I'm telling you now is that this man has come back and wants me to give him the secret of the new line!

His name is Alex and he pretended to work for the FDA when we met, but I now know he's working for Tyberry.

He's threatening to tell Mark that Molly is really his child if I don't get him the secret process.

Please, Denise. Help me. He's demanding I bring the process to him tonight. Time is running out.

Janet

Lee put the letter on the desk. She felt hollow and numb inside. Dear God, could this be true? Alex had told her that Molly's brown eyes had to come from a brown-eyed father. Was Alex that father?

"The letter was in my In basket, Lee. Unfortunately, I didn't find it until late Wednesday morning. Somehow I missed it earlier. Maybe it got clipped to the back of something by mistake. As soon as I found it, I knew Alex's application was a fraud. I knew Alex was the Tyberry spy."

The room was closing in on Lee. The ceiling seemed to have descended onto her shoulders. She held on to the desk, as though needing the extra support.

"No, it's not true! Janet was murdered by the same person who bumped me in the tunnel and tried to break into my home!"

Denise frowned. "Is this more garbage that man has been feeding you? For heaven's sake, Lee, nobody murdered Janet. She died in an automobile accident, before she had a chance to give Alexander the file. Otherwise he wouldn't have stuck around and tried to get to you."

"But—" Lee began.

Denise interrupted. "And, if somebody bumped you in a tunnel or tried to break into your home, ask yourself where Mr. Alexander was when those incidents occurred, because ten to one he was behind them!"

The weight was growing heavier. She was having trouble breathing. Where had Alex been? Had he followed her from that coffee shop in Lafayette to bump her in the tunnel? He could have let himself out her guest-room window and easily broken into hers. She had thought it strange that he was wearing his glasses. Had he faked the break-in to get her to trust him? The questions pounded inside her skull. She put her head into her hands, trying desperately to understand.

"No, Pam was hit by a green truck. And someone blew up Alex's car," she replied.

"The chemist, Pam Heyer, was hit? I didn't know," Denise said. "But don't you see? It had to be Alexander who did it. And blew up his own car. They were just desperate attempts to get your cooperation, to lead you to betray your own company."

Pam hadn't seen the driver of the truck. Could it have been Alex all the time? Lee had to think this through, but she was torn between thoughts and feelings, as though each were balanced on opposite trays of a scale, waiting for the addition of one more fact to determine the outcome.

The printer had stopped and the office was suddenly quiet. Denise got up and walked over to the machine, gathering up the rest of the sheets. Then she tossed them into the wastepaper basket.

"Give me a match, Steve," she said.

Lee looked up to see Denise take the match Steve provided and light the printout. Somewhere a nagging thought was trying to surface, to tell Denise she shouldn't destroy Alex's copy. He needed it. But why did he need it? Lee was too tired and numb to say anything else. The heavy weight of confusion was dragging her down.

She watched in a strange fascination as the flames gobbled the paper, burping up the digested fibers into smoke and ashes. It took only a couple of minutes, then the printed file was gone.

Denise walked back to Lee's desk and leaned toward her.

"You're not going to print any more copies, are you, Lee?"

Lee shook her head. "No more copies, Denise," she agreed, sensing that her voice lacked any trace of emotion. It could almost have been a computer simulation, she reflected wryly.

Denise nodded as she straightened.

"You're going to take her word?" Steve asked, clearly upset by the idea.

"The days of paranoia are over, Steve. Besides, the guard will check Lee when she leaves. I know he'll find her clean, which is not an adjective I'd ever use to describe you. Now get out of here. I'll meet you downstairs," Denise told him.

She waited until the security chief was on an elevator going down, then turned back to Lee.

"Why don't you go home, Lee? Get some sleep. We can talk to Ham together about this thing tomorrow. I know we can work something out. Alexander didn't get the file, after all. And I'll be sure to tell Ham about Steve's attack on you. It should certainly mitigate the circumstances."

Lee nodded. The weight was still too heavy to lift. She just wanted Denise to leave. She just wanted to be alone. She had to think.

"Well, I'll be going. Thank heaven this is over. Now that we've identified Tyberry's agent, we can convince Ham to stop making his silly computer changes."

"Computer changes?" Lee repeated.

"God, yes! The man has been the most paranoid of any of us! Even Steve complained when Ham insisted on changing the security software over the weekend. He had to pay the damn programmers triple time. Well, you remember. You couldn't get Alex into the lab without Steve's okay. And then Ham called Steve and kept demanding more and more changes all week! Oh well, like I said, it's behind us now. I've got to go. Do you need a ride?''

Lee looked up and tried to focus on Denise's face. Something here wasn't right—something about Ham and the computer changes. "Denise, did Ham or George know that Alex was a Tyberry spy?"

Denise nodded. "Yes, Lee. I filled Ham in on Friday night when we got the confirmation. George is the one who told me to check with Steve's contacts at Tyberry. You see, he recognized Alexander from some seminar he attended a few years back. He remembered he was with Tyberry."

"So when you mentioned Alex worked for the FDA, they both knew right away it wasn't true?" Lee probed.

"Actually, I never mentioned Alex worked for the FDA. After reading Janet's letter and calling the FDA, I knew it wasn't true. I didn't tell either of them that Alex lied on his application," Denise said.

"So Steve didn't know," Lee said.

"I didn't tell him. What's wrong, Lee? Why are you asking? We know who Alex really works for. What's bothering you?"

"Nothing, Denise," Lee said with that same emotionless voice. She sat quietly, looking at her blank computer screen, a small frown inching across her forehead, aware that Denise stood at the door watching her.

"I know this has been a terrible shock for you, Lee. I can see you cared for Alexander. But you'll get through it. You believe that, don't you?"

Lee nodded. Denise finally shrugged. "Well, I'm going. It's been a long day. Good night. See you tomorrow." Denise headed toward the elevators. One was waiting to take her down.

Lee might have said good-night; she wasn't sure. Her mind was trying to sort something out, but she still felt numb and heavy with confusion.

She looked at her watch. Could it be that only forty minutes had passed since she had left Alex's arms? An awful sadness was threatening to swallow her heart. She had to fight it.

Lee turned to the computer. Her hands played across the computer keys, recalling Janet's BABY file. Its data appeared before her eyes. She could press the Execute button and begin the program she had written only minutes before—or she could press the Erase button, and everything would remain the same.

If Alex was right and the new additive was deadly, she should execute the changes. If Denise was right and Alex had used her, she should press Erase and leave Janet's program intact. Her fingers paused between the two keys.

Was reality a world that contained a deadly, addictive additive, a murderer bent on introducing it to unsuspecting consumers, and one wonderful man who was trying to stop the evil? Or was reality a wonderful world full of tasty new products—and one evil man, bent on stealing them for his own profit?

Logically, all the evidence supported the second proposition. But emotionally, Lee found herself clinging to her belief in Alex. If she accepted that Alex was a Tyberry spy, then she would also have to accept that all her instincts were wrong. Janet had cheated on Mark, and Alex had betrayed her. But Lee's heart wouldn't let her accept such truths, no matter what the evidence.

Confusion was pressing in all around, crushing her spirit. She was being squeezed into an airless vault of indecision. The awful jaws of sadness were coming closer.

Mentally she could visualize a tiny grain of sand suspended over one tray of her confusion scale. A voice was urging her to find the evidence to support the reality she wanted to believe in, the reality that would make this world a place in which she wanted to live. Was there any such evidence?

She remembered Mrs. Windermere's angry face and how she had disregarded Mark's protests, blaming Lee for Janet's overtime. And then she remembered Janet's mother responding to Alex's comfort. Would she had reacted that way, unless he was a member of the family? A beloved son-in-law?

The grain of sand descended closer to the scale.

She remembered Alex's tears as he knelt over Janet's grave, the comfort of his arms around her after Steve's attack, the sadness in his voice as he told her of Sally's death. If the emotions he had shown and evoked in her at those times weren't real, then none of her senses could be trusted.

The grain of sand crashed down, tipped the balance and made Lee's decision. She would believe in Alex and she would believe in Janet; otherwise she would never again be able to believe in herself. She pressed the Execute button.

The terrible weight seemed to lift from her shoulders. She sighed in relief and sat in front of her computer screen for several minutes, watching the data in Janet's program deteriorate. And then some new thoughts started to grow in her mind.

No longer burdened with confusion, she was able to go back to some previous conversations, able to connect some other scattered pieces.

Janet's letter to her had been cryptic and handwritten, yet the letter to Denise was explicit and typed. Could the second letter be a forgery?

If she and Denise were the only two people who knew that Alex claimed to be from the FDA, how had Ham found out?

She remembered distinctly how he had thrown the fact into her face when he was grilling her in his library. George had mentioned it, too, when he was badgering her to dance with him. She remembered feeling surprised he knew.

But how had he known? How did either of them know Alex claimed to work for the FDA, unless...?

"So you found Janet's access code?" a voice suddenly said from the doorway. Lee didn't have to look up. She knew who it was.

Chapter Sixteen

George Peck walked over to Lee's desk. He reached down and picked up the pad where she had written Janet's access code.

"I thought it might be you," he said. "When Denise told me you knew Janet hadn't been working late, because you had checked the computer records, I wondered if you had found a way into the lab matrix. You have, haven't you?"

Lee didn't like the tone of the chief chemist's voice. She liked the look on his face even less. She didn't think answering his question would do any good. So she remained quiet.

Suddenly a hard, bony hand reached out and grabbed her shoulder, its fingers digging into her flesh. She bit back the cry that leaped to her lips.

"You're doing something to the file, aren't you? That's why it stopped in the middle of synthesizing, isn't it?"

Lee watched his thin face contort into an angry sneer. She fought the panic that his sudden attack and the pain in her shoulder were causing.

"You're hurting me," she told him calmly.

"I'll hurt you a lot more if you don't answer my question."

Lee felt the fear licking inside her and fought to keep her wits. Alex would come for her. She must play for time.

"Yes. I'm changing Janet's file. I wrote a program so that I could remove its print restriction. The program's running now."

Lee was gambling that George didn't know enough about computers to tell if she was lying or not. From his look of confusion, she thought her gamble might pay off. She kept wondering about the time. Had forty-five minutes gone by? She didn't dare check her watch and give herself away.

"How long will it take?" George asked.

Lee was momentarily confused. She was so concerned with Alex's imminent arrival that she had almost missed the meaning in the chief chemist's question. She just stared at him. He dug his fingers deeper into her shoulder, making her wince with the pain.

"I said, 'How long will the print program take?'" he repeated.

"About fifteen minutes," Lee replied.

"Damn." George was obviously upset by the information. "Stop the program! Stop it now!" he commented.

Lee shook her head. "I can't, George. Once it's been executed it has to finish the run or the file will be damaged, maybe even lost." It was all a lie, of course. But somehow she managed to say it with a straight face. George watched her closely.

"You're printing it for that Alexander guy, aren't you?" he asked.

Lee saw no point in denial. Admitting to it would lend credence to her other lie. She nodded.

He smiled. The expression on his face wasn't pretty, but at least he let go of her arm. Lee rubbed the spot where his fingers had gripped her flesh; she knew there would soon be an ugly bruise.

"I see Denise and Steve couldn't convince you that Alexander was a Tyberry spy. What went wrong, not enough evidence?" George asked, leaning on the edge of her desk.

"There was plenty of evidence," Lee responded, holding on to the arms of the chair, trying to control the fear that was shaking her insides. She must not lose control.

"Then why didn't you believe them?" he wanted to know.

"Actually, they might have won me over, if it hadn't been for you," Lee told him.

George glared at her. "What are you talking about?" he demanded.

Lee swallowed nervously. Was she foolish to point out this man's mistake? Too late for second thoughts now.

"At Ham's party, you asked me where my lover from the FDA was, remember?" Lee said.

George nodded.

"Well, only Denise and I knew Alex claimed to be from the FDA. Since you were never told, your referring to him that way could only mean one thing. You knew Alex really was from the FDA all the time. You knew he wasn't a Tyberry spy."

George looked angry and frustrated, then a thought suddenly seemed to occur to him. He shrugged. "It doesn't matter what you know...now. You won't be telling anyone."

The threat was explicit. Lee tried to swallow again, but found her throat constricted. Maybe if she could keep him talking, the time would slip by and Alex would come.

"Of course Ham knew, too. I suppose you told him?" she asked.

"Of course I told him. Everything he knows, I told him," George said.

"And you told him the truth, because you needed his authority to change the computer software. You had to close the loophole Janet found and keep Alex out of her file. You and Ham both knew the additive Janet developed couldn't take close scrutiny by an FDA chemist," Lee accused him.

He looked at her in some surprise, then shrugged as though nothing she said really mattered. "So you figured it out. Big deal. It won't do you any good now. Come on. Get up."

Lee remained seated. When Alex came for her, he would expect to find her here. She mustn't leave. George Peck smiled his ugly smile as he took a black revolver from his pocket and aimed it at her head. "I said, 'Get up.'"

Lee stood on unsteady legs.

"Where are we going?" she asked.

"We're going to stop by the lab and get the only additive in existence outside of the computer memory. I really should thank you. Since I couldn't get the damn program to print out, all I was going to be able to take out tonight was the samples. But once your print program is over, we'll get a copy and destroy the file. You see, I'm taking no more chances. This secret will remain with me.''

"And then what?'' Lee asked.

"And then we're going to pick up your friend, Alex.''

Lee moved out of her office with George and the gun behind her.

"What do you want with Alex? He can't get inside Varifoods. He's no threat to you.''

"As long as he lives, he's a threat to me. Blowing up his car and taking care of Janet and running down Pam haven't made him back off. But you'll be good bait tonight. He's got a real weak spot for you. Any man who'd sleep in a bedroom next to yours has to be a fool or in love. And Alexander is no fool.''

George's words pounded through Lee like sharp tacks on her tender nerves. The only way George could have known about their sleeping arrangements was if he had seen Alex in the guest bedroom that night. He knew about all the other attacks, too. So he was behind them. But was he the only one?

As they descended in the elevator, she began to think about the security guard on duty. Somehow she'd signal to him and get him to help. But when they entered the lobby, no guard was at the desk. Her hope had been short-lived.

When she hesitated in front of the green security screen, George brought the gun up to her ear. She put her palm onto the screen and walked out past the administrative office's electronic eye and in through the lab's. George pushed her down the hall in front of him to the lab's elevators. They stepped into one, and the doors closed.

Lee was trying to think, trying to clear her mind of fear. *Keep him talking,* a little voice told her. *Keep him talking.*

"I'm curious, George. How did you know Alex worked for the FDA? You obviously never met him at any seminar.''

"That's where you're wrong. He represented the FDA at a conference I attended a couple of years ago. I recognized him when he walked into the lab.''

"So none of this has anything to do with industrial espionage, does it?"

"Wrong again, honey. Of course it does. You don't think I'm taking all these chances to stay a lackey at Varifoods? So that the big Ham can get all the glory? This little invention is going to the highest bidder. And at the moment the highest bidder is Tyberry."

"Tyberry? You're going to give the additive to Tyberry?"

"Give? What an inappropriate word. My contact at Tyberry says he'll get me six million cash. I'll be on a plane to South America before the big Ham knows what hit him."

"You're dealing with Tyberry directly? Not through John Carstairs?"

"Of course not through John Carstairs. Everybody knows he's a Tyberry plant. No, I called the president of Tyberry directly, as soon as I knew I had something to sell. I told him all about Steve's little spy network. He was the one who arranged for Alexander's spy profile to be 'found' in the personnel computer. The false reports kept the security chief and the advertising manager out of my hair. Stupid fools."

The elevator had opened; George urged Lee out and into the lab at the point of his gun. Lee was thinking that it had been one of the seven deadly sins, after all—greed. No matter how much technology changed, people remained the same.

Lee stopped at the entrance to the lab.

"You must realize this is futile, George. The security guard is watching your every move on his monitors."

George's voice was an ugly grunt. "You think I'm a fool? Only central security can see what's on these monitors, and central security is Steve Gunn. I watched him and Denise leave ten minutes ago. And I sent the lobby guard on a thirty-minute lunch break. We have about twenty minutes left to collect what we need and get out. Now get going."

Lee still hesitated. She kept thinking that Alex wouldn't be able to find her if she went into the lab.

George was poking her back, pushing her in front of him again.

"Do you remember the last time we were together? When you threatened to go to Ham? Well, I hope you enjoyed your little moment of triumph, putting the squeeze on me. Because now it's my turn. How does it feel?"

Lee didn't answer. George grabbed her left arm with his free hand and pinned it behind her back, turning it up viciously.

"I asked, 'How does it feel?'"

Her arm hurt abominably. She couldn't stop the small cry that escaped from her lips. George's breathy laugh behind her ear told her how much pleasure her pain was giving him. Then he released her arm, pushing her toward the back where the kitchen was.

He opened the kitchen door and shoved her in first. In the dark she stumbled over the threshold, losing her balance and crashing into a counter, knocking glass beakers and other instruments to the floor.

George moved around her to the other side. He didn't turn on the overhead light, but switched on a small table lamp over the counter. He began checking the vials in front of him, using only his left hand, keeping the gun in his right aimed in her direction.

Lee stood in the opposite corner watching, trying to think of something, anything she could use to defend herself. But there wasn't much she could do with that gun pointed at her. A sliver of broken glass about an inch long lay in front of her on the counter. As unobstrusively as she could, she slipped her right hand over it and picked it up. George was intent on collecting his vials. She started to move forward.

"If you take one more step, I'll shoot you," George said.

He had obviously been watching her out of the corner of his eye. Lee stopped. Maybe she could catch him off guard. If she kept him talking, she might be able to distract him.

"You found Janet's letter, didn't you?"

He snickered. "Yeah. Something else I should thank you for. Gave me the idea of composing another one to send to Denise. Dear old Denise was just the patsy I needed to run a diversion play."

Her only defense seemed to be information. She must get more information.

"What do you plan to do with me?" she asked.

He didn't look up from his work, but put on his ugly little smile again. "You're going to have an accident. With Alexander driving. A tragic accident, in which both of you will be killed."

Lee tried to fight down the terror his words were bringing to her. Even though she had known the man meant her harm, she had somehow never believed he would go this far. The force of his words terrified her now.

All the time she had been expecting Alex to come charging in. Now she wished with all her might he wouldn't. Once Alex arrived, George would have the drop on him, and then the chief chemist would be able to carry out his threat.

She was suddenly desperately afraid. She must not let him use her as bait to catch Alex. She must think, try to persuade him out of this insanity.

"Ham will be suspicious, George. He'll know something is wrong if Alex and I are killed," Lee told him.

George laughed. The sound slithered disagreeably down Lee's spine.

"Ham couldn't care less. First, last and always, he's a businessman. You think he doesn't know that our new flavor enhancer causes cancer? He was the one who told me to kill the results of the Ames test. He'll close his eyes to your death, just like he closed his eyes to Janet's. And by the time he opens them again, the formula and I will be gone," George declared.

"So you killed Janet and stole her research. Had you altered her original design to get it to work? The new flavor enhancer was her idea. Did you bring it to life?"

He was silent for a moment, but Lee somehow knew he couldn't resist talking about the additive. It had to be the biggest thing that ever happened to him. It had to be giving him a big kick.

"She started it, all right. At first I just humored her, trying to get her off my back. I told her she could work on her pet project, as long as she didn't do it on company time and didn't try to stick me for overtime. I thought that would be the end of it. I didn't know she had found a way to beat the computer time records until much later."

"So she went ahead with the project?" Lee asked.

"Yeah. I didn't really know what she was doing, even when I caught her in the lobby late one night. She lied to me then. Told me she was waiting for a ride. She must have worked on the thing at night for a whole year, before she went on pregnancy leave. She even programmed the experiment to keep working while she was gone. Damn thing kept gathering data from all the other experiments going on in the lab and absorbed the results. She must have figured out a lot of programming stuff along the way. It was against the rules, of course, but rather ingenious."

"The program came up with the formula for the new additive?"

"With some help. We had a major power failure one day. Even the backups failed. I went in after power was restored to assess the damage. Some of the data in her program had gotten lost and, crazily enough, it seemed to make a difference. Staring me in the face were the words: Program Complete. It had produced a genetically mutated molecule. The chemical processor had been hooked up, and the first sample was already in a test tube in the kitchen."

George put the last of the vials into his pocket and turned toward her, waving the gun in the direction of the door.

"And it worked?" she asked.

"Better than even Janet hoped. Our tasters went wild. I went forward with preparing the samples for a new product line in the lab's kitchen. Nothing went out to the processing plants. To maintain secrecy, I did it all myself. Denise identified a statistically significant trial town in Iowa. We flew the samples to them."

"And then Janet came back to work? She tested it out?"

"She wouldn't accept my assurances that everything was okay. I didn't tell her about the power failure. I told her I had been monitoring her program and adapting it in her absence. It was mine now. I tried to keep her involved with other experiments, away from testing the flavor enhancer on her own. But that Friday morning she came and told me she had been reviewing the material at night, and she had just gotten the results of the Ames test. She knew it was a carcinogen. She told me if I didn't stop production, she would."

He was moving purposefully toward Lee now, gesturing with his gun for her to leave the kitchen. She had no choice but to comply. He kept talking.

"I tried to convince her that she had extrapolated the wrong data from the file, that she had gotten rusty being away so long. I know I confused her, gave her enough doubt to run the test again Friday night."

"And you waited until she left work that night?" Lee said as George waved her in the direction of his office. "You followed her car into the Caldecott Tunnel and drove her into the wall, to crash?"

George seemed almost happy at her question.

"A lucky break. Got her on the first bump. She didn't have your reflexes. Of course, the fact she was changing lanes at the time helped."

George shoved Lee into a chair next to his desk. He looked at his watch and smiled as he accessed his computer. Lee felt sick, very sick. The chief chemist went on with his story as he waited for the BABY file to appear.

"Ham called the next day and said he knew it was me. Told me I should have found another way. He could never have done it, you see. He doesn't have the guts. For all his mighty physical appearance, his position, he couldn't have done it. He's one of those that doesn't want to dirty their hands. You can bet he wanted it done, though. You can bet he'd let no one stand in his way when he had something this big to market."

Lee decided to make one more effort to reason with him, if not on moral grounds, then on the basis of logic. She leaned over the desk, trying to get through to George Peck.

"Don't you realize that its cancer-causing properties will be exposed, just as soon as the food is tested by another processor or lab? Don't you see that no matter who markets it, they'll be sued out of existence, once the truth is out?"

George laughed unpleasantly. "But that's the beauty of it all! The molecule is undetectable in the food. Looks just like it's part of a simple sugar chain. It only undergoes its chemical change when it's mixed with the saliva on the tongue. Immediately penetrates the blood vessels, enters the bloodstream in its new state and heads like a homing pigeon for the hypothalamus. So almost instantly the flavor senses are enhanced.''

Lee sat back in shock. She and Alex had been at a loss to explain how Varifoods would dare to knowingly market a dangerous additive. It was undetectable in the food! It wouldn't matter what anyone suspected. Analysis of Varifoods' new product line would have turned up nothing! God, what a nightmare this additive was!

''What have you done? I can't get this damn thing to print out! It's still running your stupid program!'' George exclaimed. She saw his eyes grow larger as he watched the screen.

Lee didn't respond. She knew Janet's research was gone now. And she felt immense relief, even in the midst of her own personal danger.

George was not at all happy with the quiet. Once again, Lee watched the barrel of the gun pointed at her face. ''I asked, what have you done to the file?''

''Janet's experiment is over, George. I've destroyed her file,'' Lee told him.

His bony features reddened with rage. He leaned over and slapped Lee's face. Lee winced at the blow, expecting more to follow. But the man's sudden anger seemed to be spent.

''It doesn't matter. I have more than enough samples in these vials to isolate the right simple sugar chain for Tyberry. It may take some time, but with these samples they'll be able to reproduce it. You see, you destroyed the file for nothing,'' he declared.

The sharp, bony fingers grabbed her again and yanked her to her feet. He quickly stepped behind her, pinning her left arm behind her again and yanking it up—hard. Tears of pain stung her eyes. George pushed her ahead of him, out the lab and toward the elevators. One was open and waiting.

George shoved Lee into it. She crashed against the wall and fell to the floor. She tried to move her left arm, but it was no use. It wouldn't respond. George had been watching her. He was smiling. He turned to the control panel and pressed the button for the ground floor.

Lee knew she had to stop this man from taking the samples and from using her to get Alex.

The elevator door opened. George grabbed her and pulled her to her feet. He had selected her left arm again. She cried out uncontrollably as the pain shot through her body.

"Shut up, or I'll really give you something to yell about. Now you're going to walk in front of me. We're going through the electronic eye and out to the street to meet Alexander. And if you don't do everything exactly as I say, I'll shoot you several times before I let you die."

Lee tried to think through the pain. Her right hand had started to bleed. Then she remembered the broken glass she was holding. The sharp end must have pricked her. She looked around for the guard, but the central monitor position was indeed empty. They were at the electronic eye.

"Put your hand on the screen," he said.

Lee hesitated, trying to move the piece of glass between her thumb and forefinger. George pulled at her arm again and she gulped down the pain.

"I said, 'Put your hand on the screen.'"

She shakily raised her hand and complied, hoping against hope that the screen would read through the glass. The electronic eye shot off. He pushed her through ahead of him, switched the gun to his left hand and spread his right hand over the glowing green screen. It was then Lee saw a quick movement—there was a shadow on the left, near the rest rooms.

"Where is he meeting you?" George asked.

He had come up behind her again. The gun was back in his right hand.

Lee's voice came more steadily now. "The car's parked a block away." She was hoping George had not seen what she had.

"Come on, then. Let's not keep your lover waiting," he said, heading for the glass entry doors.

They were just going through when the alarms went off. The evening quiet was blasted by an incredibly loud, persistent screeching. Lee stopped in her tracks, as though the deafening roar had robbed her of all ability to move. Rabid cursing assailed her ears as George swung around, taking her with him.

He shoved her back into the building, staying close behind her, using her body as a shield against whoever might be waiting. No one was in sight. He lifted the barrel of the gun until it was directly opposite her right ear. His voice was loud and sharp, straining to be heard over the blaring alarms.

"You better come out, Alexander, or I'll blow her away!"

Lee was desperately trying to think of something to do. She knew Alex had tripped the alarm purposely. She couldn't let him come out now, couldn't let him be killed.

She felt George tense; both of them had heard footsteps running from the elevators. When the sounds were almost at the corner, Lee gripped the sliver of glass in her hand and knew it was now or never. She mustn't let him shoot Alex. She reached up and jabbed George's right hand hard with the sharp, jagged edge of glass, just as he prepared to fire.

Lee was momentarily deafened by the loud retort. She saw the started face of the young guard before he collapsed into a heap. George yelled and pushed her forward, the sliver of glass still sticking out of his gun hand.

She fell to the hard tile floor, rolled onto her back, just a few feet from the wounded guard, and looked up to see the murderous stare of George Peck above her. Her death was in his eyes. The black barrel of his gun was pointed directly at her face. She watched in stunned horror as his bony finger slowly bent on the trigger.

Chapter Seventeen

Startled, Lee saw George's body twist away from her. Relief flooded her as she recognized Alex's head and shoulders. But the relief was short-lived. New fear flashed through her as she saw Alex's hand gripping the revolver cylinder, preventing George's gun from firing.

Their movements ground on in a slow, deadly dance. Her heart seemed to have stuck in her throat. She didn't dare breath as she watched the barrel of the gun slowly turn away from her in an ever-widening arc toward Alex's chest. Alex was bigger, but George already had the gun and was fighting for his life. Lee wanted desperately to move, to scream, to do something. But all she could do was sit and watch in fascinated horror.

Sweat poured off the two men; their muscles strained for control of the weapon. Lee had no idea who was winning. Neither man moved. Only the gun moved, as it inched along in a slow circle toward Alex.

No, not quite. The infinitely slow movement was now directing the gun barrel above the bodies of the two men, toward the ceiling. In a short spasm of relief, Lee realized that Alex must be winning.

Alex suddenly removed his hand from the gun barrel. The gun fired into the ceiling and made them all jump. George leaped away from Alex, his sudden action causing the revolver to drop to the floor between them. He stared at the weapon for an instant, clearly trying to measure his chances of grabbing it before Alex. But the gun was right next to

Alex and several feet from him. He quickly gave up the idea, jerked around and bolted out the glass doors.

Alex rushed to Lee's side and knelt down, folding her into his arms, gently, lovingly.

"Lee, darling, are you all right?"

Lee nodded. "You were wonderful, Alex."

He gave her a look that melted her heart. Then she heard a small groan beside her. "The guard!" she exclaimed.

They turned toward him and saw that he was coming to a sitting position.

"I'm okay. Bullet just grazed my thigh. Whatever you stuck in his hand, Ms. Lee, must have put his aim off. I thought I better play possum, so I wouldn't catch another."

They heard police sirens.

"I've got to go after him," Alex said. He looked uncertainly at the guard.

Lee could see that the guard recognized Alex's dilemma.

"Go get the creep. I'll be fine. I'm not bleeding bad. Cops will get an ambulance here." He waved Alex on.

Lee jumped to her feet. "I'm coming, too," she said.

Alex just smiled and grabbed her hand, and they ran together out the glass doors. They had no sooner reached the street than they heard the engine of George's truck start up about a half block away. Its lights flashed on. With all their might, they ran for the Fiero.

After their mad dash to the car, Lee could only hear the hammering of the blood in her ears. Alex had already started the engine, so she jumped in and closed the passenger door. As they raced after the dark green truck, she began rubbing her left arm to try to increase the circulation and eliminate some of the soreness. Fortunately it seemed to be responding.

The chase grew wild. Several times the little Fiero seemed almost to lift off the roadway and take flight. She forgot completely about her arm and simply tried to avoid being banged back and forth in the fast-moving vehicle. After several screeching turns around a number of tight corners, Alex's voice rose above the pounding of her heart.

"He's headed for the Bay Bridge. We won't be able to stop him before he gets to the other side. Hang on. I'm going to have to drive over this next island to get to the on ramp."

Lee held on, wondering briefly at the impulse that had made her join in this chase. As they flew over the center divider and jerked around a street corner, going the wrong way, she ventured a look at her companion. His face was lean and hard. An unmistakable glitter shone in the steady brown eyes.

"He's the one behind it all, isn't he?" Alex asked.

"Yes. It was George from the beginning, from the moment he realized what Janet had discovered."

"And Ham?" he asked.

"He knew about the results of the Ames test. He knew George had killed Janet."

Alex nodded in grim understanding. They tore on in silence.

Thankfully, there was very little traffic on the bridge as they weaved back and forth between lanes, trying to keep pace with the dark green truck in front of them.

The bulk of George's vehicle made it difficult for him to change lanes, but it didn't seem to be slowing him down. Instinctively he must have known he was driving for his life, because he was driving like a madman. Angry horns and squealing brakes could be heard in his wake. Lee heard Alex swear under his breath as they themselves swerved several times to avoid irate drivers.

Lee shouted out the story of how Denise and Steve had been misled into suspecting Alex. He said nothing and just stared straight ahead, keeping the green truck in sight at all times.

By the way George's truck and the Fiero were passing the other cars, Lee knew they were both way over the speed limit. Guardrails, cars, everything was a blur of metal flashes and red taillights. Even if she could have kept her balance for long enough to look at the speedometer, she decided it was a better idea not to.

In what was no doubt a new world record, the dark green truck, closely followed by Lee's Fiero, had devoured the lower deck of the bridge and begun eating up the freeway toward Oakland. Alex quickly followed when the truck turned into the lanes heading for the East Bay.

The tires squealed again, and Alex just missed the guard-rail as they entered the two-lane overpass to the 24 freeway. They careered past an old Dodge, whose horn was still blazing at the green truck that had almost run it off the road.

Suddenly yellow Caution lights began to flash by.

"What is it?" Lee asked.

"Night construction ahead. Looks like the middle lanes of the tunnel are blocked off. We'll have to stay right," Alex said.

Lee faced front. The Caldecott Tunnel loomed ahead like the black eyes of death.

The dark green truck was speeding on, several car lengths in front of them. Suddenly it switched to the far left lanes, clearly heading for the middle tunnel, right through the construction barriers.

"He's trying to get away!" Alex exclaimed.

Lee felt the Fiero swerve left, and her body was jolted forward against the seat belt as Alex hit the brakes and swerved onto a shoulder, just missing a construction worker, who was running frantically down the highway after the fast-disappearing truck.

The Fiero sputtered and died.

"Damn! We've lost him now," Alex said, trying to re-start the car.

George Peck's truck was just entering the tunnel. Lee stared in mounting disbelief as the dark green vehicle swerved into the tunnel's side wall, smashed off it and tumbled over and over in vibrating thunderbolts, deafening echoes in a gigantic drum.

"Alex!"

Alex leaned over and grabbed her arm. "I see it. Stay here," he told her as he got out of the car.

She watched him run toward the tunnel entrance. Two men in orange overalls, obviously members of the construction crew, were immediately at his side, pulling him back. Each held one of his arms. Lee couldn't understand. Why were they preventing him from going in after George?

She jumped out of the car and ran toward them, yelling, she knew not what. She had just reached Alex, who was still struggling with the two men, when an explosion broke the darkness of the night around them like a sun bursting.

The tunnel was a funnel of fire. Flames like angry, gigantic fireflies flew out of the black, burning hole. The four captivated spectators stepped back out of the blazing heat, away from the flying sparks.

The two men had released Alex. He immediately came to Lee's side and put one arm protectively around her. They could only watch the dark green truck being consumed within the fiery inferno.

"I was trying to tell your friend here, lady, that it wasn't safe," one of the construction workers said. "One of the paint trucks overturned no more than twenty minutes ago. There's paint and gasoline everywhere. Whoever was in that truck didn't have a chance. He must have been crazy, driving in there. Fool should have read the signs."

Lee was struck dumb, both by the destruction before her and by the poetic justice of it all. George had killed Janet Homer in this same tunnel a little more than a week ago. And now, in a freak accident, he had died the same way. Justice had been served.

The warm arm around her tightened its hold. She looked up and saw the reflection of the flame in Alex's steady brown eyes—and realized that he shared her unspoken thoughts.

He didn't know yet that this fire was also destroying the last evidence of the deadly additive. Janet had died trying to keep it from the public. Now Lee felt that her friend had not died in vain.

Alex watched Lee staring into the flames, a serene look on her lovely face. When she spoke, her voice was like a gentle pat on the bottom of the wind. "You can rest easy now, Janet. It's all over."

"WHO were you so anxious to call?" Alex asked as she came out of the pay phone they had driven to.

"I was getting my old boss, Dave Erickson, out of bed. I gave him an edited version of what Ham and George were up to at Varifoods, how Steve and Denise had been duped. And I told him about my conversation with George this evening. Dave was incensed."

"What will happen to Jarrett?" Alex asked.

"Dave won't do anything directly. But he'll pass the word to the others. Even without it, Ham is washed up. He goes before the board of directors tomorrow with nothing. More than eight months on the job and nothing to show for it, no new flavor enhancer and no plan for improvement at all."

Alex's eyes squinted in obvious disappointment. "It doesn't seem enough. He knew how dangerous it was. He knew George killed Janet. He turned his back on it all. He's getting off too easily."

Lee smiled. "You don't understand a man like Ham. Power is all that matters to him, and he's never known defeat. Now at thirty-four he's through. When he finds out, I'll lay odds that he'll wish he had been in George Peck's truck tonight, when it exploded into flames."

Alex smiled. "When you put it that way, I see your point. But why would he jeopardize everything by marketing the dangerous additive in the first place?"

"George told me the additive couldn't be detected in the products. It looked just like a simple sugar chain until it came into contact with the saliva in the mouth. That's when it changed into the substance you saw, the one you felt sure couldn't exist outside the body."

Alex was quiet for a moment. "It's horrible to think what was almost released on unsuspecting consumers. Are you sure Ham won't still try to market the additive?"

Lee smiled. "What additive?"

A light was switched on inside Alex's head. "You destroyed the file! That's why you were telling Jan to rest easy. You got rid of it!" he exclaimed.

She nodded.

"Are you sure they can't get it back?" he asked.

"I'm sure. You see I didn't delete it, because deleted files can be recovered. I used a variation on the virus application," she said.

"The virus application? I never heard of it."

"Well, every so often some disgruntled employees manage to infect their employer's computer system with a virus program. It attacks all the software, spreading across any network coming into contact with it. Eventually nothing works."

"And you used a variation on the Varifoods computer?"

"In a way. You see, programs have been invented to cure a virus. The sickness I gave Janet's program was more like a localized cancer. It grew and grew, swallowing up the original data, distorting it, cutting off all new input, changing even the cancer program I wrote, until all that was left was a festering mass of information garbage. Janet's experiment is gone forever."

Alex nodded his understanding as they stood by the phone booth. "In a way, it seems a shame. I wanted so much to know how it worked."

Lee nodded. "That's the scientist in you. That's why you wanted a copy of Janet's program, why you didn't just tell me to destroy it."

Alex shook his head. "No. That wasn't the only reason. You see, my boss Willy wouldn't take action when I called him about the reactions to the Iowa taste test." Alex went on to explain how slowly the wheels at the FDA turned—how he had needed overwhelming proof—how, since returning to San Francisco, they had been on their own.

"Alex, you should have told me sooner. I would have stood by you. Don't you understand that I believe in you?" Lee inquired.

Alex could see from the look in her eyes that she cared. "Yes, you've proved it. Especially when you refused to accept all that so-called evidence against me from Steve and Denise. It's one of the things I love most about you. Your belief in a . . . friend."

He had moved closer, encircling her waist with one arm. She knew she should probably move away, but she loved him so much—and time was growing short. She tried to find the words that would make their goodbye bearable. But as she tried to say them, she felt tears sting her eyes.

"Well, since it's all over now, I guess it's back to the East Coast and your job at the FDA?"

He drew her to him, wrapping both arms around her.

"I'm not going anywhere, darling. Not without you. We're a team, remember?"

"But I thought you said—" Lee began.

"I kept telling myself I wanted to keep you at a distance. I was so afraid to let myself love you and then risk losing you. After losing Sally, I've stayed away from all commitments."

"But what's changed?" Lee asked.

"I have. I've finally realized that although loving and losing are hard, living a loveless life is much worse. And you've made me realize that's what I had been doing."

His voice was tender, his arms held her gently.

"I love you, Lee. I want to marry you and spend the rest of our lives together. Just as soon as I can get a job out here, because to tell you the truth, I really don't like snow. What do you say?"

Lee looked deeply into those steady, warm, brown eyes she loved. Smiling, she looped her arms around his neck.

"Well, if it's just a job stopping you, I hear that the chief chemist position at a very reputable food processing firm in the City has just opened up. And an unimpeachable source tells me the personnel manager of that firm is madly in love with you."

She looked down at his lips. He was smiling. A real smile. His mouth was warm and full. The sadness that had inhabited it for so long was gone.

"Let's go home," he said.

Harlequin Intrigue®

COMING NEXT MONTH

#129 STREET OF DREAMS by Lynn Leslie
As a favor, vacationer Kim Campbell visited
Madame Loulou's shop in New Orleans. On a lark,
Kim ordered a voodoo doll made of herself. Twenty-
four hours later, Madame Loulou was dead, the doll
was missing, and Kim stood in the path of an
oncoming tidal wave of evil. Playwright Shane
Alexander knew they courted death at the hands of
an ambitious and powerful voodoo cult, while Kim
was to learn that love was their greatest weapon
of all.

#130 SHADOWPLAY by Linda Stevens
Someone had killed investigative reporter, Brian
Fenton, and made his death look like a suicide. But
his protégé Cassie O'Connor wasn't fooled. She'd
called in every favor she was owed to find the perfect
partner her plans required—a mystery man named
Jack Merlin whose reputation as a master thief was
only surpassed by his intensely compelling
personality. She was willing to use fair means or foul
to get him on her side, but she'd never expected his
price to be her heart.

You'll flip . . . your pages won't!
Read paperbacks *hands-free* with

Book Mate • I

The perfect "mate" for all your romance paperbacks

Traveling • Vacationing • At Work • In Bed • Studying • Cooking • Eating

Perfect size for all standard paperbacks, this wonderful invention makes reading a pure pleasure! Ingenious design holds paperback books OPEN and FLAT so even wind can't ruffle pages — leaves your hands free to do other things. Reinforced, wipe-clean vinyl-covered holder flexes to let you turn pages without undoing the strap . . . supports paperbacks so well, they have the strength of hardcovers!

Pages turn WITHOUT opening the strap.

SEE-THROUGH STRAP

Reinforced back stays flat.

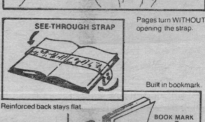

Built in bookmark.

BOOK MARK

BACK COVER HOLDING STRIP

10" x 7¼", opened.
Snaps closed for easy carrying, too.